H

Guardian

Other Books by Heather Burch

Halflings

Guardian

Book Two

Heather Burch

ZONDERVAN.com/
AUTHORTRACKER
follow your favorite authors

ZONDERVAN

Guardian
Copyright © 2012 by Heather Burch

This title is also available as a Zondervan ebook.
Visit www.zondervan.com/ebooks.

Requests for information should be addressed to:
Zondervan, *Grand Rapids, Michigan* 49530

Library of Congress Cataloging-in-Publication Data

Burch, Heather.
    Guardian / Heather Burch.
        p. cm. — (A Halflings novel ; bk. 2)

    Summary: As their mission becomes clearer, dangers intensify and tensions
    flare for half-angel, half-human guardians Mace and Raven, while seventeen-
    year-old Nikki, torn between them, desperately needs their protection from
    Damon Vessler and the powerful secret he holds.

        ISBN 978-0-310-72821-4 (hardcover : alk. paper) [1. Supernatural—Fiction.
    2. Good and evil—Fiction. 3. Angels—Fiction. 4. Love—Fiction.] I. Title.
    PZ7.B91584Gu 2012
    [Fic]--dc23   2012013069

All Scripture quotations, unless otherwise indicated, are taken from The Holy
Bible, *New International Version®, NIV®.* Copyright © 1973, 1978, 1984, 2011 by
Biblica, Inc.™ Used by permission. All rights reserved worldwide.

Any Internet addresses (websites, blogs, etc.) and telephone numbers in this book
are offered as a resource. They are not intended in any way to be or imply an
endorsement by Zondervan, nor does Zondervan vouch for the content of these
sites and numbers for the life of this book.

Cover design: Cindy Davis
Cover photography: Dan Davis Photography
Interior design and composition: Greg Johnson/Textbook Perfect

Printed in the United States of America

12 13 14 15 16 /DCI/ 21 20 19 18 17 16 15 14 13 12 11 10 9 8 7 6 5 4 3 2

To the women in my life:

First, my mom, Mary Elisabeth McWilliams.
You taught me to dream big.
Is this big enough, Momma?

Diane Burch, my second mom, and the one
who pushed me to write. And write. And write.

Melodie Adams, my mentor and friend.
You encouraged me and wouldn't let me give up.
You're truly a friend of the Halflings
and easily my best friend in the world.

Chapter 1

"We are not going in." Mace had Raven by the shirt, his hand fisted into the cloth.

Vine swallowed. Only two days ago Mace and Raven, along with their parental stand-in, Will, had rescued Nikki from her godfather, Damon Vessler—yeah, rescued. You could argue that she'd chosen Will and the Halflings, but decisions could always be revoked. As far as Vine was concerned, it was amazing Nikki was still staying at the house. Vessler was like a thundercloud on the day of a parade, hovering and waiting to strike. Vine could feel the approaching threat. So could Mace and Raven, which was one reason the two of them were seconds from tearing each other apart. The other reason was completely wrapped around Nikki herself. They both had it bad for her. And no one—including Will—knew if or when she'd go running back to Vessler.

And all of those factors caused Vine to stay alert. He'd even left the house without the bag of candy he'd spent an hour carefully packing after Zero discovered the location of a possible Omega Corporation storage facility.

Raven shoved Mace away from him. "If we can get inside, we can find out what Omega's hiding. Why would a science lab need a giant warehouse?"

Mace's shoulders dropped marginally. Vine could see he was trying to calm down, and that Raven's smug smile wasn't helping. "We were told to observe and report back to Will."

"This isn't Will's journey, Mace. It's *ours*. And the sooner we find out why Omega wants Nikki, the sooner this whole nightmare is over."

At the mention of Nikki's name, Mace's eyes changed. The strange blue-green color darkened into a bubbling sea of frustration, and Vine watched Mace's right hand flex.

Of all the days to forget gummy worms.

Mace and Raven were probably pretty evenly matched as far as Halflings go. It'd be a brutal fight—and Vine was ready. He'd stepped between the two once or twice. But their anger was boiling like a lava pit, and all that hostility was about to release somewhere. It wouldn't be at each other. Vine wouldn't allow it.

Mace's fingers relaxed, but his eyes remained harsh and focused. "We also risk being caught. This place is crawling with men from Omega."

"Exactly," Raven argued. "We need to find out what's happening inside or this trip was a waste."

It wasn't a trip; they'd simply gone to the edge of town on a surveillance mission. When they saw a van with the Omega emblem on the side, they confirmed what Zero had suspected: The lab was more than a harmless research facility. Their job was done.

"And if we go inside, we could ruin everything. We're leaving."

An engine whined above them, and the three boys ducked deeper into the tree line as a small private plane circled overhead. When it landed at the adjacent airfield, the boys relaxed. Sort of.

Raven challenged Mace with a look. "I don't take orders from you."

"You don't take orders from anyone. You do whatever you want without even a thought to how it could hurt others."

Raven angled closer. "Are you talking about Nikki? It's not my fault she didn't pick you, bro."

That's when the fist flew past Vine and sank into Raven's jaw. Stunned for a moment, Vine waited for Raven to retaliate, but the return punch didn't come. Instead a slow, devious smile formed on Raven's lips. "It's not my fault you lost. Get used to it."

Raven walked away.

Mace stared down at his hand, then at the ground. And Vine's heart ached for him. How many times would Mace have to relive Nikki's refusal to get romantically involved? She hadn't chosen Raven; she just decided not to be with Mace. Since their last date on homecoming night, the two of them had stayed apart, but it wasn't hard to see they were both miserable.

She hadn't gotten any closer to Raven either. She avoided him like she avoided everyone. But it didn't take a Halfling's senses to see her resistance was crumbling.

Vine wanted to say something to alleviate even a little of Mace's pain, but there just weren't words. Instead, he placed a reassuring hand on Mace's shoulder. "Everything's falling apart," Vine muttered. The words popped out unrestrained.

"Let this be a lesson, Vine."

Even now, Mace was watching out for his "kid brother." They weren't actually related, of course. Not by blood. Like all Halflings, their family was due to providence, destiny. And Vine was grateful he'd been given a wise older sibling. Two, actually. Raven was just as smart—he simply chose to go after instant gratification sometimes rather than follow wise counsel. Vine had learned from both of them. What to do … and especially what not to do.

Falling for a human was on the latter list. It had been the Achilles heel for both boys. If Mace and Raven lived through their broken hearts, maybe things could get back to normal. They'd survive, at least. Nikki'd sworn to Vine she wouldn't get involved with either of them. He hoped she was telling the truth.

Nikki heard the voices right after that unmistakable sensation of heaven breaching earth. Lightning particles danced across her fingertips and she knew something ethereal was happening downstairs. She left the room—her sanctuary, her hiding place from the boys—and paused at the top of the stairs. The air in the room below was electric. So much so, she wasn't sure she could enter. It was reminiscent of the first time she'd met Mace, Raven, and Vine. Back when she had normal things like a family and a real home.

Now she was an orphan. But best not to dwell on that when there were so many more important issues, like how she nearly was the cause of Mace—and Raven, for that matter—losing his one chance at eternity. A good eternity. Everyone would spend eternity somewhere, she now understood, but for Halflings there was no salvation, only obedience. Either by choice or by rebellion, all half-human, half-angel beings would either rise or sink. She nearly sunk the two she cared for most.

Last night she'd found Vine with tears in his eyes, sitting alone on the back porch. He knew as well as she did that she held the power to destroy Mace and Raven. What she hadn't realized until then was how strong that power still was—and what it was doing to the rest of the house. She promised Vine she wouldn't lead either boy on, and that she would do everything she could to keep them on the side of the Throne. Now she had to concentrate on keeping that promise, even though it only made her feel deader inside. She truly was alone. But though the solitude cut like a razor against her heart, it was a vacation compared to the thought she'd send either one to hell. That she couldn't bear.

Nikki blinked and put one foot on the first step, intent on dealing with whatever awaited her downstairs, when she heard Will's voice slice through the haze of regrets and promises. She tried to piece the conversation together. All she could understand was a ship had sunk.

The heavenly angel's words were filled with concern. "Is the crew of *The Journey* all right?"

"All accounted for," a voice replied.

She could practically feel Will sighing with relief. For a heavenly angel who wasn't equipped with human emotions, Will sure seemed to experience them.

"Why has this news brought you to my door, brothers?"

His brothers? More heavenly angels? Maybe that's why the room felt so alive with the essence of heaven. She shifted her weight just enough to make the stair creak. Nikki's eyes closed at the sound. *How could I be so stupid? Eavesdropping on heavenly angels.* She felt the gravity of their stares, though she couldn't see them. A few heavy moments passed.

"Come," Will said. "Let's go into the kitchen where we can talk."

Stupid, *stupid*, *stupid.* She was lousy at the stealthy thing. Maybe she should have studied ninjutsu instead of karate.

"Who was that?" Vine asked Will as two heavenly angels disappeared from the house.

Will didn't answer.

"Things going okay here?" He reached across the counter and grabbed the bag of candy he'd forgotten earlier.

"We may be leaving." Will's expression looked pained.

Vine frowned while several thoughts splashed through his head. Leaving Missouri, this journey? "Why, and where would we go?"

Will faced him, hands resting against the countertop. "The two angels who were here informed me a transport ship went down at the hands of *The Journey.* They think we need to accompany Sky, Dash, and Ocean to Europe."

Vine needed a sugar fix and fast, because that just didn't make sense. "We're on a journey already, Will. Why would we need to interrupt this journey to start another one?"

"There's no reason at all."

"You're not making sense."

"It makes perfect sense. *The Journey* is part of our journey." Will forced a smile. "Ironic, isn't it?"

"I don't mean to complain or anything, but don't we sort of have enough going on? That warehouse you sent us to was

12

crawling with guys. Something's happening there ... or about to happen. We need to be here, Will. We need to watch Omega."

"True. More than you know."

"What's that supposed to mean?" Vine pulled the Ziploc bag open and scoped it for the candy he wanted.

"The angels also informed me that Omega is pulling in several new scientists. Experts in genetics. A whole new team, in fact."

"And those same winged dudes think we should leave?" Vine scoffed.

"Yes."

"You sure they're on our side?"

A deep frown cut across Will's face. "Yes."

"How can you be so positive?"

"Just before they arrived, heaven whispered and told me to prepare for an ocean voyage."

Vine sucked on a Sweet Tart. "I don't think it's such a good idea. In case you hadn't noticed, Mace and Raven are at each other's throats right now." He plopped into a kitchen chair. "Being trapped on a boat together is the last thing they need."

"It's exactly what they need," Will corrected. His gaze traveled to the window and the yard beyond. "Go tell the boys. I'll inform Nikki."

"Man, I'm not sure which close-quarters combination will be worse. No one's going to be happy."

Chapter
2

My parents are dead. My home has been emptied by the only man who is a link to my past, I'm leaving the only town I've ever known, and I'm still being hunted by demons.

Sometimes, Nikki went over those things, rotating them through her mind, holding on to what she knew to be her reality. Sometimes it helped. Sometimes it only made her feel crazy.

As if those little facts weren't enough to send a seventeen-year-old over the edge, Nikki was about to climb onto a boat and sail across the ocean with multiple beings, none of which were human. *Half-human counts*, she decided as she crossed the gangplank. Only one week ago she'd stood in the middle of a park with those beings—Will, Mace, and Raven—on one side, and her godfather, Damon Vessler, on the other, forcing her to make a choice. Had she made the right one? Damon had left so many messages on her cell, she finally stopped listening to them and buried the phone in her suitcase. The suitcase Will bought for her because she owned, well, almost nothing now.

Nikki glanced back at him. He nodded her onward to the belly of the boat. *An ocean voyage. Great.*

Her gaze found Will again and sought assurance. They shared a look for a brief moment, her eyes questioning, his reassuring—just like always. There'd been lots of those looks. Will kept a close eye on her and, like a mother hen, gently nudged her in whatever direction he deemed necessary at the moment. At *this* moment, that direction was an eighty-foot luxury sailboat. At least it wasn't some ancient fishing vessel with a layer of sunbaked fish guts on the deck. Nikki's stomach turned, reminding her not to think about things like dead sea creatures and their entrails.

"Don't be nervous, Nikki," Will said.

"Difficult not to be."

"Find peace in the storm." Will was always full of brilliant—albeit abstract—wisdom. "If you're so concerned with each next breath, how will you ever be able to look ahead?"

She frowned.

"One day soon, your ability as a Seer will be tested, and you'll be called on by the Throne. There is a purpose for you, Nikki. But as a Seer, evil is drawn to you. It's important that you begin to understand your gifting."

And this was supposed to help her feel better. *Try again, Will.* Suddenly, his encouraging look ticked her off. She'd spent time with him over the last several days and had discovered that she both loved and hated him in equal measures. No, that was unfair. She loved him. She hated this stinking situation she'd been thrown into. It was all *way* over the top of Mount Freak, and let's face it, she wasn't much of a climber.

She used to be. But that was before her parents were killed. Mace and Raven had been with her that night, and had made peace so she could concentrate on surviving the loss of her mom and dad. But in the last few days, the boys' relationship—rocky to begin with—had eroded as they all tried to avoid each other in the big house on Pine Boulevard.

Apprehension twisted her hands into fists. Now they'd all be on a boat together. For days. And though there would be others on the yacht too, she knew she'd run out of places to hide.

Nikki would keep her promise to Vine. She'd stay away from Mace and Raven, even though there was a gaping void inside her. The two boys had once filled that empty hole. But no more. She was strong without them. She just had to keep reminding herself.

She wished the female Halflings would arrive. Vegan and Winter always made her feel like less of a freak. Hmm. Funny that she, *the human*, should feel like a freak. But surrounded by winged heavenly creatures, how else could one feel?

Nikki'd never sailed before. Not a lot of opportunity to do that in southern Missouri. She stopped on deck to look up at the giant mast puncturing a cloudless blue sky. While she'd meant to look over the ship, her eyes were drawn to the blue expanse above. She'd flown with Will to the South Carolina launch site while the Halfling boys flew themselves—one advantage of having wings—and though the group left Missouri at the same time, she'd lost track of Mace, Raven, and Vine almost as quickly as they hit the air. Any chance Nikki got to see them in flight drew her full attention and caused that fluttery thing in her chest. Moth to a flame. Which, she knew, never ended well for the moth.

How often in a lifetime could someone watch three hot teenage boys sail through the air like eagles? Dipping and soaring on the thermal currents …

Off to one side of the mast, she spotted a seagull. It dove for the water, and Nikki couldn't stop herself from running to the edge of the rail to see what it was after. The bird took flight as she halted and grabbed the railing. A thin fish wiggled in the bird's beak.

"Likely to see dolphin later." The voice, heavy with an Australian accent, made her jump.

Nikki turned to find herself face-to-face with yet another hot teenage guy. His eyes were the blue of the sky and his skin was deeply tanned.

"What?" *Way to impress him with your witty repartee.*

He nodded toward the cobalt expanse of rolling waves beyond the marina. "If you think a seagull finding breakfast is entertaining, wait until we run across a family of dolphin. Babies and all, jumping right outta the water." His last word came out *wah-duh.* Accents were so cool. She ran across very few of them in Missouri—which made them even more captivating. Then the guy smiled. *Wow.* A row of perfect white teeth. He *had* to be a Halfling. That cute, that tall, and that ...

A voice from above interrupted her thoughts. "Not as entertaining as the school of amberjack we found last week."

Nikki squinted, head tilted back, and tried to get a fix on the voice. She gasped when she saw him suspended there. One hand wrapped around a loose rope while the other tied something. He wore long shorts, a white tank, and his bare feet dangled precariously a good thirty feet above her. His partially obstructed view of her must have caused him to push off the wooden post, because in a moment's time he was sailing in a high arc like an acrobat. Nikki lifted a hand to her head to block the sun's glare from her view of the boy who *flew through the air with the greatest of ease.*

He tipped an imaginary hat to her.

Nikki waved.

The Aussie said, "Yeah, I'd agree the amberjack were cool, but—"

"Everyone's seen dolphin, brother. It's not that big of a deal." Again, the boy swung past. He was as tan as the first, but with darker brown hair laced with golden streaks, the kind reserved for surfers and, apparently, acrobatic sailors.

He released the rope and plummeted to the ground. Nikki screamed, clamping her hand over her mouth. He landed at her feet in that felinelike way Halflings had, balls of his feet absorbing the impact and knees deeply bent. The boy straightened slowly and held a hand out in greeting.

When she stood there motionless, he plucked her hand from her mouth, inserted his palm into hers, and pumped several times, jolting her out of her shock.

"You must be Nikki? Right? Is it Nikki? We've met the other females. So you must be …"

"Nikki," the older one finished for him with an exhale. "Excuse my brother. He's had too much caffeine this morning."

Okay, there were so many things she needed to say. First of all, how could they be Halflings and be brothers? She didn't think that was possible. Will told her Halflings had only one offspring. And there was the *other* thing he'd said. Yes, she definitely needed to deal with that first. "Oh, I'm not a female."

His eyes blinked in an unspoken question, brows rising to peaks on his forehead.

She shook her head. "I mean I am, but I'm not a *female*."

He continued to hold her hand and glanced downward over her body. It was a quick look, but still it set her cheeks on fire.

"He's not great with the ladies," the older boy said, then

clamped his hands over theirs and broke the hold. "My name's Sky. It's great to meet you, Nikki."

An Aussie sky. I've always wanted to see one of those. "You too, Sky. I meant that I'm not a ..." Her words trailed. What if they weren't Halflings? Should she even say the word *Halfling*? Maybe she'd blow their cover. If, of course, there was a cover. She really should have questioned Will more about this trip. At least she wouldn't forget his name; Aussie Sky, eyes like this cloudless afternoon.

Sky's smile brightened. "You're not a Halfling. We get it. But you are a Seer, so forgive us for our excitement. We don't come in contact with a lot of Seers."

She nodded, hoping the bobbing of her head would somehow force the disjointed thoughts back in line. It didn't work.

"My brother here, the caffeine-induced jittery one, is Dash. You'll meet Ocean later. We're on a skeleton crew this trip since several of us got pretty banged up last voyage and are in the midplane. So don't be surprised if we expect you to earn your keep."

Nikki swallowed a lump that had lodged in her throat. "I don't want to hang from the rigging."

Sky and Dash shot a confused look to each other then laughed.

"Right." Which sounded like *roy-t.* "We'll find ground-level stuff for you. Maybe you can scrub the fish guts off the deck."

Nikki actually felt her face turn green.

Will stepped toward the group. "Dash, Sky. Good to see you two fit to go. I heard about your run-in."

Dash gestured to the mast. "Should have seen it, Will. I thought we were going down for sure. But we pulled out. Saved the crew aboard the titanium transport too."

Will turned to Nikki. "An illegal shipment of titanium was making its way to the States. It was to be used for wingcuffs."

"Wingcuffs?"

He nodded. "Titanium brackets that clamp around a Halfling's midsection."

Dash motioned around his ribcage. "Weakens us and makes flight impossible. The ship gave us a pretty good fight."

"What happened to it?"

"It's resting," Dash said.

"At the bottom of the ocean," Sky finished for him. "No loss of life, though. We're pretty careful about that."

With the whole "kill a human, spend eternity in hell" thing, she supposed all the Halflings were pretty careful about that. "But your crew was injured?"

"Yeah, all but the best." Dash rocked back on his heels.

"All but those in bed asleep, he means."

Nikki angled to see the owner of the deep voice. He was maybe an inch or two taller than Sky and Dash, but looked slightly older. Like the other two, his skin was gloriously darkened by the sunrays, and his eyes glinted with wisdom that seemed out of proportion with his age.

"Good to see you, Ocean," Will said, shaking his hand.

"Your bags arrived last night. We'll be provisioned and ready to leave by tomorrow morning, although it could be a bit rough as we've got some weather coming in. The boys?"

"They're on their way. Should be here shortly. But I haven't heard from Vegan, Winter, and Glimmer."

"They were here, but decided to go back to get something."

"Really?" Will's chin dropped, punctuating his intrigue. It was that *heavenly angel* thing he did.

Ocean chucked a nod toward the gangplank.

They all followed his gaze.

Poor Zero. He was being half dragged, half shoved by three females who looked tired of the game. He clutched a laptop to his chest, and his words were heated—though inaudible—as the four of them approached the boat.

"Oh, this is classic," Dash whispered.

Nikki gave him a questioning glance.

"Zero's afraid of the water."

Awww. The tall, thin, icy-eyed controller of the Halfling network looked as out of place as a tractor in a shopping mall. White knuckles gripped the railing as he mounted the steps that would carry him onto the ship. His other arm held the laptop even tighter. He said something and Glimmer rolled her eyes. Vegan spoke to him, and even from a distance Nikki recognized soothing words of encouragement.

Once his feet were firmly planted on the deck and he'd moved away from the railing in a kind of one-foot-forward shuffle, Zero stood in the center of the boat looking around. His eyes fell on Nikki. "Oh, *you're* here?"

So much for feeling sorry for him. She'd forgotten how acerbic he could be.

Glimmer flashed a quick smile that didn't reach her eyes.

Vegan and Winter both crossed the deck to Nikki and sort of trapped her in a surprising girl hug. She maintained her stoic position—motionless and wordless. She wasn't a big hugger.

Zero laughed. "Get used to the sisterhood, Nikki. It appears you've been inducted."

"So where are Mace and Raven?" Glimmer asked, seemingly ignoring Sky, Dash, and Ocean while her body language read her awareness of them and her golden eyes took in everything on the boat.

For some reason, her question irritated Nikki even more than the Vegan and Winter love fest. Why hadn't Glimmer asked about Mace, Raven, *and Vine*?

Because she wasn't interested in Vine. Mace and Raven … that was another story. It shouldn't bother Nikki. It shouldn't feel like fingernails along a chalkboard down her back. But it did. Scraping, screeching fingernails dragging along, until …

Until she imagined herself trapping that flirty girl in a headlock.

She could feel a scream of frustration building in her throat. Nikki swallowed, forcing it down like bitter medicine. This was not the way to start a voyage. Usually, when things got to her, she set out on her motorcycle and let wind and speed work its magic. Here she'd have to deal with Glimmer because there was no escape. Hello, it's a boat. She threw a longing look to land then to Zero, and understood why he clutched the laptop so tightly. If her bike was here, she'd be doing the same thing. And a motorcycle on a boat was about as much use as a laptop on the ocean. Zero caught her looking at him and sneered.

Nikki felt ensnared in a bad reality show. So this was to be her life for the next, oh, she had no idea how long. Maybe they could sell the show idea to MTV. Reality with a supernatural twist. It'd be a hit. She could see it now: Will acting fatherly; Sky, Dash, and Ocean sending her to clean fish muck; Winter and Vegan and their girly "Let's be best friends" squealing; Glimmer and her ice-dagger stares; Zero and his sneers; Vine and an unending supply of candy. Had she left anything out? Oh yeah, Mace and Raven. The real twist in the program.

It was going to be a long trip.

Chapter
3

Nikki stood on the deck of *The Journey* as the boys approached.

Vegan had ushered Zero into the depths of the boat, Glimmer was off somewhere—probably doing her nails or applying another layer of lip gloss—and the "crew" was doing all sorts of *shippish* things readying for departure or disembarking or deportment or whatever they called it. Nikki rested her head against a post, hands gripping the railing as she watched Mace, Raven, and Vine cross the marina lot. Even from a distance, she could see the thread of tension wound tightly around Mace. It seemed to intensify as he drew closer to the ship.

Vine walked between the two other boys and tried, unsuccessfully, to grab something from Raven. Nikki squinted and leaned over the railing to see what it was. A bag of candy dangled beneath Raven's fist. When Vine lunged for it, it was snatched from reach. Vine could fly. He could just launch himself at it. And maybe that's what he'd intended to do, until his eyes scanned the area and found too many people in close proximity. Raven waved a finger at him as if to say, "No."

The air carried the sound of their laughter to her. Boy games. So silly—and so desperately needed, she fought the urge to laugh as well. She was smiling, something she hadn't done much of in the past few days. And there'd been little laughter either.

Vine tried to engage Mace in the game, but he'd have none of it. Nikki watched as his spine straightened, his shoulders expanded, and a deep inhale lifted the muscles of his chest.

Her heart broke, and the steel-like barriers she'd worked hard to construct fell.

He was preparing to board. Preparing to see her in the close confines of a ship where they'd spend days on end.

When Vine tried one last time to pull Mace into the fun, Raven's interest quelled. He tossed the bag at Vine with such force, the younger boy had to jolt back to keep it from hitting him in the face. So this had been Vine's existence since her arrival. Trying to keep peace and keep the boys from killing each other. She'd been so busy avoiding life, she'd failed to notice. Poor Vine.

No wonder she'd found him that night on the back porch with tears in his eyes, his white-blond hair wrapped around his shoulders like a blanket and his knees drawn to his chest. The night she promised him she'd stay away from Mace and Raven.

"They made it. Good," Ocean said, stopping beside her. "You settle in okay, Nikki?"

She nodded, not bothering to look at him. Her eyes were glued to Mace. "Yes. I didn't bring that many clothes, so everything fit in the trunk under the bunk beds."

"Sorry you four girls have to share a cabin."

"It's fine." And even if it wasn't, did it matter? She was trapped on a boat with no way to cope, no sense of home, and no privacy. Why not add sharing a barracks-type room with girls she barely knew? One of which couldn't stand her, and the feeling was mutual.

"Nikki," Ocean said, his voice dropping, "there is a purpose to this voyage."

Okay, that drew her attention. She forced her hair from her face, where it had danced in her eyes, moving in tandem with dangling ropes, edges of sails, and everything else not fastened tightly to the boat.

"Will wouldn't have brought you on if he didn't have a good reason."

True enough. When she'd questioned Will about the heavenly angels and their visit, he changed the subject, saying the boat would be a fabulous place for her to get some training as a Seer. Whatever *that* meant.

Ocean gestured with one hand. "Look around you. Will, the boys, the females. Even Zero, who loathes the water."

Unruly strands smacked against her hand, fighting desperately to be released from her grip. She tried to hold them firm but felt her persistence slipping. She could no more hold her hair out of the wind than she could erase the destruction she'd caused. "But Will didn't know Zero was coming."

"Exactly. Which makes it that much more interesting."

Really? She was having a hard time finding it interesting. Irritating. Aggravating. Even terrifying. But interesting? No.

He planted his hands on his hips. "You're a Seer. What do you see?"

Her eyes slid to the gangplank. *Mace. And Raven. And a gulf of hatred that now separates the two.* "I don't see anything,

Ocean. I know you said you and Sky and Dash were anxious to meet me, but I'm going to be a huge disappointment. I didn't know I was doing it—seeing the other realm and all. I only see it when I draw. I'd always thought ideas were coming from my imagination until hell hounds actually arrived and chased me through the woods. When I questioned Will about it, he said my drawings have the ability to create a doorway for the supernatural. The hell hounds I first encountered crossed over because of me. So my being a Seer doesn't help anyone. It just creates more danger. For everyone."

"Well, that explains why Will wants you on the boat."

Nikki gathered her hair at her nape and tucked the bulk of it into her collar. "What do you mean?"

"Demons and hell hounds have been cast to the dry places. They crave water but aren't successful at finding it or navigating through it. A big body of water creates a lot of difficulty for them. There's nowhere for them to go if they leave their part of the midplane. It's fairly unlikely any would choose to land on the boat—they're weaker when they are out of the dry places. Plus, with all of us on here, it would be certain death."

"So it's safer to train here."

"For a time, but creatures from the pit are resourceful. Eventually, they will think of a way to attack."

"Great," she mumbled.

Ocean's warm blue eyes smiled down at her. One tanned hand left his hip and landed on her shoulder. "Try to relax. Maybe even enjoy the trip."

As Mace appeared on the deck with Vine behind him and Raven trailing them both, Nikki was sure that would be unlikely. Of all the things this trip would be, enjoyable seemed impossible.

26

Her stomach tightened, and she slipped behind a post when Ocean stepped forward to greet the boys. Tilting slightly, she peered around the edge of the wooden hideaway. Mace hadn't noticed her. He was busy greeting Ocean and introducing Vine. Then Sky made his way over from the helm, where he'd apparently been checking strange electronics with even stranger names like *Loran* and *Depth Finder*.

Sky, Dash, and Ocean had certainly been nice enough, and had made her feel welcomed. But as the group of six Halfling boys chatted about things like the trip and the weather, her eyes stayed trained on Mace. She hurt for him. For all he'd been through.

She'd been avoiding eye contact—any contact, for that matter—for so many days, she'd almost forgotten the planes of his smooth face. Strong but tempered with a gentleness that came as much from within as without. His jawline, his straight nose, and those full lips that had kissed her hands after they were burned in a laboratory fire …

As if he knew her thoughts, his tongue darted out and moistened his lips. He gave Sky a half smile after some comment about swabbing the deck. They were all laughing now in that good-natured way guys had, while she was a million miles away, tucked behind a wooden post. Her fingers began to ache. As she raised them to eye level, she realized she'd clamped them down, trying unsuccessfully to capture his touch and that electric sensation of his mouth gently kissing away her pain. She needed to force her thoughts in another direction, because she didn't know how much a heart could take.

Raven was there too, but her eyes remained on Mace, at least until she could stand it no more. It was almost unsettling to see such a large group of Halfling boys. Each tall, lean, their six-foot-plus frames and strong shoulders coated in long muscles. To outsiders, the boat could easily be the site of a photo shoot for some top designer's clothing line. But while human models needed to work hard to appear so perfect, Halflings couldn't help themselves. Flawless features. No brow waxing needed. Hair that fell perfectly into place. What one would expect from beings who are half angel.

Finally, Nikki chanced a look at Raven. He was staring right at her. She pulled back and sank beside the post, pressing her shoulder into the wood. But his face, his eyes, even the almost vulnerable expression were still there. In the dark, safe place behind her tightly closed lids, his image stayed fixed. And without even watching him, she knew his gaze had searched the ship for her while the others talked.

He always searched her out.

They'd been on the boat for only a few minutes, and already she felt emotionally stripped. Nikki judged the distance to the stairwell leading to the safety of her room. Could she make it without them noticing?

Will joined the group of boys, creating a sort of giant angel wall between her and the gathered crowd. Escaping might be possible. But when she heard the conversation, her feet froze and her body snapped to attention.

"Do you think they will find us?" Will said, concern in his voice.

"No. We turned the crew over to the Coast Guard five hundred miles from here. But Will—" Ocean's words were thick with apprehension. "The last time we sank one of their ships, they retaliated."

"How?"

"They bombed a hotel in Southern France."

"Why there?"

"To send a message. Our operation is based out of France. I have no idea how they found out, but we've avoided sinking other transports since. We certainly didn't mean to sink this last one."

"But since it happened, you think we should expect the same sort of retaliation."

"Afraid so."

"And now we're on the ship with you," Will said. "Interesting that the Throne would choose to send us. As well as a Seer."

Her? He must mean her, but she was of little use to anyone. *That* had been clearly established. Nikki bit her bottom lip. Sometimes she forgot that the world of men and angels—the world of evil and good—was as real as the disaster that was her life. Guilt for being so consumed with her own personal problems sifted through her system. If they—whoever *they* were—chose to retaliate, people's lives were at stake. And Ocean, with his wise manner, felt responsible for those lives.

It was time to stop playing the helpless victim. It wasn't like she could sit behind her post the entire voyage. She would cooperate with what Will wanted her to do—learn about her gifts—so this trip would end and Ocean and his crew could return to hunting bad guys or terrorists who make wingcuffs or whatever. All she needed to do was set her mutilated emotions aside. Nikki straightened her spine and stepped out.

Raven's midnight-blue gaze hit her, and a smile tilted one side of his face like he knew exactly what she intended to do. And without warning, she was trapped. It felt as if a cold, thick blanket pinned her.

Raven's smile widened ever so slowly while the other Halflings turned to see what he was looking at.

Why couldn't she move? Even her eyes felt pasted to him. She tried to open her mouth, but no words came out. What words did she have anyway? *I'm glued to the deck and can't even move my eyes?* Oh, she was a brave one.

To the right of Raven, Mace stood statue-still. There was a sound from him, something between a sigh and a cough of disgust. But for once her gaze wouldn't go there, even when she willed it to shift.

From the corner of her eye, she saw Mace look to Raven then to her, then back to Raven.

No, no, no, she wanted to scream. If only this force field would release her. She didn't even want to imagine what Mace thought of her behavior—her staring at Raven, him smiling back at her. Her mind worked; why couldn't her body obey? *It's not what you think. I'm not staring because of him, I'm just … Just what?*

When Mace spun from the group and headed toward the front of the ship, the spell finally broke. Her gaze traveled around the boys. Sky and Dash looked confused. Will wasn't making eye contact with her, but there was a distinct hint of disapproval, and Ocean and Vine both had pitiful little smiles of condolence—almost worse than the disapproval. Raven grinned victoriously. *That* burned her stomach. In a fury, she turned from the group and ran to the stairwell.

"Is this it?" Vegan asked her.

Nikki was stretched out on her bunk with hands locked behind her head, wondering if she could stay in the cabin for the entire "several day" journey. That was another thing Will had been sketchy on. He'd never answered her with specifics, just said, "Oh, several days."

To avoid Vegan's face, she glanced over and located the bow and quiver full of arrows standing in the corner of the cabin. She mentally traced the outline of smooth wood and once again wondered why the weapon was there.

Vegan rested a hand on Nikki's bunk. "Nikki, did you hear me?"

"I'm sorry. What?"

"Are these all the clothes you brought?"

They weren't just all the clothes she'd brought—they were all the clothes she owned. Her godfather, Damon Vessler, had emptied her house right after her parents' death The very thought of his lackeys rifling through her parents' things, going through her stuff—from her artwork to her underwear—tossing it all into boxes, and hauling it away …

She'd never forgive Damon. And yet he'd been calling her constantly to tell her all her belongings were safe and sound in the big basement of his house. That he'd moved it all to help her. And he wanted her to come back. *Come home*, he kept saying in the pleading, pathetic messages he left. *Home. Ha.* There was no home anymore.

"You need more things to wear," Vegan said, her bracelet-clad wrist flying into the air as if that decided things.

"Why?"

On cue, Winter and Glimmer entered the room.

Vegan reached into the trunk she'd slid from under Nikki's bunk and scooped up an armful of clothing. "This is all she has."

Glimmer, who usually reserved only dirty looks for Nikki, first gasped as if she'd witnessed something horrible then jumped up and down. "Yay, shopping! I've wanted to hit the mall since we got here. Plus, I already heard Ocean say we can't leave until morning, and there is no way I'm staying on this boat longer than I have to." Her short, golden-brown curls bobbed as she plucked a few clothing pieces from Vegan. She squinted as she scrutinized them. "Normally I'd say let's add to her summer collection. But, uh, I think we might just want to start from scratch."

Nikki leaned up on her elbows. Was there no sense of privacy here? Oh yeah, she'd already established that. At the same time, if anyone could help her wardrobe, it was these three. They always looked magazine perfect. But not like her best friend Krissy, a fashion princess whose clothing recommendations were uncomfortable and hard to move in. The Halflings looked great but still seemed like they could maintain a range of motion. Sort of important when your vocation includes hand-to-hand combat with demons and hell hounds.

"What style do you like, Nikki?" These were the most—and the friendliest—words Glimmer had ever spoken to her.

Who'd have thought she and Glimmer would bond over clothing? Nikki straightened. "Uh …"

Three sets of golden eyes waited.

Style of clothing? She didn't know. Now that she thought of it, Vegan, Winter, and Glimmer did seem to have their own styles. Glimmer wore a set of white shorts, a stretchy top with some gold rhinestones on it, a gold-trimmed cotton hoodie, and wedge sandals that made her legs go on forever.

Vegan wore faded jeans that were frayed at the bottom and a heathered forest-green long-sleeve T. Gold hoop earrings complimented the look.

Winter had on a black shirt and skinny capri jeans. Very

classy and elegant, almost like she could breeze into a country club and fit right in. And all three of the girls had those gold-and-silver bracelets that looked like sheets of thin metal twisted together. She'd not seen anything like them.

When she didn't answer, Winter spoke up. "Something comfortable, but cool."

Vegan dropped the clothes and turned her full attention to Nikki. The bundle fell to the floor and the bed, and a few garments even landed on the tiny end table separating her bed from Vegan's.

Before she could protest, Nikki was being dragged from her bunk. Winter made a little twirl with her finger in midair, and Nikki obliged by spinning in a slow circle, arms outstretched.

"Will's going to undoubtedly be working on her martial arts skills, so she needs to be able to move easily." Vegan's eyes were scrunched in thought.

So much concentration over textiles.

Winter nodded and swiped her dark hair over one shoulder. "Exactly. Definitely pants with a little spandex in them."

"Jeans," Glimmer said in a harsh tone that could end all conversation. "Nikki is a jeans girl. She won't wear anything else. We have to find stretchy jeans, probably skinny, because she has those great legs. And we can give her some real style by choosing gorgeous tops and shoes."

Nikki blinked her surprise and left her arms out, though the scrutiny was over. She was overwhelmed. First, that they were that interested in helping her determine a personal look, and second, by Glimmer's admission of great legs and the whole *jeans girl* thing.

Glimmer put her hands on her hips. "And no more flip-flops! You need proper sandals."

33

Winter lowered Nikki's arms with the gentle touch of her ice-cold hands. Nikki tried not to react, but goose bumps spread over her upper body.

Winter turned to the other girls. "Glimmer, we're on a boat. She's going to need flip-flops."

Glimmer brushed a hand through the air like a queen dismissing her lackluster court. "Fine, but only one pair and they aren't to wear every day. Got it?" She pointed a gold-polished fingernail at Nikki.

"Got it," she mumbled.

And with that, they were off to the mall to reinvent Nikki Youngblood.

Chapter 4

"I'm still a little unclear about the whole money thing," Nikki said as they left the mall. Her arms were aching after lugging heavy shopping bags from store to store.

"We have what we need, Nikki."

She raised her arms, bags dangling on each side. "I need these?"

"Desperately," Glimmer said.

Winter slid a couple of bags from one of Nikki's arms. "We serve the Throne. The Throne is hardly broke."

Nikki stopped in the middle of the parking lot. "It's just weird, you know? Think about it. You serve the Creator of everything, and he makes sure to give you shopping money. Doesn't that sound a little strange?"

Each girl shrugged.

"No," Vegan said. "Sounds like normal life."

"There's nothing normal about the life you all lead."

Winter slipped a couple more bags off Nikki's arm and

handed them to a reluctant Glimmer. "The Creator chose to take us in. And though we don't know our eternal fate, we do know he's given us all the tools we need to live victoriously now."

"But you don't know your future? How can you stand it? I mean, for most humans the whole idea of eternity—eternal life—is pretty abstract. But for you …"

"You have to know the nature of the one you serve. We have no promise of tomorrow. But we know the character of the One. Our ability to do what we do is rooted in our faith in him."

Nikki looked down. Strappy sandals encased her feet. She wiggled her toes. "I've never had faith in anything except what is tangible. I doubt I ever will."

Vegan took the last of Nikki's purchases, leaving her hands free to rub the creases on her arms. "You will."

"I don't think the Throne will have much tolerance for me. I've made a huge mess of things so far."

Awkward silence. They all knew she was referring to Mace and Raven.

Glimmer pointed across the parking lot. "Let's go bowling."

Vegan turned to her. "Did you just say bowling? That was random."

"We can't, Glimmer." Winter looked at her watch. "Will is expecting us."

"Not for another hour or so. Come on. This is our last night on solid ground for who knows how long."

Vegan smiled, nodded, and waited for Winter to decide. After a long pause, Winter headed toward the bowling alley. "Fine," she sighed. "Do you think we should let Will know?"

"No," Glimmer replied. "He already told us to keep Nikki close. We're doing that."

He'd also reminded them that because she was a Seer, evil

was drawn to her. Just what she needed to feel comfortable and safe.

Five minutes later, they were standing at the counter inside the bowling alley. "I've got two lanes available at the far end," the attendant said, pointing to one side. "Men's league takes most of the other lanes." He motioned behind him. Yep, the place was brimming with guys.

Winter pulled out her money and paid for their shoes. All three of the Halfling girls chose sixteen-pound balls. Glimmer was frustrated because all of the heavier ones had large holes to match. "What is with this? Does everyone have fingers this fat?"

"You can use my ball," Vegan said, picking up a brightly colored green, brown, and neon orange globe.

"Uh, no thanks. It's ugly."

Vegan feigned shock and cradled the ball against her chest. "It's not ugly. It unique."

"Uniquely ugly," Glimmer said.

As soon as they started playing, Nikki noticed the amount of attention the Halfings had drawn from the men's league. In all honesty, Nikki'd never seen a girl lob a bowling ball the way these three could either. A few of the men made comments as they passed to go to the restroom. Without so much as a word, the girls deliberately—Nikki was sure it was deliberate—started getting fewer and fewer strikes.

Nikki thought back to the bow and arrows resting in the corner of their cabin. "Glimmer, while we were shopping, Winter told me the bow and arrow is yours."

"Yes?"

"I just … I've never seen it before. Is it new?"

Glimmer's chin dropped a degree. "Uh, no. It's not new. I've had it with me all along."

"What?"

Winter leaned over and dropped her voice to a whisper. "Nikki, Glimmer had them on her back when you first met us at the guys' Victorian house."

Nikki was sure she would have remembered that. "I didn't see anything."

Winter smiled. "But you saw it in our cabin? That's good."

"Or crazy," Nikki said.

Glimmer reached over her shoulder as if pulling something from a backpack. "Hold out your hands."

Nikki obeyed and watched as Glimmer's fingers clasped around nothing but air. She rested her hands over Nikki's, then released the grip, and Nikki felt something drop into her grasp. Shocked, Nikki stared down at the arrow. "Where'd it come from?"

Glimmer's warm fingers brushed hers as she took the arrow back and rested it on her shoulder. "They're a spiritual gift. Like our wings, so they aren't visible unless you look through the eyes of your spirit. Oops, my turn." Glimmer hopped up and headed to the lane to get her ball.

Nikki pulled in a breath and looked hard; crisscrossing Glimmer's back was the bow and a quiver full of arrows.

She was the only Halfling who carried a weapon—at least as far as Nikki knew. Glimmer lined up to throw her bowling ball—a plain gray one she'd found on the last rack of choices. Arms locked in place, eyes zeroed in on the target. Nikki'd never seen Glimmer shoot her bow, but sensed she must be a deadly force.

A shiver ran the length of Nikki's spine. Just before releasing the ball, Glimmer glanced to her left toward the men's league and all those eyes watching her with interest. She huffed out a sigh and tossed the ball half-heartedly at the pins.

Thwack. Two pins remained.

She dropped onto the seat beside Winter. "I'm bored with this. Let's go home."

"We're in the middle of a game, Glimmer. Besides, bowling was your idea."

Glimmer rolled her large, golden eyes. "We're not in the middle of a game. We're just trying not to draw attention."

"At least I have a shot at winning now," Nikki added. Huh. Being pinned by three female stares was pretty unpleasant. *Okay then*. She faked a yawn. "Actually, I'm kind of tired myself. I wouldn't mind leaving."

Glimmer flashed a quick, appreciative smile. It was slight, barely a quirking of the cheeks, but it was nice to get that look rather than the nasty ones she was used to.

Vegan shrugged. "Fine with me."

Winter nodded. "Okay, let's go back and torture Nikki. We'll make her try on all her outfits."

A few minutes later, they were making their way to the marina with packages in tow. No talking, no chatter. It seemed the bowling alley—or, specifically, having to stop the real competition so they'd seem "normal"—had stolen the night's joy. Which Nikki hated, because she'd actually had a good time at the mall, being ordered around by three girls determined to turn her into Cool and Comfortable Barbie instead of the Overdressed and Awkward version Krissy always seemed to create.

They rounded the corner and entered the marina parking lot. Lights twinkled on the water, where boats of varying size rose and fell with the gentle swells. The sound of waves breaking against wood filled her ears. Nikki paused. Beyond the marina a dark, rippled world stretched forever. A new world, one she'd never experienced. "Wow," she mumbled.

Her companions stopped and glanced back at her. "What's wrong?" Winter said.

Nikki brushed a hand through the air. "It's beautiful. I'll fall asleep tonight being rocked by the ocean."

"A bit overwhelmed, are we?" Winter smiled. The others remained silent, taking in the marina and the variety of motor- and sailboats.

Am I overwhelmed? After a few moments' thought, Nikki shook her head. "No. Teenagers with wings are overwhelming. Being chased by hell hounds is overwhelming. Finding your name in a computer at a laboratory that may well be trying to bring about the end of the world, now that's—"

"Overwhelming," all three girls answered.

"This is …" Masts pointed to the sky as if directing attention to the blanket of stars above. If she had a canvas, she could capture it in paint. "Magical."

They stayed quiet for several moments, letting the coastal breeze lift their hair and travel over their skin. Nikki closed her eyes and tilted her head back, drawing salty air into her lungs. The smells of the ocean seemed even more intense, but it only added to her pleasure. For the first time since she'd arrived, the idea of enjoying this journey seemed possible.

Someone was talking; an intrusive voice laced with anger and a complete disruption to the moment. Nikki opened her eyes to find Mace stomping toward them. Vine and Zero were on his heels, and Raven brought up the rear, moving with none of the others' intensity.

Mace stopped dead at her feet. "What were you doing?"

Vegan's hand fell on Nikki's arm as if to pull her from the

trajectory of Mace's words. As she did, Winter stepped between Nikki and Mace, almost protectively. "She was with us."

The challenge was evident, and Nikki saw the slow burn in Mace's eyes as they narrowed. His hands were fisted, his lips a tight line, and he looked about ready to explode. "Nikki is our charge." He took a step closer and started to reach, but Vegan closed the space between them, stepping in front of Nikki before saying, "And she is just as safe with us as she is with you."

"No, she's not." The words were a growl from deep in Mace's throat.

Glimmer stepped between them as well, creating a wall to keep Mace at bay. "Why not? Because we're girls?"

Mace turned his attention to her. "It has nothing to do with that. She's safest with us because she's our responsibility."

"Then where were you when we decided to leave?" Glimmer cocked her hip and her head. "I didn't see you rushing to offer to take Nikki shopping. In fact, you haven't even said a word to her since you got on the boat."

Glimmer was right. He hadn't talked to Nikki. He also knew he couldn't continue avoiding her. And that recognition must have shown on his face, because Glimmer continued her irritating rant. "Some protector you are. Nikki didn't even have enough clothing to be on a boat for a few days, and what do you do? Oh, that's right—nothing. You're too busy with the guys to even notice what she needs. Don't get mad at us for doing your job when you dropped the ball." She shoved an index finger into his chest hard enough that he was forced back a step.

His eyes left Glimmer and found Nikki tucked behind the wall of females, staring at the ground. Mace's throat began to ache. He should apologize, say he's sorry to all of them, especially Nikki. He'd done nothing for her since he'd arrived—except make her feel like more of an outcast than she probably already did.

He started to open his mouth, but the quick jolt of Nikki's head stopped him.

She swallowed and met him eye to eye as one arm rested on Glimmer's shoulder and the other on Winter's. "It's okay." But it wasn't. She was fighting every instinct within her in order not to yell at him. The evidence skated across her features and was replaced by a determination he could only admire. "We shouldn't fight. We have to work together."

The admission knocked a bit of the fight out of all of them.

Nikki chewed on her bottom lip and looked away. Oh, dear Lord, she was trying not to cry. Mace felt like scum.

She forced a small smile. "I should have given the boys a chance to go with us. I'm sorry, Mace." She swallowed what must be gall in her throat. Her voice cracked on the last word, destroying him, but she soldiered on. "Vine, Raven, I should have told you. Forgive me?"

Mace wanted to sink into the sand and shells of the parking lot and disappear. Little pains shot through his chest. She was taking the hit herself to keep peace among the Halflings. And it worked. The evidence of shame was glaring. Uncomfortable glances, dropped heads, tinges of red across cheeks. None more so than him. He'd just been so angry when Will told him they'd gone.

But had he given her any choice, really? Who wants to wake a sleeping bear?

When he realized she was walking away, he called, "Nikki."

But she held a hand in the air to silence him. "Don't." Bitterness coated the word. Head high, her feet carried her to her new home while four males and three females seemed at a loss. Of all of them, Nikki'd been the only one to act like an adult. If Mace's job was tough before, now it had just become impossible.

Nikki stood in the galley shortly after sunrise. Ocean had instructed her to work there for the morning—which really irritated her because she'd wanted to watch the boat pull away from land. Everybody works on this vessel, he'd reminded her.

Hands on hips, she glanced at the number of boxes that needed to be stored. Why her? She didn't have a clue where food should go in a floating kitchen. After opening a cupboard— after several unsuccessful searches elsewhere—she got her answer. Each tightly closed door housed specific provisions, and each section was labeled with black marker. "This won't be too hard," she said quietly, and started opening drawers and the yet-unsearched cupboards to familiarize herself.

Ocean had said he'd send someone to help as soon as they left the dock. It couldn't be too soon; there were a million boxes.

"What are you doing?"

She was so into her work, the voice made her jump. *Mace's* voice. Again.

She turned to face him. Standing just inside the galley doorway, he wore a white tank and loose jean shorts. He looked amazing. His feet were bare, and the wind had fixed his hair into its usual style, but messed up, like fingers had roamed through it repeatedly. For a moment she let herself imagine her own hands doing the job. *Whoa, there.*

Heat rose to her cheeks, but he wasn't looking at her. He was staring in awe at the kitchen. She wondered why—it seemed dark and cramped to her. Her eyes trailed the space. Surely he wasn't impressed with what she'd accomplished so far. Cabinets, cupboards, and drawers held only a minimum of supplies—left over from the last trip, she supposed. "I really haven't done anything yet."

"Nikki, we're about to pull away from the dock." His words were stiff and tinged with a bit of panic.

"I know, and I wish I didn't have to miss it."

His eyes widened and he headed straight for her, voice rising. "We're about to *pull away* from the dock."

Then it registered. Horror stricken, her gaze bounced around the kitchen again, seeing not supplies, but future flying projectiles. "Oh no!" She lunged toward the nearest counter and began slamming doors—some of which popped back open. She used her knees, feet, and even rear end to close drawers and cupboards.

Mace started on the other side and must have been doing better than her, judging by the slams she heard. Hearing the motor rise, they flew into high gear. And by the time they felt the first surge of movement, the only cabinet left open was across the kitchen from both of them. To her horror, it was filled with cups and glasses.

Mace's eyes met hers as the motor rose again and both of them were thrown forward. She pushed off the counter as the boat lurched back and forth, and the cups rose to teeter on their edges then fell into place. She jumped into action, Mace at her side. His outstretched hands filled her vision. *We'll make it*, she thought. But the boat lunged again and sent the jostled cups out in a flurry toward them.

Both were grabbing and reaching like mad as glass after glass and mug after mug flew like buckshot toward them. Arms full, Nikki used her head to slam the door shut.

A long pause of relief. An exhale of all that air. Eyes returning to normal size. And then … laughter. First it bubbled from Mace, then from her. They both sank to the floor, breathless and loaded down with unbroken cups. "That was close," Mace said and started setting his armload down in a neat row on the floor. He began a second row with hers.

"Good thing you came along when you did."

He chuckled.

And it warmed her from the inside out. It was so good to hear a chuckle, a laugh, anything from him that represented joy instead of pain.

"Ocean would have killed us!"

"Us?" He gave her a sidelong glance. "This was all your doing."

She smiled over at him. "I never would have admitted it."

He winked and her heart stuttered.

"Well, he shouldn't have sent you down here alone, anyway. He hadn't meant to. Zero was supposed to be here, but he's pouting in his cabin."

"Why?" Though she was thankful she didn't have to work with Zero.

"Ocean wouldn't let him bring a case of juice boxes onboard. Ocean told him there wasn't room. Zero flipped."

"Poor Zero." How she could go from disliking him to feeling sorry for him so quickly amazed her. But Zero was like a little kid—a naughty little kid with killer computer skills, but still. "Juice boxes are his lifeblood. I can't imagine him taking that too well."

"He didn't. In fact, he threatened mutiny when Ocean started questioning him about the case of PopTarts."

Her hand flew to her face. "No. Ocean didn't take the PopTarts, did he?"

"No, but he told Zero mutiny was punishable by death and trying to sneak juice drinks past the captain could end in keelhauling."

"What's that?" Before he could answer, Nikki realized she and Mace were having an actual conversation that wasn't filled with tension.

There was a *little* tension, she had to admit, but not the bad kind. Sitting there, side by side on the floor, legs stretched out before them, she could feel some of the old spark. They both wore shorts, his long, hers a shorter pair Glimmer had chosen for her at the mall. She'd put on her wedge sandals—again, Glimmer's pick, but they were actually comfy and cute and really did highlight the lean muscles in her calves and thighs. When she glanced at Mace, she saw he'd noticed.

He looked up, nervously. "Sorry. You don't usually wear sandals. They're, um … They look … Are they new?"

He likes them. A warm pool emptied into her stomach. She refused the warning voice that told her he shouldn't like them and she really shouldn't feel all mushy inside because he did. Nothing had changed. He was still a Halfling and she was still a human and that made this all wrong. "I got them at the mall. Glimmer picked them out."

"She sure jumped to your defense last night."

The whole nasty scene flooded her mind. "I'm sorry about that, Mace. It seems like everything I do ends in a war."

He scooted close enough that his arm and hers rested beside one another. When she breathed in deeply, they touched. She angled toward him so they touched on every breath.

"Don't apologize for people wanting to fight for you, Nikki. You're important. More than you know. We all acted like spoiled babies—me especially. You were the one who deserved an apology."

"Did you really think I was in danger?"

Mace's head fell back to rest on the kitchen cupboard. He breathed in and out, his eyes fixed on the galley ceiling. "No. Do you mind if I explain something to you?"

So formal. But that was Mace.

"I've always tried to do the right thing."

This, she knew.

"I've never been impulsive. I think things through. But with you, I tend to let my emotions run me. And sometimes, they make a mess. Does that make sense?"

It did, and as Nikki pondered it she realized Mace was a mystery. She'd thought he was the easy one to figure out, but he wasn't. He was the loose cannon. Whereas Raven could be counted on to do the impetuous thing. Every time.

His lungs filled slowly as if he were trying to control every sensation, both internally and externally. He smelled like the air outside, fresh and salty. She'd missed the sound of his voice, the soothing vibration of his words. He said something she couldn't quite make out. "What?" she asked, feeling as though she really needed to hear whatever he'd uttered.

"I was upset because you'd left and I wasn't with you. I was jealous, Nikki."

Slam! She crashed against the kitchen wall just as hard as if she'd been physically hit. What it meant for her, for him, for *them*, she wasn't sure. But he'd wanted to be with her. Even after that awkward episode on the deck with Raven. Even after telling him on homecoming night she didn't want to be with him. The same night her parents died.

This was bad. And good. And too much to figure out right now because Mace was leaning ...

He scooted a fraction closer so his head tilted toward her, and all that salty scent came rushing at her. Closer and closer.

Off in the distance, a door opened and closed, but Nikki barely heard it. Mace's cerulean eyes were locked on her and she couldn't breathe.

The warmth of his fingers intertwined with hers. A quiver ran up her arm, setting her skin ablaze.

"Well, Captain will be pleased to know you two have rearranged the cups."

That now irritating voice, thick with an Australian accent, interrupted her blissful moment. She refused to drag her eyes from Mace.

"Not sayin' I'd have chosen the galley floor for storage, but I never claimed to understand Yanks," Sky said, his casual tone laced with humor.

Mace let out a long, surrendering sigh and rose from the floor, leaving a cold void beside her.

"It was Nikki's idea," he teased and threw a wink down to her. "Never argue with a woman about a kitchen. You'll lose every time."

Nikki blinked up at him. *What just happened?*

Sky dusted his hands together. "Well, if what I just saw was punishment, sign me up."

Ugh. Nikki felt nauseated. Maybe it was being the object of this discussion, or maybe it was the movement of the boat.

48

Either way, she needed air. The kitchen that only moments ago was like an oasis of comfort suddenly became a stuffy, oxygen-depleted closet.

"You look green," Sky said, concern and a bit of amusement twinkling in his eyes. "Come on, let's take her above."

Sky and Mace each offered her a hand up, and together they headed toward the stairwell. "Should I stay down here and finish the job? Ocean will expect it to be done," Mace said.

"Nah. What can he do? Fire you for insubordination? The supplies will keep. Everyone should get to watch land shrink away."

Mace stopped. "Still, Ocean is counting on us. I'll stay down here and keep working. Take care of her, Sky?"

Nikki's stomach churned. "I don't feel well."

Sky hurried her along. "Nikki, it's time for you to learn about one of my favorite sailor's traditions."

"What's that?" she said.

"Introducing the contents of your stomach to the sea."

Chapter
5

She hadn't vomited. Yet. But at least the wedge sandals lifted her to the perfect height to hang her upper body over the railing. Being above deck helped ease her stomach, however, as did feeling the wind rush through her hair, drying the sweat on her temples. She'd never known herself to be seasick. But she'd never been on the ocean in a sailing yacht, either.

"Are you going to be this antisocial for the entire trip?" Raven asked, leaning over the railing to stare down at the water with her.

"Not in the mood for your sarcasm right now, Raven." The boat rolled over waves as they made their way through a pass. Sky had warned her it would be a bumpy ride until they cleared the jetties. White peaks smacked the side of the boat like tiny explosive water bombs. Every now and then, one would reach high enough to coat her face in a spray of seawater. It felt amazing.

"Just for you, I'll try to resist all cynicism."

He threw her a patronizing glance before returning to his

study of the water below. Oh, she hated that look. Not the patronizing one—the hidden one, the one only she seemed to see. The extreme longing deep in his dark-blue gaze. It was that bottomless yearning that made Raven who he was. And on many levels what made him hard for her to resist, because she shared his profound need, felt its intensity. Simply put, she lived it. It's what made them different from everyone else.

And what made them the same.

Nikki wasn't sure if her stomach was completely settled or if this new sensation was masking its upset. Raven was the only one she'd met who mirrored her own tortured soul. Two misfits, two outcasts, one common quality: misery.

He leaned closer. Too close, but that was part of Raven as well. "I've been worried about you."

She barely heard the words he whispered against her hair. Nikki closed her eyes and slid a few inches away. Why couldn't he leave her alone? Why couldn't he stop looking at her with those eyes that read through her cover stories and peered straight into her soul? He saw the confusion, the deception. Saw that she was a contradiction of life.

Within moments his hand was on her back, warming a spot in the center. *And why can't he maintain his infuriatingly moody personality when I need him to?* Instead, he changed, chameleon style, to exactly what she needed—and exactly what she didn't want.

The hand gently slid up and down her back.

Nikki strained against it, but the last time he'd reached out to her like that—after she'd slayed the hell hound that killed her dog, Bo—flooded her mind. She'd left Mace heartbroken at the football field hours before, essentially telling him she'd chosen Raven.

She hadn't. The choice had been meant to protect them both: Mace's soul was on the line and she couldn't bear to be the cause of its ruin. She and Mace had tried unsuccessfully to break things off before, but every scenario ended in … well, like the incident in the galley. So she'd done the only reasonable—albeit deceitful—thing she could. She led him to believe she loved someone else.

It wasn't completely a lie. She really did love Raven, but it was different. At the time, she believed Raven was safe. He'd spent plenty of time helping earth girls fall for him, and he knew how to walk away unscathed. She wouldn't be the cause of his destruction. She'd just be another girl to add to his list. *And yet.*

He'd held her gently, comforting her after she killed the hell hound. He'd stroked her hair and her back while she cried. His voice had closed out all the pain, and she remembered the sensation as his soft words feathered against her cheek and ear.

And she remembered the realization he was praying. For her.

That revelation had rocked her. Had he prayed like that before? Did he do it often?

The sails grabbed the wind, and the rustle knocked her back into the present. She straightened her spine and faced Raven. "I need time. I'm still trying to deal with what happened to my parents. Please don't ask me to sort out my feelings for you and Mace on top of that."

The long strands of his dark blond hair flew around his forehead and slammed against his cheeks. A hint of a smile appeared, but only for a second. His eyes trailed her face, moving methodically over her features. "I can give you time." An entire conversation silently passed between them.

"Will you?" she said, finally.

"As much as you want. No matter how long you take, the outcome will be the same. You and I were destined to be together, Nikki. Eventually, you'll realize that like I have and stop running."

Running. She'd like to run. But girls on boats had little room to run, and humans who fell in love with Halflings had few choices. None of which led to a happy ending.

Time, she could use. And maybe a solution would present itself before she destroyed her guardian angel.

Both of them.

Will worked with Nikki on her martial arts skills for the remainder of the morning. She was getting her sea legs, and Ocean had instructed her to watch the horizon whenever possible to lessen the queasiness. It seemed to be working, but the coastal sun was warmer than she was used to, and by noon she'd worked up a sweat. General sailing labor was going on around her. They worked the boat in shifts: girls in the galley, boys on the deck, and vice versa. Nikki'd slid out of her sandals when Will called her over. Good thing; the movement of the boat coupled with her sweat and the heel of her shoes could have been a deadly combination.

"Are you ready to begin?" Will asked. He didn't seem to be sweating at all. An angel thing, she guessed.

"Begin what? You've been working with me for the last two hours." He'd asked to see some of her blocks and strikes, and had recognized the style immediately, even tweaking her form. Sensei Coble would be proud.

"It's time to begin the most important lesson you will ever learn."

"Ever, huh?" She brushed her arm across a slick forehead. "That's a pretty long time."

"I walked the earth when only wood and mud-fashioned houses existed. I've seen her lands crumble into the sea while others emerged from the depths. I've witnessed every war and every victory there has been, and I can tell you, without a doubt, this is the most important lesson you will have the privilege to learn. Ever."

Wow. What was it about angels and the monologues? It was staggering, though. To think Will, a heavenly angel and guardian to the male Halflings, had roamed the earth for all of recorded time. And to do that without ever dropping a bit of sweat—go figure. The Halflings were capable of sweating, at least. Nikki had to corral her concentration to keep from glancing behind her, where Mace and Raven worked with their shirts off. *Really nice view out here on the ocean.*

"Are you ready?" Will said.

It seemed too good an opportunity to pass up. "May I ask a question first?"

"Certainly." He gestured with the palm of his massive hand. Her eyes narrowed. "Remember, a heavenly angel can't lie."

His eyes narrowed in response to hers, and he crossed his arms over his chest. "It's hardly necessary to remind me. Lying isn't a part of my makeup. Go ahead."

"Why are we on this boat? Besides the heavenly angels showing up and telling you we needed to come."

"You mean the conversation you were listening to?"

"Uh, yeah."

"You need—"

"And don't say I need training. I know that's part of it, but there's more."

"Your perception is growing. Good." His intake of air seemed to suck the oxygen from everywhere around her—quite a feat when you're continually slammed by fresh gusts of wind. Will's gaze traveled across the deck, and Nikki was sure he was going to refuse to answer. But then he began to smile, and she glanced behind her to see what he was smiling at.

Mace and Raven were at the far end of the boat, one on one side of a horizontal post, one on the other. They moved in tandem over some giant lever, while their muscles flexed and released. A sheen of sweat covered their skin.

"My Lost Boys needed to learn how to work as a team again."

His Lost Boys. His … sons. So that was it. The confines of a ship would bridge the gulf between Mace and Raven. It made perfect sense, really. And Will's plan seemed to be working. "Pretty smart, aren't you?" Nikki said, her attention divvied between the boys and Will's pride as he watched them.

"I'm experienced, but that should never be confused with natural intelligence."

"Whatever. Sounds like splitting hairs to me." Nikki rocked back on her heels. "You're without a doubt one of the best fathers I've ever known."

Will's eyes darted to hers, his face falling into concern.

"What?" She wanted to step back, but with the railing so close there was nowhere to go.

"I'm not their father," Will said, and it seemed as though speaking the words was almost … painful.

She gestured with an upturned palm. "I know you're not their real father, but as *you* know from all your time on earth, an adoptive dad can be much more of a father than a biological one."

Wide fingers fidgeting, shoulders jerking slightly, a tiny head shake. It was weird to see a heavenly angel so … out of sorts. But really, if Will didn't think of himself as the Halflings' father, well … That was it. He did. She knew he did. "Look, you don't have to admit anything to me."

He scratched his head, nervous tension flying off his body like showering sparks ready to combust. "There's nothing to admit. I'm a caregiver. The boys are in my charge. I am commissioned to do my best by them."

Nikki laughed right out loud. She hadn't meant to, but all that energy seemed to gather around her, and when she breathed it in, it took over. "I'm sorry, Will," she said, swiping a tear. "I know they aren't your sons. They aren't even brothers." Neither were Sky, Ocean, and Dash, she'd discovered. Though that's what the three called each other. In fact, they called Raven, Mace, and Vine *brother* as well. No one was safe from the title. On occasion even she'd been referred to as brother by Dash. Nikki had given him a playful-but-dirty look the second time. He'd mumbled that she'd been the one to say she wasn't a female.

"Humor is a great tension reliever, so I'm told. But make no mistake, Nikki. The boys and their ability to work together is only one small part of this journey. Much of what will happen in the next several days holds you as the central piece. This is no game."

And just like that, all the joy dissolved.

Will moved away from her, maybe to give her time to absorb. Instead, she shook it off and followed him to the front of the boat, where he wrapped his hands tightly around the railing.

"Where are we headed?" she asked. The blue expanse of ocean stretched beyond forever. "Where *is* this voyage taking us?" There was a new gravity to her tone, but she didn't care. Life was nothing if not volatile.

Her question pulled Will's attention from the water. "France. We'll pull into port there then make our way to Viennesse."

"But you don't think this voyage across the sea will be without struggle, do you? Will, what do you think is going to happen?"

"I don't know," he admitted. "It was important to the Throne that we be on the boat. Now that we are, I only sense that we should be … ready. You, especially."

He really didn't need to drive that point home any more. Maybe a change of subject would be best. "You said Viennesse. That's your ancestral home, right?"

"Not mine. The Halflings'."

Ah, yes—as a full angel, Will's true home was heaven. Except not anymore. He'd been demoted. One day, she'd need to ask him about that. "Do Halflings split their time between an earthly ancestral home and the midplane, except when they're on a journey?"

He nodded.

"Are there houses in the midplane?"

"Not as you know them. It's similar to earth, but being there … well, a human would liken it to camping."

"Only without the bugs?"

He faced her. "Shall we get back to your lesson, or are you going to badger me with inquiries all day?"

"No, you're off the hook. Let's get to this ever-so-important lesson. What is it, exactly?"

Will cupped his hands as if cradling a beach ball. His brow tilted into a frown, creasing his smooth forehead, and his eyes closed tightly. Pure energy seemed to cluster about him like metal shavings to a magnet, and Nikki stepped back until she bumped against a pole. Will's hands tightened slowly until a silvery ball took shape between his cupped fingers. It became more concentrated as he tightened his grip. When he stopped, a round, silvery globe with tiny blue lights trailing inside it rested on his upturned hand.

Her mouth hung open and was quickly dried by the sea air. "What is that?" Intrigue forced her closer. A ball. A silvery ball appeared out of absolutely nothing.

"It's faith."

As soon as he said it, Nikki knew she was in trouble. She had faith in what was tangible. And this was not only intangible, it was untouchable. When she reached for it, her hand passed right through.

If this was the great lesson she needed to learn, she was certainly going to be a huge disappointment. Again.

"Nikki, come on over," Winter hollered across the deck. "Sky is briefing us on what they know about Omega Corporation."

Thank you, Winter! Raven wanted to say. He'd wanted to call Nikki over to the group for the last several minutes, but knew she'd reject the offer if it came from him.

She'd avoided the pack of Halflings sitting in a circle near the center of the boat, choosing instead to scrub a clean railing and oil a glistening teakwood deck. Will's lesson had left her intrigued, amazed, and determined—and all of those things left Raven unable to concentrate on the conversation. It didn't help that sweat clung to the edges of Nikki's hairline, making his fingers itch to touch the moist strands and brush them from her face.

Every now and then those light brown eyes of hers would meander to the small globe of faith Will had left floating above the railing at the front of the ship. Her eyes would narrow and that methodical mind of hers he loved would go to work.

She crossed the deck at Winter's words, and Raven caught a blast of Nikki's scent—life and promise. He breathed her essence, filling his lungs again and again. Man, she looked good with her long hair loose and scattered by the breeze, skin glowing in response to the sun, and her face alive. Really alive. Like the day she took him to Arkansas on the back of her motorcycle. Nikki was freedom. Freedom needed to be protected. Nurtured, even. And he was up to the task. One thing he wouldn't do was let Mace put her in a cage. Because Nikki—brave as she was, the girl who watched as four hell hounds attacked her—was also scared to death when it came to heart stuff. He'd be careful, something that didn't come to him naturally. But he would win—something that *did* come to him naturally.

"Have a seat, Freedom," he said, sliding a couple inches toward Glimmer. The circle of Halflings looked over at him, but several bodies scooted to make room for Nikki.

"Freedom?" Nikki echoed, wrinkling her nose.

"Yeah. New nickname for you."

She shot him a biting look and sat on the other side of Glimmer, forcing the whole group to shift again.

But just before she blinked away her frustration, Raven saw a moment of approval splash across her face.

Unintended, no doubt. But still. Her scent shifted his direction when the wind changed. He tried not to look obvious as he took it in. Like life, like everything he should be entitled to. Like everything he would one day have. He'd give her time. But it wouldn't hurt to hurry things along every now and then.

59

"Ocean and the crew sunk two boats loaded with titanium. What we didn't know is Ocean thinks they are connected to Omega Corporation," Mace said. He'd acted nonchalant during the exchange between Raven and Nikki, but a note of irritation threaded his words. Good.

Nikki's brow furrowed. "So, Omega is studying electromagnetic pulses, they are possibly doing genetic testing, and now this? Oh yeah, and my name was on one of their computers."

Vegan crossed her legs and stretched back until her weight rested on her palms. "Not *possibly* doing genetic testing, Nikki. They're bringing a whole new batch of genetic scientists. And don't forget, we've seen the horses at the laboratory in Arkansas. No normal horses look like that. So, we have proof of what they've done. Just no information on what they plan. Or how, and if, you're involved."

"Dr. Richmond might know," Nikki said.

Raven tried to drag his attention from Nikki to the task at hand. Difficult, but not impossible. "I don't know if he can give us answers on the computer records, but when I went to Richmond's house, he was working on a DNA splicing project."

Vegan nodded. "And we know he worked with the horses when he was a scientist for Omega, but that was years ago."

"And he still visits them." Several eyes cut a trail to Raven. "He didn't admit that, I figured it out."

Winter's gaze remained on him, as did most of the others' sitting in the circle. He felt the sear of their stares, all the questions, and only he had the answers. Was it cruel to make them wait? Probably, but who cared?

Finally, he shrugged. "His shoes, the manure … Trust me, you don't want any more of an explanation."

"What else did you learn at Richmond's house?" Winter asked.

"His daughter is hot."

The girls rolled their eyes.

Oh yeah, girls were always jealous. "Seriously, I mean, this girl is amazing. He's got a picture of her on a beach somewhere, and you know, I could almost smell her coconut suntan lotion."

Vine dropped his voice and leaned in. "Has anyone *else* noticed the smell of coconut lotion when Will comes around, or is it just me?"

Glimmer tilted her head to the side. "I thought maybe Will had some new beachy cologne or something."

Raven scoffed. "Beaches smell like dead fish. I don't think they make cologne in that scent."

She crossed her arms over her chest and split him in two with her dagger eyes. "And I thought your favorite scent was manure."

"This isn't helping," Vegan said.

Vine nodded in agreement and took a bite of red licorice.

Raven continued. "The horses could be just the beginning. Omega could be gene splicing any number of creatures. Humans, Halflings."

"That would account for the wingcuffs. There was enough titanium to make thousands." Sky leaned his weight against a post and locked his hand around his bent knee.

"So, should we assume Omega is trying to splice human and Halfling DNA? And if so, for what purpose?"

"An army," Zero said as he approached the group. He stood there, hovering above them, silver-white hair quivering in the wind. Raven liked Zero; he was one smart-mouthed guy. But honestly, the dude freaked him out a little with those milky-white eyes and corpse-pale skin. Too many PopTarts, too many juice boxes, and not enough sunlight did *not* do a body good.

Winter motioned with an upturned hand for him to continue.

Vegan donned a huge smile and scooted over, crowding Mace and making a place for Zero to sit.

Zero sneered down at the spot and remained standing. "I found some formulas in one of the Omega files. There weren't any specific explanations, but I think they had to do with Halfling-human splicing."

"No." Now Will approached the group. He did indeed smell of coconuts.

Zero gave him a dirty look.

Will also stood at the edge of the circle, feet shoulder width apart, arms akimbo. "Halflings are Halflings and humans are humans. I don't believe the two could be combined by gene splicing. It simply isn't possible. The best that could be expected would be to mask the angelic qualities, and that would only work for a short time. The angelic strength would eclipse the human and ultimately destroy it."

Vine shook his head. "But the original Halflings came from an angel-human union. So you must be wrong, Will."

Will stared at him. "A *union*. Breeding, not splicing."

"Okay, so we can rule out human-Halfling DNA splicing. I guess we don't have to worry about an army from that source," Vine muttered.

"Then no army at all, because, as we all know, Halflings are capable of having only a single offspring," Winter interjected.

Will raised a finger. "Not *all* Halflings. There have been anomalies in the past. Very few, but some."

Zero inched a little closer. "Will, what if a specimen were mostly Halfling, but the human DNA just filled in a few missing pieces?"

Will shook his head, a frown almost wrinkling his forehead. "I just don't see how human anything could be introduced and not be eclipsed."

"Would it matter if the DNA *was* eclipsed?" Mace asked. "Angels have the ability to recuperate rapidly."

"Cell recovery?" Will said.

"Why not?" Mace said. "It would work with the horses too."

Several gasps created their own little vacuum. Winter leaned forward. "Mace, you aren't suggesting the horses could have spirit horse DNA."

But Raven knew that's exactly what Mace was saying. It was written all over his face, even when he shrugged. "Just a thought."

Glimmer looked at Raven. "Why do you think Richmond's basement laboratory experiments have anything to do with Omega?"

"I don't know. But they do."

Glimmer's curls shifted in the wind, catching light. *She's pretty if you can get past the razor tongue and steely eyes.* "You're going to have to spend more time with him," she said, but he sensed a quick moment of recognition in her eyes, where she'd obviously read his mind about the whole thinking-she's-pretty thing.

Great.

Glimmer tipped one shoulder and blinked heavy lashes at him. "You seem easy to talk to—maybe Richmond will confide in you."

As if that hadn't been his plan all along. "Yeah, well, I'm on a boat in the middle of the ocean right now, so that's going to be difficult." Raven shot a dark look at Will.

"You're where you need to be, Raven."

"Whatever," he mumbled. One thing was certain. As soon as Will backed off this whole *let's go on a cruise* thing, he was headed back to Missouri, back to Dr. Richmond, and back to the fight.

Chapter
6

Zero was mumbling and hunched over his laptop as Nikki approached. Her movements were slow, the kind she imagined a person would use when trying to capture a wild kitten.

"Stop!" he yelled, and raised a hand.

She froze.

"Stay right there." He dropped his arm, crouched his head a little closer to the monitor, and went back to click, click, clicking away at the keys.

She waited, listening to the almost melodic sound of his fingertips against the keyboard. It would be soothing if she didn't know he'd eventually open his mouth and ruin the moment. "What am I doing just standing here, Zero?" she asked when the seconds stretched.

"Obscuring the sun," he answered without so much as a pause in his typing.

Nikki nodded. "Wow, I've really got to go on a diet, eclipsing the entire sun and all ..."

His silver gaze lifted up for a moment. "You do look a little thick."

Nikki shifted her upper body, and the sun slammed him in the face. Silver hardware flashed, he growled, and she returned to standing still as his sun blocker.

"Women are evil," Zero muttered, pressing his palms into his eyes.

"I hear Ocean is going to stop the boat later and everyone is going swimming," she said cautiously.

He visibly shuddered.

"You know, Zero, I could teach you how to swim. I'm a really strong swimmer."

He slammed the laptop closed. "What makes you think I can't swim?"

Those silvery irises bore into her. But she'd thought about this discussion and wouldn't back down. "I'm not saying you can't swim, but you don't seem to like the water. If you're afraid of …"

"I'm not afraid of the water," he spat. He pointed over the side of the boat, then to the laptop. "Water and electricity, they don't really get along. I *hate* the water, I'm not *scared* of it."

"Okay," she said. "So you know how to swim?"

His hands closed into fists. "I don't, and I don't care to learn." Each word shot toward her like poisoned arrows. She should walk away, but she couldn't. She liked Zero. At least she did when she wasn't busy hating him. Nikki stared over the edge of the boat. *Endless blue, above and below.* "Well, if you change your mind, we'll be off having fun."

"Tell you what," he said as she'd started to walk away.

"Yeah?"

"You teach me how to swim right after I teach you how to fly."

Suddenly, she didn't care if he could swim. In fact, she'd like the opportunity to drown him. "You know, you're not the only one who isn't happy about being trapped in the middle of the ocean."

"I'm not the one complaining about it." Sharp features and his unsettling gaze stared her down. "Why don't you just stop playing games and tell me what you want?"

Count to ten, Nikki. Just count to ten. "You're a jerk, you know that, Zero? I was just trying to help, and you make it seem like I came over here with some hidden agenda."

She spun from him, but he reached up and grabbed her arm. "Didn't you?" Zero's grip tightened.

"No," she threw back at him.

He squeezed harder. She could wrench away—she knew how to break a grip—but Zero was a Halfling. It was unnerving being trapped by him, his eyes calculating every thought inside her soul. "No," she said again, feeling a distinct need to defend her actions.

He continued his scrutiny.

"I didn't have a hidden agenda … did I?" Then it occurred to her. She was hoping to ask Zero if he could check back home and see if there was any new information on her parents' case. Was she really that conniving? To think that she'd offer to do something nice for him in return for information about her mom and dad. "Maybe you're right," she murmured, and pulled ever so gently out of his grasp.

Zero's voice echoed behind her as she walked away. "Come back. I was just jerking your chain." He laughed, but Nikki kept going. "Nikki!"

Who am I becoming? She'd never been manipulative before. Then again, maybe she had, but no one ever noticed—including her. Now, surrounded by half-angel beings, her true colors were easily visible. When long, bony fingers clamped on her arm, she jumped.

Zero spun her to face him. "You know, you really kill the fun of hacking your data when you're so busy beating yourself up."

"I'm sorry, Zero. But you guys see right through me. It's creepy and way too revealing."

His top lip curled up as his brows tipped down. "It was a joke, Nikki. You were trying to be nice, and I didn't let you. Man, you need to lighten up."

"I'll try," she offered, but it was weak at best.

"Come on," he said, and led her back to his laptop. They sat in the nearby deck chairs. "There's no new information on your folks."

Her heart sunk a little. "How'd you know?"

"Vegan asked me to check things out for you. I just had to finish updating Ocean's navigational systems first."

"Thank you." No news, but the fact that the Halflings were concerned warmed her heart. "I really apprecia—"

"Yeah, yeah, whatever. Look, don't go getting all mushy on me or I'll have to go back to ignoring you."

She nodded.

Zero clicked a few keys then turned the laptop toward her. "Here ya go."

She looked down at the screen, but had to adjust it to see. No wonder Zero wanted her to block the light. "What is it?"

"Math assignment. You can scroll through. I've got all your classwork on this laptop. Can't promise how long the battery will last, so save often when you aren't plugged in."

"I don't understand, Zero."

"I tapped into your school's files and lifted your assignments."

"Lifted?"

"Yeah, I liberated them."

She shook her head, confused.

"I appropriated them. Filched? Embezzled?"

She had to wonder if these were terms Zero often used to describe his work. "You mean you stole them?"

"If you want to put it that way." He tilted his head, causing him to resemble a huge, white, curious bird. "Hardly a crime to steal homework. Answers maybe, but stealing questions? My conscience is clear."

Her finger trailed the edge of the monitor. "Why?"

"When this is all over, you'll want to go home, right? So I asked Vegan what she thought, and she said it'd be good to get your homework for you so you don't get behind. Good job on the straight As last semester."

His words were blurring into one massive realization. *Home.* A tiny slice of home rested inside the laptop. And Zero and Vegan were responsible for giving it to her. Her nose tingled. Oh, she detested that. Normally she'd hate for anyone to see her eyes get misty, but right now it just didn't matter. Other things, important things, were happening around her. "Thank you, Zero."

He shrugged. "No big deal." But Zero was fighting back a smile about as successfully as she was fighting back tears. A giant wave slammed the side of the boat, and tiny droplets of water stung Nikki's face. She protectively cupped her arms around the laptop.

"See what I mean?" Zero said. "Water equals evil."

Nikki laughed. "And Zero equals not such a bad guy."

Jumping off the side of a boat into the water ... what else could feel so good? The heat from the sun, the whoosh of wind past his ears, then the cool sting of the sea. Rather than surface, Mace stayed under until his lungs began to ache. Down here, there was no need to keep constant watch over things. Or at least that's what he chose to believe.

Was it possible for someone under twenty to have high blood pressure? 'Cause he'd fit the bill for sure. It was like he was fueled on stress these days. And as Mace rolled onto his back to look up at the round, glittering sun, mottled through twenty-some feet of water, he had to wonder if the stress would also ruin him.

The rays hitting the sea's surface were too intense to look at, forcing Mace to close his eyes. A gentle swish of his arms kept him in place as, slowly, his body lifted toward the surface. There were probably fish below, a rainbow of colors and designs, but he didn't care. Maybe he'd inspect the sea life later; now, all he wanted was the soothing silence and the press of liquid salt against his skin.

Something caused him to open his eyes. Through a distorted, floating wall of seawater, Nikki watched him from the railing of the ship. Even from his position beneath the waves, he read the concern on her face. It caused him to smile. When he did, water flooded his mouth. A swoop of his arms and he was topside, tossing hair from his face, spitting seawater, and gazing up at her, because, let's face it, looks like that were scarce.

Her fingers had dug into the railing, and when he finally reached the surface she released a huge breath. Her chin dropped a degree, and she rested her forearms on the rail as if settling in to watch a movie or something. The faintest of smiles was on her face. Man, that hit him in the gut. Nikki was content. And that was rare.

Without warning, an urgent desire to get to her overwhelmed him. But this wasn't a safety thing, or a rescue thing, just a … seize-the-moment thing. Like time was running out on them.

Time was one commodity Mace couldn't control, master, or lead. It was rebellious and not inclined to listen to his suggestions. But he'd learned a thing or two about time, the biggest of which was don't waste it. Once on the ocean surface, Mace snapped his wings open, introducing each feather to the cool water. A second later he was airborne, rising to meet Nikki at the edge of the boat, wings heavy laden but heart riding high.

He paused in flight and faced her, water running in trails down his chest and back. Droplets from his wings showered her with every gentle beat. Each time, she closed her eyes and tilted her head back as if inviting more. "Aren't you going to get in?"

"I was," she said. "Until I saw you drowning."

"You thought I was drowning?"

"Yes. Don't scare me like that."

Reach out and grab her. The thought surprised Mace so much, he tried to shake it off, but it persisted. His hands responded first. And …

"Don't scare you like that? How about if I scare you like this, then?"

She squealed as he lifted her from behind the railing and into his arms. Her hands clamped around his neck. Slick as he was with water, she couldn't get a good grip. The loose hold caused her to press against him. Very nice. Why hadn't he done this before?

70

"Uh-oh, not sure I can hold on." He loosened his grip marginally, causing her to squeal again and sort of climb a few steps up his legs. Even better. The motion left her partially on one side of him so that her arm could drape around his neck for a perfect grip.

"Stop it," she said, but it was mostly a throaty laugh.

"Sorry. Did you want me to let go?" For an instant, he dropped his hands from her.

Her arms tightened around his neck again, pulling their faces close. "No!" She glanced down at the water some twenty feet below.

There was no danger, of course. This was a game—and she seemed happy to play it. That fact alone sent Mace's heart into a tailspin. Homecoming night she'd told him she didn't love him. Clearly, Nikki was a liar, only trying to protect him. Admirable. But futile. He carried her a little higher as the sea air worked its magic to adhere their touch. What was slick became glue. Mace concentrated on pumping his wings softly to raise her above the tallest point of the ship. He was giving her a bird's-eye view, but her eyes never left his profile, as if it were completely different this near. Her gaze, like hot coals, scorched his skin. He didn't make eye contact for fear of breaking the spell, but in his mind he pictured her sharp concentration, studying every line and angle and curve that encompassed him above the throat, dissecting each with her artist's eyes.

"I wish I could draw you right now," she said on a long, slow exhale. "Will made me promise not to draw anything without his supervision."

He couldn't stop his eyes from trailing to her.

But she didn't notice. Her attention was on his jawline; eyes slightly narrowed, mouth barely open, head tilted.

She shifted and then her fingertip ran the plane of his jaw. The tiniest frown creased her forehead as her finger tracked his features.

Did she have any idea what that did to him? Probably not. She was too busy analyzing her subject matter. That was the thing about Nikki: she was fully devoted to whatever drew her attention as if it was the only thing on earth. She was a 100 percent kind of girl. Except where he and Raven were concerned. And eternal punishment aside, that reason alone told Mace she didn't belong with Raven. Sure, he piqued her interest. And on some levels, Nikki might be a little like Raven right now. But that was due to circumstances, not due to who she was on the inside. Nikki was a warrior, not a rebel. She was a leader, not a dissenter.

Her palm flattened against his throat. Mace's body responded by tilting his head to give her more access. "I can feel your pulse."

Ya think? Nothing more came to mind, so he swallowed instead.

"It's racing," she said.

Are you trying *to kill me?* "Yeah, um, exertion, I guess."

"Exertion? What, am I getting fat or something?"

He gripped her small waist, drawing her even closer to his side. "No, Nikki. You're not fat."

"Zero says I'm a little thick."

"What? Nikki, if anything you're too skinny. If it wasn't for the muscle you've built doing karate, you'd blow away in a strong wind. And why would you listen to Zero about anything? Other than the best antivirus software." He tilted his head side to side. "And maybe the best juice boxes."

She laughed. "I think all this *girl time* is having an ill effect on me."

He nodded and hoped she'd keep her hand against his throat. "Uh, yeah. If you're starting to worry about your weight and clothes, I'd have to agree. Those females are trouble."

Her hand remained, but its pressure changed. What had been an exploration became a caress. "And what about you boys? Are you safe?"

Mace's wings stopped for a moment. "No," he said, and even he could hear the sadness in his voice. "I wouldn't say that."

Her fingers slipped away slowly. But instead of closing him off, she settled in by laying her head against his shoulder, her ear against the throbbing pulse in his throat. "I would. I'd say I'm safe with you, Mace. You're my guardian." She drew a deep breath, lungs filling with air, filling with him. On the exhales she whispered, "My guardian angel."

Chapter
7

New scientists, shipments of wingcuffs, and Omega's warehouse a buzz of activity back in Missouri. Mace's attention needed to be on the new information instead of on this, but he couldn't help himself. He had a present for Nikki. He'd intended to tell her about it when the others were swimming, but he'd been completely leveled by her guardian angel comment. Now, three hours later, he wasn't sure why he was pacing in his cabin, why his palms were sweaty, why his stomach felt like he'd eaten bait for dinner. Enough! He snatched the box and went in search of her.

She sat tucked in one of the galley's booths, head resting on her palm, so engrossed she didn't notice him enter until his shadow blocked the sunlight streaming over her through a porthole.

She looked up, and that warm smile spread across her face. "Hi."

His insides became molten. "Hi." One hand was behind his

back, and with the other he pointed to the novel she was holding. "Is it good?"

"Yeah. It's a steam punk, but not as much adventure as I'd like. It's funny at least." She placed the well-worn book on the table and wrinkled her nose. "I read it about a year ago, and it seemed like nonstop action then."

"Well, the excitement level in your own life has kicked up a few notches."

"A few? How about I'm not even on the chart anymore?"

"In a league of your own."

"It's lonely at the top."

"So they say."

She laughed softly and pointed to his bent elbow. "What's behind your back?"

"A present for you."

She perked up. "Really?"

"Mm-hmm." Mace bit his cheek to stop the grin that threatened to take over. His hands were sweaty again. *I'll wind up handing her a sweat-drenched box she'll have to wring out before opening.*

"Is it an action-packed novel?"

"Nope. Even better."

Her little hands reached out. "Gimme, gimme, gimme."

He set it on the table by her book and tried not to hold his breath.

For a long moment she stared at it. A barrage of emotions scattered across her face until she finally settled on confusion. But there was a distinct smile too. "Why did you give me this?"

Mace slid into the seat beside her and began opening the camera box. "I know Will warned you to draw only under his strict supervision, and I know how much you love drawing.

I've seen you studying things on the boat. The curl of the sails, angles of the helm … other things. Drawing is your way of keeping the world sane."

She nodded. "What keeps the world sane for you, Mace?"

"Nothing."

Her mouth tilted into a downturned bow.

"Nothing until you."

Her face beamed then turned suspicious. "Liar. You didn't need sanity until I came along."

"I didn't need a lot of things until you came along." The air around them thickened with all the unspoken things between them. "Anyway, I know you miss the freedom drawing gives you, so I did a little recon—"

"Recon?" she said.

"A little research, and from what I can tell, photography is kind of close to drawing."

She nodded, but her mouth straightened into a line as if she planned to cross-examine him. "So your *recon* revealed that photography is like drawing?"

"From what I gathered, a lot of artists photograph their subjects before they draw or paint."

He was pretty sure she was biting back a full smile. "And why do you suppose they do that?"

Was she baiting him? No fair. He already felt like a fish on a line, helplessly being reeled in. "Best I can tell, it's for composition. Maybe color too, but mostly composition. I'm no artist, but I'd think you'd still want to make sure your subject matter makes for an interesting design."

"Hmm." She pressed her lips together, and the motion created a dimple on the left side of her cheek. He fought the urge to kiss it. Instead, he said, "I would think a camera could be really helpful. You know, in a capturing-the-moment kind of way."

"Definitely." She bit her cheek again. "What else did your recon teach you?"

"Zoom. I picked another camera first, but after talking to an artist—"

"What artist?"

Okay, he'd had about enough of the third degree. "Do you want this camera or not?"

"Yes! Of course, yes. I'm just blown away that you went to all this trouble." Nikki grabbed the box and tore it open.

"Like I said, I know how much you miss drawing. I don't want you to feel like everything has been stripped away from you."

This brought her head up. Nikki tucked hair behind her ear and practically whispered, "A lot has been taken." Her fingers toyed with the ripped edge of the box. "But a lot has been given as well."

She leveled him again. Mace lifted his hand and stroked her cheek. "It's amazing that you can see it that way."

"I have to or …"

"Or what?"

"Or the darkness will take me."

Mace's arm closed around her protectively. He understood what she meant; whether human or Halfling, darkness was a reality for all of them, seeking to devour every soul. And sometimes you just wanted to let it. The problem was Nikki had a destiny. Mace recognized the markings of a leader upon her. If any of them thought that one day she'd return to her old life and pick up where she left off, that was a joke. She'd been drawn into the battle of battles, and he feared neither side was willing to let her go. There was so much she needed to learn in order to survive in this world. And he was a pretty good teacher.

When the moment's intensity grew to be too much, Mace helped her finish opening the box.

"This is just amazing. I mean, how long have you had this? You must have bought it in South Carolina." She rolled her eyes. "No wonder you were so ticked when I got back to the boat the day I went to the mall. You were out buying me a present and I'd gone shopping with the girls. I'm sorry, Mace. I had no idea."

"Oh, uh ..." Prickly heat crawled up his neck. He tugged at his collar. "I didn't exactly buy it that night."

She stopped. "You already had it before that?"

"Um, not really."

Nikki set the box on the table, camera half exposed. "When did you buy this?"

"Last night."

Her eyes widened. "What? We're in the middle of the ocean! Did you swim down to the Super Center in Atlantis or something?"

"No." He really hadn't wanted to explain all the details. "I flew back to South Carolina last night while everyone was asleep."

There was that barrage of emotions again, flitting across her face. Nikki opened her mouth but no words came out. Instead her head shook from side to side, and then she threw her arms around his neck and hugged him so hard it almost hurt. *Girls are insane. They laugh when they're embarrassed, they cry when they're happy, and they try to choke you to death when you do something nice for them.*

No wonder guys don't understand them. Nikki loosened her grip and settled in, resting her head against his chest.

Now *that* he understood.

Over the next four days Nikki photographed practically everything on the boat. Vegan and Dash had become a two-person spotting team of any and all things interesting and picture worthy. They'd even dragged her out of bed one morning to capture a particularly beautiful sunrise. Apparently Vegan and Dash both had an interest in photography. And with Zero's interest in all things Vegan, his mood had sunk from grumbler to full-on grouch.

When Nikki wasn't snapping pictures, she worked on developing her level of faith, though she still couldn't touch the faith ball. What had once felt like a challenge had become complete frustration.

Mace had told her over and over to think it through. Once again he was posted at the railing, sitting cross-legged as the ball mocked her. Though he'd basically made himself her personal coach, Mace wasn't much help. He seemed to be growing more and more frustrated with her lack of ability—like the earth's rotation depended on her. Which was a scary thought.

It made her angry, his persistence. And it made her want to be with him all the more—which made no sense at all. But in the deepest part of her being she knew he felt an urgency to help her become … whatever it was she was supposed to become. He wanted to help her be a conqueror. And an infuriating part of her found that endearing.

"You know it exists because you see it. Listen, you can even hear it," Mace told her.

It was true. The faith ball gave off a low humming sound.

"Close your eyes. See it in your mind?" Mace said.

"Yes."

"Hear it?"

Its gentle song called to her. "Yes."

"Now reach out and touch it."

She reached, fingers hungry to hold the elusive orb. Her heart rate increased. Even with her eyes closed, she knew she was almost there. Seconds later she felt something against her skin, against her fingertips. Her eyes opened to find Mace's hands. She'd reached right through the ball. For the fourth straight day.

Mace gave her a pitiful smile. "We'll work on it later."

"No! I need to do it again." She forced her attention on the ball, but again she failed.

"Nikki, it won't do any good if you're annoyed when you try. We'll do it later."

Annoyed? She was far beyond annoyed, because with each passing day she felt everything slipping from her. Emotions gurgled up from the box she'd locked them in. "Why don't we just say what we're thinking and stop pretending everything's going to be okay?"

Evil was waiting to strike. She sensed it, and she worried Mace did too. It was likely the reason he was so intent on helping her master the faith ball.

"What do you mean?"

She threw her hands out. "All of it, Mace. You, me. We try not to act like a couple, but melt whenever we're together. You want to help me, but it's out of fear. I'm going to cost everyone their lives if I don't get this stupid ball thing. And it's impossible for me. I. Don't. Believe." She pushed up from the deck.

After a long time, he stood. "It's not impossible. You can do this, Nikki. It just takes …"

"Faith?" she spat. "That's the whole problem. I have none.

I'm trying, but even as I reach out I'm thinking *round, silvery glowing balls don't exist.*"

Will had overwhelmed her with the little announcement she'd be called on by the Throne. *The Throne.* He'd also wrecked her emotional equilibrium when he told her, "This is no game." Was the safety of the entire ship on her shoulders? It sure seemed so. And she, the *chosen* one, was unable to do a simple thing like touch the round, glowing sphere. To make things worse, Mace was losing his patience with her. Losing his patience with the whole thing. The most sickening part was his reaction seemed to be the catalyst that made her want to fall into Mace's arms. Oh, she was one messed-up girl.

Mace's voice, soft and encouraging, cut through her thoughts. "Just because something is outside your realm of experience, that doesn't mean it doesn't exist. And you know that. Look how far you've come."

She became statue-still for a moment. "What do you mean?"

"Well, six months ago you wouldn't have believed half-angel beings roamed the earth. You wouldn't have believed there were hell hounds or demons, right?"

True. She had come a long way. Mace's smile diffused a tiny margin of her frustration, but even that couldn't erase the impending doom that colored every waking moment. She looked behind her, where Will was smearing lotion on his chest. "Or heavenly angels." She watched Will for a few seconds. "Is he still trying to—?"

"Get a tan?" Mace nodded. "As far as we can tell. I think he's trying to hide it though, so don't say anything."

"So that is why I smell coconuts whenever he comes around."

"Yeah. And as far as us, Nikki, you and I will do what's right. Not by our standards, but by a measure far above our desire to be together. Because that's how we're both geared. We're hardwired for it."

She stared down at the wavy pattern in the teakwood deck. Was she hardwired to do the right thing? She used to think so, but now ... Now she just didn't trust her character. A big part of her wanted to be reckless and say, "Hey, whatever happens, happens." And she hated that reaction. She needn't admit it to Mace. His face reflected her insecurity.

Nikki gestured toward the angel behind them. "Will's as pale as he was the day we left."

Mace nodded. "Apparently angel skin doesn't tan easily."

"You guys have all gotten darker." Her gaze started to roam over his exposed skin, but she stopped herself at his pecs. Hard to drag her eyes away from those muscles, but she managed. *Hardwired to do what's right. Uh, yeeeeaaah.*

He cleared his throat. "Half-human. Guess that makes tanning possible."

The slight movement caused the amulet around his neck to shift. It was different from the one Vegan had given her back in Missouri, but fashioned in the same manner. Nikki stepped to him and reached to touch the necklace. Anything to redirect the conversation. "I remember the first night I saw this." Her finger trailed the cord as her mind went back. Mace had doused his shirt in the water to soothe the burns she'd gotten on her hands after going into a blazing laboratory because someone was trapped inside. As she stroked the short necklace, her fingertips lightly grazed his skin.

"I'm so sorry for everything you've been through, Nikki."

"The camera helps take my mind off of things." She stood only inches from him. Heat from the sun rose from his body and pushed against her. "I'm just glad you're here," she said, words so soft they could almost be swallowed by the sound of wind and waves. She mostly hoped they would be.

He flashed a devastating smile. "I promised to see it through."

And that's when all her solid, commitment-filled decisions came crashing around her. She ached to move closer, but she wouldn't. Especially now, being so brave and hardwired to do what's right. The fact was they were like two boats helplessly trapped in the same whirlpool. Being together only meant sinking faster.

She needed to get away from him immediately.

When she moved to step past, he trapped her hand, flattening it against his chest. "We can do this," he said, and she understood what he meant. All too well.

"Can we?" Her eyes closed and she allowed her body a moment to enjoy his nearness: fingers on her hand, his skin so warm, his heart pounding beneath her touch. His breath came in sweet waves against her cheeks.

Too many unwanted realities rushed to the surface as they stood there, the biggest being the closer they got to each other, the farther away she felt from conquering the darkness that threatened. Darkness was an unfortunate truth for both of them, one that couldn't be denied and one that wouldn't go away. And sadly, one whose appetite only grew with time.

How could standing with the girl you love feel so desperately lonely? She was right in thinking everything was on the line. Not just him, not just his eternity, but her very safety. Fact was, she was still in danger, and a boat ride across the ocean didn't change that. Breaking one rule meant breaking more. Hadn't he learned that the hard way? And breaking the rules could only mean one thing: failure.

He'd put her in danger by trying to be too close to her. They had to watch their emotions. If they didn't, Nikki might pay for the mistake with her life.

He might have been willing to gamble with his eternity—no matter how stupid that was—but he could never gamble with Nikki's safety, especially now. Her fate could affect ... well, the world as they all knew it. He'd never been surer of anything, and in his entire life nothing had ever frightened him more.

When the wind grabbed her hair and thrust it at him, he pulled in her scent and tried to remember his commitment.

"Mace," she said.

"What?"

"I'm ... really scared."

His hands instinctively found their way to her upper arms. "You're trembling, Nikki. What's wrong?" He searched her face. Her eyes were liquid honey, but so haunted in their depths it seemed the very color might drain from them.

"I don't know." Her words were small. "I don't *know*. I feel ... wrong inside. Like something awful is going to happen." Her gaze darted around the boat but focused on nothing. "And I don't feel like myself. I can't sleep at night, but I'm not really tired the next day. My ears are so sensitive to everything, sometimes I just want to clamp my hands over my head so I won't hear it all."

He gently rubbed her arms to soothe her. "Has Will been working with you on your ability as a Seer?"

"Yes."

"Maybe you're tapping into that power."

"Maybe. But whenever he instructs me to draw, there's nothing except this burning urgency to master it. I've tried to sketch, but nothing happens. It doesn't feel the same as when I drew the hell hounds in the woods or the laboratory on fire."

"What did it feel like then?"

"Electric. Almost living. Like the pencil was alive in my hand. I just connected and the drawing happened."

He raised a hand to her cheek. "Don't worry. When you need to see, you will."

"I hope you're right. Because if you're wrong, I'm no good to anyone here."

"I'm not wrong, Nikki." He dropped his lips to her forehead and pressed a gentle kiss onto her skin. And that was close to tempting fate. "Come on. Let's go swimming."

It was the second time Ocean deemed it safe enough to stop the boat for them.

Nikki could barely believe the sight around her—Halflings flying, swooping, then crashing into the water. Were they always such daredevils? Probably. Even the girls flew to the crest of the mast and swan-dived into the ocean. She reached a conclusion: Halflings were fearless.

But Nikki couldn't seem to concentrate, no matter the glorious display. All day long she'd felt as though tiny fingernails were clawing her insides. As the day dragged on, the sensation increased until she was forced to climb out of the water and remain on deck, watching the winged creatures float around her, and occasionally rubbing her hands over the goose bumps on her bare arms.

Raven's dark gray wings blocked the sun and created a

V-formation shadow on the deck. She'd been aware of his gaze going to her whenever he performed some death-defying feat. The other boys mimicked him—excluding Mace—each one trying to outdo the last.

He was dripping wet when he stepped onto the deck beside her. Tipping one wing, he shook water onto her skin. "You look hot," he said with a mischievous grin.

She caught the double meaning. "Thanks for cooling me off."

"Anytime." He flipped his hair from his face, but strands of it clung to his wet cheeks. "Swim with me," he said.

She shook her head. "No, Raven. I just want to sit out here on the deck for a while."

He tipped his head to the sun for a moment. "Come on. I want to show you something."

She pinned him with her eyes.

"I'm serious. You're gonna love this." His dark blue eyes glistened and a tiny dimple in one cheek became visible. "Listen."

At first, she only heard the sounds of the others: wings fluttering, laughter, the boys taunting each other. Beyond that, she could hear water and wind, and the gentle hum of the faith ball. Then … Yes, there was another sound. High-pitched, echoing. "What is it?"

He reached for her hand.

She recognized the sound, but from where? "What is it, Raven?"

"Come on, I'll show you, but you have to be quiet. If the others hear, they'll scare them off."

She knew better, but she reluctantly slid her hand into Raven's.

He led her to the opposite side of the boat and pointed down, where a group of dolphin swam just below them. Nikki sucked in a breath when one jumped out of the water and landed with a splash.

Raven wrapped his arms around her waist. "Hang on."

Before she could react, his wings snapped open, and they were hovering just above the water line, feet dangling in each rising wave. "Here," he said, reaching into a pouch fastened to his waist. "You want to feed them?"

She nodded, but couldn't exactly speak as two dolphin vied for her attention once they saw the small fish. Raven kept a tight grip on her waist. She wound an arm around his neck and maneuvered just enough to feel comfortable letting go with the other arm, then held the fish out. A dolphin jumped, and she dropped the bait into his waiting mouth. As it fell back into the waves she let out a quick breath that actually had a tiny squeal hidden in it.

"Pretty cool, huh?"

Her head bobbed and she looked at him. She immediately regretted the eye contact. Raven's midnight gaze, aflame with her excitement, made her feel flush. He was smiling a most un-Raven-like kind of smile. Genuine, happy. Free.

She swallowed.

His hands flattened against her back.

"How'd you know they were here?" she asked, attempting to lessen the closeness, the intimacy.

But being locked together, faces only inches apart, made that impossible. "They've been following us. I've been hoping to get this close for a few days, in fact."

Nikki smiled. "Will they stay with us the whole trip?"

"No," he said, and something painful entered the depths of

his gaze. "Eventually they'll go back where they came from and we'll never see them again."

She realized her heart was pounding. Not just pounding, hammering, and she knew he wasn't talking about dolphin anymore. And without as much as a warning, Nikki was sad. Because the Halflings had become such a part of her life, and one day she'd return home. The idea of never seeing them again … well, it just seemed impossible. Her arms tightened around Raven's neck. It was an attempt, though a useless one, to hold on to what she was sure to lose.

"Sort of makes you want to make the moment count, doesn't it?" His eyes searched hers. "It's different when you know you only have a short time."

Why, why did he have to do this? Did he want to destroy her completely? It wouldn't be any easier for him and Mace to walk away than it would be for her. But eventually time would rip them apart; of that, she was sure.

Neither she nor Raven had broken their gaze, and her pulse began to skitter and her throat constrict. She knew how Raven felt about her, or at least how he *believed* he felt. "You said you'd give me time."

His mouth twitched into a smile, but the sadness lingered in his eyes. "You? I wasn't talking about you, Nikki. We were talking about the dolphins."

When he pumped his wings, she could feel the agitation— and the truth. But he tried to hide it, something she appreciated greatly. She was barely sorting through her feelings for Mace; she couldn't begin to sort through the twisted emotions she had for Raven.

"You want to pet one?"

Without hesitation she said, "Yes!"

He helped her readjust so she was safely against him, then gave her another fish. "Here, stand on my feet and let go of my neck."

She obeyed, and with a gentle wave of his wings she leaned out away from him.

"I've got you, so just relax." His hands were tight around her, fingers against her hipbones. "Hold the fish with one hand, but don't drop it. When the dolphin comes up, raise the fish and reach to his head with your free hand." Raven lowered them a little deeper into the water.

"Okay," she said on an exhale. Within a few seconds, a dolphin came up out of the blue and hovered face-to-face with her. First shock, then awe overcame her, until she remembered her instructions. Slowly, she raised the bait and reached to stroke the dolphin's smooth skin. Finally, she dropped the fish in the dolphin's mouth, and it made some clicking sounds then disappeared into the water. "Wow," she said.

A moment later, her body was resting against Raven's. She hadn't even noticed until she felt the muscles of his chest moving in tandem with his wings. For a moment it seemed like they were right back in the woods with the dead hell hound they'd fought, and Raven was her shelter again. Her head rested on his collarbone.

"I lied to you, Nikki." With his lips against her ear, there was barely any need for a voice.

Her eyes slammed shut. She didn't need to hear that tone, that low, honest one that he reserved for her.

"I lied to you about your painting."

The broken pot. The proof she and Raven were so much alike, and the representation of the one thing that Mace could never understand.

"Your painting doesn't represent life draining from a broken pot. It represents hope. Even something broken can be mended." He nuzzled deeper into her hair. "Even something broken can have the promise of a future."

She struggled to answer. To say *something*. But what? Raven had seen through all her great defenses, all her carefully constructed masks. Raven knew who she really was. And wanted her anyway.

Mace, in contrast, saw her through rose-colored glasses, and she could never begin to live up to his expectations.

Nikki opened her eyes. Around them rolling waves crested and fell. It would be a mistake to look at Raven, but she tilted her head, eyes trailing up until she found him.

She saw real love reflected in the blue of his gaze. "I know you're scared about what's on the horizon. But I'll be here for you."

It was an oath. A promise. And it broke her heart because she couldn't promise to be with him. "Raven, I—"

But he didn't give her a chance to answer. Raven closed his mouth over hers in a gentle, sweeping kiss, his lips soft but hungry. His mouth lingered for only a second before he tilted back and studied her, searching for something she didn't think she could give. Nikki was surprised to realize her hand had slipped up to rest against his throat. With her elbow bent, her fingers fluttered against the ends of his hair. *Why can't my body obey my mind around him?*

Raven dropped another kiss on the tip of her nose. "Don't worry. I'll still give you time. But I'll also occasionally remind you."

"Remind me?" she echoed.

"Yeah, remind you that with me, you don't have to pretend

to be something you're not. You're free. And the smell of free-dom is good on you."

A sound came from the edge of the boat, and Nikki looked up. Several sets of Halfling eyes were on her and Raven. She squirmed to move away from him, but it was too late. Mace turned from the railing and disappeared.

"Dolphin," Glimmer said.

A second later, Nikki heard a splash as the Halflings dropped into the water.

Chapter
8

The confines of the cabin had become too much, forcing Nikki to grab her blanket and leave the sleeping Halfling girls for fresh air on the deck. *Four a.m. and wide awake. Great.* They'd reach their destination in one more day, and still she couldn't feel the faith ball.

She opened the door and wind blasted her, disrespecting her personal space. It pressed against her sweatpants and T-shirt and almost ripped the blanket from her shoulders.

Nikki offered a faint wave to Sky, who stood at the helm. He waved back but didn't say anything, so she meandered toward the front of the ship.

Raven was standing on the bow tossing the faith ball into the air, catching it, then tossing it again.

"If I didn't know better, I'd think you were taunting me."

He turned to face her. "I thought I smelled you."

"Ugh. How many times do I have to ask you to stop saying that? Besides, you're lying."

He caught the faith ball and held it still. "What?"

"You couldn't have smelled me. I'm downwind, and with the breeze as strong as it is, there's no way."

"Sensed you, then." In the star-brightened night, his eyes sparkled like they held their own universe inside.

"Or maybe you just heard the door shut."

"Maybe."

"I smelled *you*, though. As soon as I stepped outside, your scent came right to me."

His eyes narrowed playfully, but not before they flashed a moment of concern. "Really? You smelled me?"

She rocked back on her heels, bare feet cool against the wooden deck. "Yep."

Raven left the ball and moved toward her. Which always made her nervous, because she never quite knew what Raven would do.

He stopped inches from her. "What do I smell like?"

"What? You don't believe me?" She took a tiny step back.

He took a step closer. "I just want to hear what you think I smell like."

Nikki closed her eyes and pulled a deep breath in through her nose. And with it, it seemed Raven invaded every cell of her being; a beautiful scent, an inviting scent. One part snow-capped mountains and one part black pepper. "You smell like danger, Raven. Like trouble."

Water hit the side of the boat in a gentle rocking motion. "What else?"

The movement of the boat on the water and the intensity of his question—not to mention being so filled with his fragrance—made her wish she'd stayed in the cabin. The wind was colder at night, and Nikki pulled her blanket tight around her shoulders. "That's all," she said, and it didn't even remotely sound like the truth.

"What else?" Raven insisted.

Nikki started to turn and walk away, but once again her feet wouldn't obey her mind. She wouldn't tell him what else he smelled like. She wouldn't even think it again. In fact, she'd forget the sensation that accosted her, forget the one word it brought to mind. Forget that it was exactly what he'd said to her.

"What else?" he said again.

Freedom. Like the first rev of her motorcycle, or the wind on a summer day, rich and alive and filled with possibilities. Like rain after a long drought. It took all her strength to step past him and go to the faith ball now hovering waist high. With all her concentration, she reached for it. Nothing.

She willed herself to concentrate yet harder. Still nothing. Her hand passed right through.

"Do you really think that's going to work?"

She ignored him and went over the things Mace had taught her about faith. *It's real. It's touchable. The ball has mass and weight. Reach out. Feel it.*

"Stop, please. It's embarrassing."

Her eyes flew open in an attempt to scorch him. "Do you have a better way?"

"Uh, yeah."

"Fine. Teach me."

He shook his head.

Her mouth dropped open. "You stuck-up—"

"Watch it," he said, holding a finger in the air.

She swallowed her insult, and it scratched all the way down.

"Look, it's not that I *won't* teach you. It's that I *can't* teach you."

Her anger searched for an outlet. "And that, Raven, is exactly why I'm wasting my time here with you." She turned to go back to her room. At least it was quiet there.

"No one can teach you."

His words stopped her mid-stride. She angled to look over her shoulder at him. "What?"

He jerked his head, motioning her back.

"I already regret this," she mumbled.

Raven tossed the ball a couple of feet into the air and caught it. "No one can teach you because you can't *learn* it. You have to *feel* it. From within. Faith has to become a part of who you are. It's not a separate item. It's woven into you." As he spoke, he moved so her back was to him. With one quick motion he stripped the blanket from her, leaving her feeling bare in spite of the sweats and T-shirt. A heartbeat later, Raven reached around her, holding the faith ball in front of them. "You can see it, right?"

"Of course." His arms were warm against her where they scraped her shoulders, creating a little harbor of safety against the night wind.

"If you can see it, you can feel it. But you can't feel it *because* you see it, or you've missed the whole point."

"Okay," she said.

"Put your hands on mine."

Nikki draped her arms over his and placed her hands on the outside of Raven's. More warmth. More warning that this was a bad idea.

"Now, close your eyes and tune in to the faith at your fingertips."

She did, and for the first time there was a fluttery sensation along her fingers. "Is that you moving?"

"No. You feel the vibration of faith. Can you hear it?"

The hum was louder and almost sounded in rhythm to her body, her heartbeat, her inhalations. "Yes."

"It's becoming part of you." But as she thought back on Mace's instructions, it all started fading.

"Don't lose it," Raven said, and slid his hands to the outside of hers.

"I'm trying to hold on."

"You're trying too hard. Forget what you've learned! It's about the heart. You can't learn it with head knowledge. It's heart knowledge."

The hum returned, the sensation quickened. "Okay, it's back."

"Now put your hands out and close your eyes."

Reluctant to let go of the ball, she released it on one side and held out a flattened hand, then repeated with the other.

A slight movement, then Raven asked, "Which hand is it in?"

She could feel the vibration and weight in her left hand. Her eyes opened. "My left!"

"Close your eyes!" Raven demanded and placed the ball in her right. He repeated the action several more times, each correct answer building her faith a little more. "Now, toss it into the air."

Eyes still closed, Nikki obeyed. She felt the weight of the ball leave her hand for a few seconds, then *smack*. It was right back in her palm again. "I did it!"

Raven's smile was broad and genuine—her personal smile. "You did. Do it again."

This time Nikki left her eyes open and watched as the silvery-blue globe sailed into the air and dropped into her hand. "So, none of that stuff Mace was teaching me mattered?"

Raven nodded toward the ball. "Did you learn it from him teaching you?"

"No."

"Then it didn't matter."

She tossed the ball again. "Thanks, Raven."

"Anytime."

Raven didn't fight the grin that stayed plastered on his face as he watched her walk to the door that led back to her cabin. *Turn around*, he urged. She reached for the door handle. But before slipping inside, she cast a long look over her shoulder.

Oh yeah. His heart thumped.

Her long, dark hair flew in all directions compliments of the wind. Gone were those shadowy, hollow places under her eyes that had been there since she'd gotten the news about her mom and dad. And there was a lightness to her, because tonight he'd given her something no one else—including Mace—was able to give her.

"What are you doing?"

Rarely did *anyone* sneak up on Raven. But he'd been preoccupied with Nikki and let his defenses down. He turned toward the voice but said nothing.

Winter stepped out of the shadows to the right of the ship's bow. Dressed in a long, flowing black garment, she resembled a gothic witch, especially with her dark, swirling hair and pale skin. "What are you doing, Raven?" She repeated the words softly, but there was a distinct bite to her tone.

One he didn't appreciate. "Not much. You?"

She exhaled and looked back to the door Nikki'd disappeared behind. "That's not fair and you know it."

"What?" She was really starting to irritate him.

"Nikki. You let her think her faith made the ball touchable."

"But she was finally able to touch it, wasn't she? So what does it matter?"

Winter tossed her head, sending hair over her shoulder. Trapped in the light of the moon and a billion stars, she looked … pretty. The breeze caused her long gown to cling to her legs. Red-polished toes peeked from the hem. His gaze returned to her face and found a frown.

"It matters because you can't borrow faith. You have to find it in yourself."

"Really? Thanks for the lesson." He turned away from her and leaned against the railing. "Why are you even out here in the middle of the night?"

She moved beside him and leaned too, mimicking his posture. "I heard Nikki get up, and I've been worried about her. Plus, I'm a light sleeper."

As she spoke, Raven couldn't stop himself from looking at her. In the planes of her face, in the gentle edge of her eyes, pain long forgotten—or pushed away—lingered. He wondered how old Winter was, and why her skin felt like ice. She seemed older than the other females, but he knew next to nothing about her. *What are you hiding?* Most guys would coax her into a conversation slowly. Which might be a good idea, because suddenly he felt like he needed to know more about this girl. "So," he began. *Choose your words carefully.* "What's up with you? Are you, like, really old or something?"

Winter's eyes widened and angled to stare at him. Her mouth was open slightly, but no words came from it.

Way to go with the slow and subtle approach. He shrugged. "You don't look old or anything, but you don't carry yourself like a teenage girl."

Her lips came together and she ever so slowly turned back toward the water.

Raven took a deep breath. "Sometimes, admissions are hidden in words. 'I'm a light sleeper.' That's all you said, but your eyes told a different story. Maybe something happened that's hurtful, but it happened so long ago you didn't think you'd need to hide the pain anymore."

Winter gazed out at the night, but her shoulders dropped marginally, telling him he'd struck a nerve.

He shrugged. "Maybe you didn't even think it hurt anymore."

Still silence.

Raven dropped into silence too.

"I was ... captured once." Her voice was steady but low. "Tortured. For days. Maybe weeks. It was a very long time ago. I've had a hard time getting used to sleeping belowdecks."

"The small, confined space?"

"Yes. And the smell of wood. Or oil." Winter shook her head, and her long hair fanned around her like darkened smoke. "I don't know. It's something in the room, I guess. I never sleep much, but it's been worse on the boat."

"Some wounds take a long time to heal."

She looked over at him. "And some you just learn to live with."

"That's hard enough to do for a single lifespan. We have several to remember our mistakes, our regrets. Our pain."

A faint smile touched Winter's face. "But also to remember our victories. The people we saved, rescued."

Raven tilted a little closer to her and tried to pierce her with his gaze. "Why don't I see *that* reflected in your eyes?"

A sound that wasn't quite a laugh escaped her lips. "Easier

to remember the bad stuff, maybe? Hold on to the good in each journey you take, Raven."

He turned and looked back at the door where Nikki had disappeared. "That's what I'm trying to do."

"But also remember, journeys end. And we have to walk away. Don't do more damage than good."

Anger shot through his chest. *Just when I was starting to think I liked you.* "I'll try to remember that. Thanks, Mom."

"Nikki is a human."

"Really? I hadn't noticed."

"One day ..."

"I get it. One day she'll return to a normal life."

Winter shook her head. "No, she won't."

What did she mean? What did Winter know about Nikki's future?

"Don't look so worried, Raven. What I mean is, how would you ever expect Nikki to return to a normal world after being swept off her feet by an angel who's determined to make every moment she spends with him a breathtaking adventure?"

He didn't like the feeling that settled in his stomach, and he wanted out of this conversation. But he stayed.

Winter went on. "The dolphins, the faith ball. Every second she spends with you is one spectacular moment followed by another. You've made sure of that, but you can't keep it up, not even for one lifetime. Sooner or later the shiny new penny looks just like all the others. And where does that leave you?"

He laughed without humor. "Suddenly, you're worried about me?"

"I've been worried about you all along. Because one day Nikki will grow old and die. But you, Raven ... Unless you're murdered, you'll have until the end of days to remember what it felt like to not be the new toy anymore."

What did Winter know about who he was? Nothing. She barely knew him.

"I'm not trying to hurt you. I'm just speaking from experience. I couldn't live with myself if I wasn't honest about it. Nikki's a mistake, Raven. Don't turn it into a tragedy."

With that she walked away.

Raven pressed his lips together hard, trying to reject the words she'd said, but they refused to be silenced. They flew through his mind, bouncing off one another, each accusation growing as the collisions increased.

Nikki isn't a mistake. Nikki is freedom, and possibly my only chance to be content.

The roll of the waves had increased as the wind shifted direction. *At least that's what she is right now.* But what about later? When the new wore off? How would she feel about him then? He thrived on the moment, but what happened when the moment lost its charm? Was there anything, any lasting thing that would hold Nikki's attention and affection?

Something tingled in his nose. Raven's hands clamped into fists as he stared up at the stars through watery eyes. "This is why you're a loner," he mumbled. "Anything else is just too painful."

Chapter
9

Nikki woke with sweat pouring off her body. On instinct, she grabbed the sketchpad and charcoal pencil on the table beside her bunk, then scooted on the bed into a dim streak of light coming in from the porthole. The room was a suffocating mix of hot air and Glimmer's perfume; she worried she might vomit, but she forced down the pressure in her throat and put the pencil to her sketchpad. Her hands were trembling, making the first few strokes jerky and uneven. Slick with perspiration, her arm stuck to the pad while she drew. But as the lines took shape, her breathing slowed to a normal rate. She swiped her brow with her free hand, not wanting sweat to run into her eyes and obscure her view of the drawing. For days she'd felt something strange happening in her mind. Now, the answers lay in the lines and angles forming on the page.

The small round window was over her shoulder, but taking the time to open it for some needed airflow would slow her progress. She noticed the room was empty, and wished the girls had left the door open even a crack—a quick glance up confirmed it was closed tight. Nikki marveled at all that fresh air above the ceiling that had no inlet to the room.

The entire bed was wet from her fevered dream. A nightmare of something horrible. She remembered falling, a giant metal music box slipping and then crashing. *Why is it so hot in here?* Nikki swiped her forehead and focused on the picture. She ignored the stale, suffocating air.

A mass of mangled lines originated at one corner of the page. Tracks stretched from them, crisscrossed rails intersecting like a ladder. *Train tracks!*

The realization fueled her, though her hand ached from the tight grip and intense force behind each line. Within minutes a train began to take shape beneath her purposeful strokes. As the sketch became clear, her apprehension grew. Short puffs of air became all her tight lungs could handle. Her eyes darted from the mass of tangled lines in the corner of the sketchpad to the center where long boxcars filled the page. The picture cleared. It was definitely a train.

And it was about to crash.

"Where?" Will said, his eyes searching Nikki for answers she didn't have.

"I don't know." Her voice squeaked, close to panic.

She'd gathered a crowd when she'd run up the stairs screaming for Will. Now the entire crew was staring at the picture, as well as at her, and they all wanted the same answer as Will. But she *didn't* know. Nothing else came to her mind, though she'd tried to continue drawing.

Will studied the picture. "What's this?"

She looked at the spot he pointed to. "A road sign, maybe?" She concentrated on the small square. Numbers, letters, but nothing conclusive.

"Zero?" Will said.

"I'm on it." He disappeared behind her.

"Can you draw more?" Will asked her.

She shook her head. "I don't think so. There's just nothing else."

Ocean stepped into the center of the crowd and pointed to the drawing. "This is it, Will. This is what I feared."

"Retaliation?"

He nodded. "My guess would be to start searching in France. If the titanium shippers are trying to send a message for us to back off, this would certainly be one way to do it." He pointed to the paper. "The train's about to hit the section of track that's mangled. How could that happen? Only a bomb could twist a track into a silly straw."

"Which means there's no way the wreck is an accident." Will nodded. "Vine, go tell Zero to narrow his search to France, then spread out from there if needed."

"I'm here," Zero said, carrying his open laptop with one hand while feverishly tapping the keys with the other. He settled onto the deck and motioned for Vine to block the sun. Vine got in position, even snapping his wings open to create a perfect shadow over Zero.

Around him, the rest of the crew stayed silent, waiting for Zero's words.

He shook his head. "Nothing. No train wrecks reported. And I've checked globally."

Will's eyes returned to the sketch. "Maybe it hasn't happened yet."

Nikki stared at him. *Hasn't happened?* Did he think she could draw the future?

Mace stood behind her and placed a hand on her shoulder. "Nikki, when will it crash?"

"I—I don't know."

"As a Seer, you glimpse into the realm of the spirit. While the heavenly realm is tightly connected to the earthly realm, it doesn't always move simultaneously." Will looked at her the same way he had when they'd begun training. "You may have caught a glimpse of something that is in the near future. But we need to determine which one it is."

Okay, like she really needed more pressure right now. "I don't know what train it is or where it is, or ..." She shook her head, causing the sets of eyes on her to jump and jolt. Panic rose. It burned in her stomach, escalating with each breath.

"Just try to think." Mace's words were soft, but tinged with urgency.

Think. Just focus. But when she tried, her mind blanked. "I don't know!"

Zero left the computer screen long enough to snag the sketch. His silver eyes seemed to analyze every stroke. "What's on that sign? The letters and numbers—read them to me, Nikki."

She shrugged from Mace's grasp and stared at the words above Zero's finger. But the page was a blur.

"You can do it," Mace coaxed.

She shook her head, and a fat tear slid down her cheek. "I can't. They aren't clear." Her heart beat so hard it was making her nauseated. *People's lives could be at stake and I can't read my own writing.*

"You wrote them, Nikki. You've got to be able to read them."

When she didn't answer Mace, just looked at the paper blankly, she felt him move away. Nikki watched as he stepped to the railing and stared at the horizon. Was he giving up on her?

Then she felt warm hands flat against her back. She'd know that touch anywhere, and with it, calm descended. The heat of Raven's body was like a wave of peace over her. Lips against her ear, he whispered, "Close your eyes, Nikki."

She did and felt a few more tears trickle down her face.

"Imagine the picture in your mind. Can you see it?"

She nodded.

"Do you see the sign?"

"Yes," she croaked.

"Tell me what it says."

"There are two sets of letters, but I can't read them."

"That's okay. Just tell me the letters one by one."

"A-l-s-a-c-e, and V-o-s-g-e-s. Yes, Vosges. Then the numbers twelve, five km … or maybe that's one hundred two, five km. I'm not sure."

"Good job," he whispered.

Her eyes opened and she turned to him. "Did I tell you what was on the paper?"

His upper lip curled. "No. There are only six letters on the paper. You just told us what was on the whole sign."

"Got it," Zero said. His fingers stopped clicking keys. "It's near the Rhine River in France. Vosges Mountains. Looks pretty remote, Will."

Will pointed to Ocean at the helm. "How long until we make landfall?"

"Less than an hour. What do you want to do?" Ocean asked.

"We can't wait. Zero, try to discern what train line that is and get a message to them that the track is out. We'll leap from

106

here, then Ocean and Zero can catch up to us once the boat is in the harbor."

Zero shot Will a look, but must have decided not to argue.

Mace made his way back to the group. "Nikki, you'll be safe in the harbor. Just stay on the boat and out of sight."

"What?" Her anger flared and she shot a questioning look to Will. "I'm going with you, right?"

"If we come upon a train wreck, the Halflings will need to focus their attention on helping the wounded. I can't guarantee your safety."

Mace's hand began to fall on her shoulder. She pushed it away. "I don't care about my safety. I'm the one who found the train. I'm going."

"You can fly with me," Raven said.

Daggers flew between him and Mace.

"She will fly with me," Will corrected, and stepped between the boys. "She's right. We need her there, as she's the only link to the wreck." He turned to Nikki. "I just wanted you to under-stand the risk."

She gave Mace a defiant stare, but guilt followed as his eyes liquefied into worry.

"I'll be careful," she offered. "I promise to stay out of the way."

He tried to nod, but the gesture was more like a flinch. Every muscle in his face was tight. Nikki hated the fact she'd caused him so many of those looks. Sometimes it seemed all she did was hurt Mace. Over and over and over again.

When did Raven become so sensitive? Mace pumped his wings

harder, knowing the adrenaline and anger would fuel his flight. He was mad, but had no one to blame but himself.

The one time Nikki needed a soft touch, he'd pushed her too hard. Raven, ever the opportunist, had snaked right in there and helped Nikki. Man, it was so difficult sorting his feelings where she was concerned. He was all about getting the job done and done right, and he was all about protecting Nikki. But every obstacle that came along became one more thing he stumbled over. Worse, with each fumble his grip tightened a little more. It almost made him sick to realize, but to keep Nikki close he'd have to be a little more like Raven. Live in the moment, let his emotions override his brain. *But only a little*, he reminded himself, *because Raven is the worst kind of dangerous.* One that assumed no responsibility. The way Mace saw it, Raven was the inevitable fall, and he was the waiting net.

And Nikki was slipping.

Mace tried to force the image of Raven and Nikki together in the water from his mind. Surrounded by dolphins, her hand against his neck, and looking like there was nowhere else she'd rather be. And the kiss. Raven's lips on hers like it was his right.

She hadn't turned away. Hadn't tried to stop him. She just stayed against his chest, head tilted up to his, kissing him.

Mace pulled in a long breath, and as he let it out released the situation from his thoughts. Right now he had to concentrate on what they would find at the scene of the train accident. He glanced left and right to see the other Halflings moving at the same accelerated pace as him. He located Vine in the mix. His white-blond hair flew like a miniature cape behind him, and determination set his face. He was preparing himself for what they might see. Mace hoped Vine was ready for his first big test since tapping into his angelic power. Fighting demons and hell hounds was one thing. Human carnage was another thing entirely.

Will flew with them, although as a heavenly angel he could certainly fly faster. But unless authorized by the Throne, Will couldn't intervene in the accident, which, selfishly, suited Mace just fine. Nikki would be with Will, and that meant she'd be safe. Even though Will had told her he *couldn't* assure her safety, perhaps he'd hoped she'd choose to stay on the boat. Will probably figured she'd be a distraction to both Mace and Raven. Maybe he was right.

Raven touched down in the valley, where a mass of mangled metal foreshadowed the disaster to come. The surrounding hillsides gave the lush landscape an Old World charm, and if not for the tracks and a narrow road beside them, it would appear untouched by man.

"Where's the train?" Glimmer asked as she stopped beside the track. Her glistening wings tucked behind her as she turned to study the metal, hands on her hips.

A hillside stretched behind them, cut only by the strip of track that ended in a twisted clump of metal near the spot where they stood. Raven had noticed the eastern side of the track dropped off a mountainside. This was the worst possible scenario and probably carefully chosen by the enemies. If it hit with enough force, the train's propulsion could topple the whole thing right off the cliff.

"Let's get organized," Mace said. "Can we bend the track back into shape?"

"No way." Vine grabbed one rail and tugged hard. "Even if

we could, we'd never get it straight enough to keep the train from derailing." Dash grabbed the same piece of metal, and as both pulled it creaked and moved but remained kinked.

"He's right," Dash said. "The train is still going to jump the track. No way around it."

"Listen!" Mace held a hand up.

A whistle blew, and its urgency threw them all into high gear. Mace's eyes darted to Raven's. "It's coming."

Think, Raven, think. "Vine, Dash, go down the track. Try to get the engineer's attention."

"There isn't time for it to stop," Sky said, pointing to a flash of black iron and steel snaking through the countryside and coming closer. Before Raven could stop them, Vine and Dash disappeared in the direction of the oncoming train.

"Maybe they can slow it down."

The others began pulling and tugging the metal, but too much of it had warped into an irreparable mangle.

Will landed beside Mace with Nikki in his arms. The massive guardian angel placed a hand on Mace's shoulder.

Mace pointed to Nikki. "Will, get her on the hillside. If she's down here when the train hits …"

But Will was frozen. His face read deep concern. Mace didn't seem to notice, but Raven did. "Will, go."

The verbal order snapped him back from wherever his mind had traveled. Just before he left, however, Will's lightning-blue eyes settled on Raven. This look held neither the reprimand nor admiration Raven expected to see. It almost resembled a good-bye. Will and Nikki disappeared from sight and materialized on the next hill over.

Raven's entire body felt bathed in ice water. At the very beginning of this assignment on earth, he'd stood outside of his room listening to Will nag about the importance of protocol. For once, Mace had been the one in trouble. He'd broken the rules and gone after Nikki.

The look on Will's face that day was too much like this one. And Raven knew even then what it meant. This journey would take the life of either him, Mace, or Vine.

He wondered if today would be a good day to die.

Chapter
10

There was a time when Raven would have welcomed death, to be removed from the tug of war that was his existence. But that was before Nikki. She'd made it worth staying, and changed everything almost from the day they'd met. Besides, it was a lie anyway. If he died—and wasn't offered mercy—eternity would be far more hellish than anything he'd experienced on earth. And Raven had a strong suspicion he'd not be offered mercy.

The train rolled closer, and he knew what had to happen. Before he could shout instructions to the group, Mace beat him to it.

Hmm, at least we agree on one thing. Raven snapped his wings open and jumped in front of the train.

Off to the right, where Nikki stood on a hillside, he could hear screaming.

Nikki clamped her hands over her face as both Mace and Raven jumped onto the train track. From her vantage point, she could see the scene clearly, though her eyes begged to look away.

Her hands flew forward as if she could reach out and snatch them from harm, even though she knew it was impossible. The two Halflings she loved were flying straight toward certain death.

Sparks flew from the track, and she squinted through tears to see what caused them. More wings came into view, and she realized Winter and Glimmer had grabbed the side of the train, their hands digging into the metal and their wings fighting to slow the forward momentum. Both girls were being dragged along but continued to hold. Soon the others arrived as well. Sky and Dash dropped to the far side of the train as if they planned to copy Glimmer and Winter's tactic. Vine dropped to the front of the train, and though there was nothing for him to stand on, he faced off with the metal monster and pumped his wings feverishly in a deadly game of chicken.

Nikki clamped her hands onto Will's shirt, crumpling the material against his chest. Beneath his clothing, she felt the mass of muscles, *angel* muscles. Her fingers gripped tighter. "Help them, Will!" she pleaded. "Go help them."

His eyes were hollow, dulled by some internal force. He looked down at her but spoke no words.

Her plea became an order. "Help them!" But somehow she knew he meant to stay right there no matter what happened. Fury clawed its way into her throat and out through her hands. She lashed out and hit Will's chest with a fist. "What's wrong with you?" she screamed. "Go help!"

But he was a statue—a giant, cold marble statue refusing to engage and ready to watch his Halflings die. The only thing moving was his face. Will's chin quivered and something glistened in his eyes. "I cannot help them," he said.

Nikki shoved off of him and returned her attention to the train. The brakes were screaming now, and it had slowed some, but not enough. Impact was imminent. Wings that had been strong and steady now flapped at uneven speeds. The Halflings were wearing out and the broken track was coming closer.

Why did I have to sketch that train?

As the back of the third car came into view, Nikki noticed faces pressed to the windows. They must have felt the change in the train's speed and were now gazing out, and the faces she could see were a scattered blend of confusion and concern. *All those people.*

The front of the train was engulfed in feathers, all working to slow its speed. It looked as though they could lift the first car right off the ground with all that angel power, but behind it was another car and another and another. Clouds of dust rose around Winter and Glimmer. Their feet were probably raw from the onslaught of gravel and dirt, and Nikki wondered why they didn't stay airborne.

She sucked a breath when she realized. The girls were trying to dig their feet into the ground to slow the forward push. It had to feel like being stuck in a meat grinder.

Despite all the effort, nothing was working. The train's momentum continued barreling it toward the broken track.

Sky suddenly appeared atop one of the cars, his wings spreading and catching the wind. From the hillside she could see his expression, one of pain and fierce determination. Where his wings met his back, a tight cord of muscle strained under the pressure. It looked as though his wings could be ripped from his body.

But it was working. The train slowed marginally.

Nikki beat her fisted hands against Will's chest, this time out of excitement. "It's working! The train, it's slowing down." She screamed it, first at Will, then at the Halflings. "Get on the roof," she yelled with her hands cupped around her mouth.

Sky looked up at her as if he heard, then hollered something. One by one, the Halflings on the sides began making their way to the top. They spread out until they stretched over the first two cars, their glow making them look like lightning bolts wrapped in flesh. The wind pressed against them with such force, it flattened Glimmer's curls to her head, but the feathered parachutes of their wings were counteracting the train's momentum.

But where were Mace, Raven, and Vine? Her breath was short spurts now, as fear and apprehension stole her momentary joy. The Lost Boys were still at the front of the train. And the broken track was nearly upon them.

"No," she whispered. But as the train and the car-sized mass of twisted metal became one, the whisper grew to a scream. "No!" Soon she was sobbing and hiding her face as metal scraped and crashed against metal. It went on forever, the sound of the crash and the human screams, the shuddering and screeching as steel compressed and was refashioned. The very track groaned in protest as car after car reverberated with the impact.

Nikki buried her face in Will's shirt. But there was no strength in her body. Her head spun, and had it not been for the frozen grip of her fingers, she'd have dropped to the ground.

The solid wall she leaned on wavered. She forced her eyes up to Will's face. A vein in his throat throbbed. Worse, his eyes were empty. Lifeless, staring not at the train, not at her, but straight ahead as if trapped in time.

Then a tremor from his chest, a stifled quake as his unblinking eyes filled with tears. Nikki's fingers unwound from his shirt and she stepped back. She heard a scream from below and recognized it as Vegan's voice. She started running.

"Mace!" she screamed, closing the distance to the wreckage as she raced down the hillside. Her heart pounded, but her feet skidded to a stop when she saw him. Nikki fell to the ground, legs unable to obey her desire to get there, to get to him. Mace was motionless and flat on his back beside the train.

Vegan screamed again, but the tone wasn't one of anguish; it was a cry for help.

Nikki struggled to her feet and forced her legs to begin moving, this time with more power.

"I'm coming, Vegan," Mace yelled, but he was only able to push himself up a few inches before falling back to the ground.

She ran to where Mace lay and threw herself over his chest, wrapping him in a fierce hug. She jerked back up to her knees and ran her hands over him while she sobbed. "I—I saw you. You—were between the train and—and—"

"Shhh," he said, trying to wrap his arms around her. "It's okay. I got out of the way. We all jumped right before impact."

Nikki's gaze traveled from side to side. Her hair clung to her wet cheeks and she pushed it away. *We all*, he'd said. There on the ground, Vine and Raven were stretched out, breathing hard but moving. She offered a relieved smile to Raven, but he looked away. Though he'd tried to hide it, she'd seen the sorrow in his eyes. She'd gone to Mace. Not him.

Nikki swallowed hard. She wouldn't apologize for fearing Mace had died. She clamped her hands on his face. "But you're okay?"

He grinned beneath her touch. "I'm okay, Nikki."

The tears were starting again, but she tried to force them back. She began to tremble, and the shaking only worsened as Mace placed his hands over hers. "Hey," he said in a whispered tone. "It's okay. Nikki, I'm all right."

But the tremors grew. "I thought— I thought I'd watched you die." The floodgate opened and became two steady streams beneath her eyes.

He took her face in his hands. "I'm fine." Mace sighed and cast a glance around them. "Nikki, I need you to get back to the hillside. We have to start helping the wounded."

Her hands dropped to his shirt and tightened in a death grip. He couldn't expect her to just jump up and leave after … after … But of course he did. This was Mace, after all. "I could help. I could stay down here. You need my help." Panic drove her words.

Mace shook his head as he stood. "No, Nikki." His voice was soft, but final. "You'd just slow us down. I'm sorry."

Fear and relief turned into embarrassment. She sat there for an instant feeling the prick of pain accompanying his words. She was a useless, helpless human.

Slowly, she rose and headed toward the hillside trying to ignore the screams from the people inside the train. As she passed Raven, she thought she heard him say, "I'd have let you help."

Nikki watched from the hill. Mace was probably right. She didn't know how to handle the questions the people were undoubtedly asking about how the train had slowed, where the group of rescue-teenagers had come from, and why they seemed to have wings. What could Nikki do? Just get in the way. Just slow them down. After all, she was only a human.

As time wore on, and she'd tired of pacing, Nikki angled her attention to Will, who was waiting quietly, solemnly, beside her like a sentry. Below them the Halflings worked their way through the passenger sections of the train. One crashed train car then the next, all the while pulling survivors from the wreckage. She counted fifteen passenger cars, and the Halflings were sifting through them at lightning speed.

With each passing minute, she felt more inadequate. "Humans are powerless," she spat.

Will's inquisitive gaze turned on her. "No, they're not." Such conviction drove his words, she had to look at his face to see if he was serious. He was.

She shook her head and looked away.

"Nikki, humans wield one of the most powerful forces in this realm."

She crossed her arms. "Which is?"

"Prayer."

"Prayer?" she said, half-mocking.

"Everything that's done is done by petition. A great battle wages for the lives and deaths of those below." Will nodded toward the train.

"If there's such a great battle going on, why can't I see it?"

His mouth quirked a smile. "Perhaps you haven't petitioned to do so."

She threw her arms up. *Fine.* "I'd like to see the battle," she said to no one.

When the sky darkened around her, Nikki crouched for a moment. A cloud blotted the sun, and she had to wonder if a silent airplane or a huge blimp floated overhead. When she looked up, she saw something filling the sky in a circle above the train. Ominous gray-black clouds were hovering, gathering, but something kept them at bay. Another circle created a barrier between them and the train. Each cloud was independent of the others, and when she squinted she realized they had shape. Not quite human shaped, but close, like a person's distorted shadow.

"Show me more," she whispered, reverence entering her voice.

The scene above cleared, and she watched the barrier circle become beings of light. Silver warriors blocked the dark clouds by holding swords of chiseled sunbeams. The brilliant glare was so intense, Nikki's eyes watered. She rubbed the moisture from them then tipped her head to look again. "What is this?" she finally uttered.

Will didn't answer, but his attention drifted to one section of the large circle of what she now knew were angels. A being maneuvered through the dark shapes. He was bigger than the others, darker almost, as if he himself were a cavernous void, a black hole. The other menacing creatures cleared the way for him.

Icy coldness seeped through Nikki's clothing, stroking her skin and causing her to shudder. "What is that?" she whispered.

"Death. He's come to claim another."

Nikki's heart skipped and her focus trailed to the train. The Halflings had maneuvered many of the wounded to a grassy spot where they laid each person down gently before returning to the train to search for more.

Will pointed. "He's come for the boy."

Nikki followed his gesture to the small child stretched out on the ground, his mother crying beside him. "No." Indignation arose within her. "No, he can't have him!"

Will shrugged. "There's nothing you can do to stop him."

The ugly, lumpy cloud had made his way to the edge of the angelic wall. Even from below she could feel the smug sense of superiority it oozed. Her eyes fanned to the boy again, still clutching a bright yellow toy truck. Blood smeared his forehead from a wound along his hairline. "No, you're wrong. I can pray."

Will's brow rose.

She closed her eyes, but no words came. She really didn't know how to pray. Will had called it a petition. All she knew was that a petition was a heartfelt plea. *The heartfelt part won't be a problem.* She threw a glance to the tiny hands clasping the toy, hanging on as if the truck represented life itself.

"You might want to hurry," Will said. "He's breaking through."

Nikki's eyes closed to slits and she looked up. The dark being pressed against the angelic army and pierced a hole in the perimeter.

She clamped her eyes closed and dropped to her knees. *Pray,* her heart screamed. But her mind kept spinning. Was this part of the big picture? Did the Halflings pray? Stupid question—Raven had done just that in the forest after she'd killed the hell hound. He'd held her and stroked her back, and it was like the words flowed out of him. What did he say? *Oh, I am really bad at this.*

"Pray from your heart," Will said.

She nodded, clamped her hands together, and petitioned the Throne. Nikki didn't know how long she prayed, but her knees ached from the press of rocky ground beneath her. When she opened her eyes, the sky seemed a little lighter and death was gone. "I did it?"

Will smiled down at her. "You weren't the only one praying." He nodded to the boy's mother. She held him in her arms, rocking him back and forth and weeping.

"The sky is lighter."

"Yes. Some of the darkness was forced to flee. Imagine if everyone down there was praying." Will's storm-blue eyes sparked. But something else flickered there too. A challenge.

And Nikki knew what she had to do.

Chapter
11

Mace caught her in his grip as she ran past the last passenger car. "Nikki, why aren't you up on the hill?"

He supported her arms, grasping her elbows, and she let her weight rest on him while she tried to catch her breath. "I had to come. Look." She pointed to the sky.

Mace stared overhead.

"People are praying, and death isn't taking any more prisoners today."

A slow smile spread on Mace's face. "You're dealing with this whole *clash of realms* thing really well. You should be proud."

"Well, I'm not. I'm leveled by it. *Angels*, Mace. I saw *angels*." She thought a moment. "I mean, I always see an angel when I look at you. And there's Will. But these were white-clad, sword-carrying *warrior* angels floating in the sky." Nikki felt the blood drain from her cheeks.

Mace's grip tightened. "Hmm, maybe you aren't dealing with it as well as I thought."

Tiny spots appeared before her eyes. She shook her head in an attempt to scatter them, but the spots remained.

"Deeeep breaths," Mace said.

She nodded, but her lungs were light as a feather and they didn't seem inclined to accept the oxygen her deeeep breaths were offering.

A voice came from the right. "Mace, I need your help." It was Vegan. Or maybe Winter. Strange that she couldn't tell. Strange that everything felt so dreamlike and foggy.

"Sit down," Mace instructed while his arm encircled her waist, lowering her to the ground.

Once there, he released her. He was talking, mouth moving, words coming out. Something about being right back. *Okay*, she thought. And hoped he heard. He must have because he disappeared in the direction of the Vegan/Winter voice.

Nikki rested her forehead on her knees and tried to calm her speeding heart. She'd grown accustomed to the hammer blasts in her chest over the course of the day. But really, that couldn't be good for a system. *Get a grip. Everything's fine.*

She glanced around. Wounded were still being taken out of the railcars, the heavenly army was still holding back the clouds. Off to the right Mace and Vegan were dragging someone from the last car. A noise to her left drew her attention. A black, lumpy cloud lumbered toward her. It'd taken shape, and its fat, grotesque legs, one bigger than the other, carried it in a sort of awkward, loping run. Holes in its misshapen head framed white eyes. No irises, only a tiny pupil. Nikki stood as it approached her. But it didn't see her. When she glanced over her shoulder, she discovered its milky eyes were focused on Mace.

"No!" she screamed.

Death continued running as if she wasn't even there.

"No," she said again, this time with more force and holding her hand out to stop it. "God, please, don't let this happen!"

It skittered to a stop at her feet. Milky eyes turned on Nikki as if trying to focus. The creature's odor closed around her while the being found a new target. Her. She felt consumed by the monster. Black hands reached toward her throat, but its touch was everywhere, and Nikki was instantly submerged in its vat-of-snakes embrace. Her skin crawled in response, and she desperately sought a way to gain release. She opened her mouth to scream, but could only suck in a breath of the creature. Something slid across her tongue then down her throat. She wanted to clamp her mouth shut to close it off, but it was too late. It fisted and tugged as if pulling, ripping her soul from her body.

Nikki tried to hold on, but her sanity was slipping from her. The creature smiled a toothless grin and once again a cracked, bleeding tongue darted out as if he intended to lick the side of her face. She was immobile. Death puffed hot breath into her face.

Behind her, she heard the words, "You have no authority here."

And as quickly as it had leeched onto her, it released her from its grip.

Nikki felt the weight of Will's presence warming her back, persuading life to return to her.

The creature opened his mouth wide and an anguished screech split the air. She clamped her hands over her ears.

A moment later, it was gone.

She blinked and sagged to the ground as life pooled back into her. "What just happened, Will?" Around her, everything looked normal: Mace and Vegan placing a brace against the contorted door of a passenger car, a green pasture dotted with Halflings and humans, Will.

"You met death and overcame it."

Fear had disappeared with the creature, leaving a strange emptiness when it went. She stood. "Uh, you overcame it. Was it really killing me?"

"No. Just trying to intimidate you."

"Well, it worked. It was after Mace." As soon as the words left her mouth, Nikki heard the groan of metal. She turned and watched as a beam broke directly over Mace's head.

It wasn't that Mace feared death. He understood eternity, even had a healthy respect for it. But the idea of a dark infinity was enough to shake anyone. The humans didn't know how good they had it. All they had to do was make a choice.

Of course, he hoped for light, for mercy, and had made every choice in this life to do his best to be worthy of such grace. But ultimately that decision rested with the Throne. He wasn't human. He wasn't offered the mercy seat as they were. Yet Mace knew the grace of the One he served. And because he did, he'd had no reason to fear death.

But the look on Nikki's face as he heard her scream, and as he felt the shifting of the beam above and the wind as it dropped to him … that, he feared. And something, some deep force, threw his hands into the air, and he caught the beam before it crashed against him. He lowered it to the ground as it whined in protest. And as it fell, so did Nikki. She fainted in a heap at Will's feet.

Without stopping to think, Mace jogged the distance to her and pulled her onto his lap. He rocked her gently back and forth and thought of what a horrible day this was for a human to endure. She awakened wrapped in his arms. And then she cried. Great, heaving sobs. One hand stroked her hair, moving the tear-moistened strands from her face. The other stayed tightly fitted around her waist; an assurance, a promise not to let her go.

"Mace, there are a few more wounded." At some point Vegan had come alongside him, and she didn't sound altogether pleased.

He closed his eyes a moment. Back to work. He heard the other Halflings working to situate the remaining injured and dressing what wounds they could with torn strips of clothing. "Are you okay now?" Mace whispered, because Nikki needed to be okay. A seed of anger and indignation rooted into his heart, a seed that was connected to her. Because she'd lost her parents, her home, even her dog. Because she'd had to watch him almost die, because she was being hunted by evil creatures no teenage girl should have to think about. And for all those reasons, she needed to be okay right now. He would never let iniquity settle in his heart because she was destroyed by what he brought into her life. He'd always been okay with the destiny chosen for him. But he wasn't okay with this. And iniquity, though it could be a fire able to warm the coldest soul, was also a one-way ticket to hell.

Mace. Holding her. His beautiful face resting above hers. He asked her something. Was she okay? Nikki read every worry in his face and nodded. He *needed* her to be okay.

So she was.

She pulled a breath and with it drew her courage. "I've watched you die twice today." As soon as the words left her mouth, she wished she could grab them and shove them back in. This isn't what he needed right now. He needed someone strong, someone able to stand beside him, not crumble at every challenge. "But I'm okay. Vegan's right. You have to help the rest of the wounded."

Mace's eyes conveyed approval. His fingertips traced from her temple to her jaw, until his index finger trailed over her lips. "That's my Nikki," he said, then his lips were where his finger had been.

She thought she'd already run the gamut of sensations in the course of this day, but the press of his mouth to hers created a new barrage of feelings. Her awareness heightened as she felt the shockwave rock through his system. Mace deepened the kiss, barely, but somehow monumentally. And Nikki knew as soon as she pulled the breath he released into her lungs that there'd be no going back. They'd just crossed a line. She wouldn't apologize for this. It felt right being in his arms. To truly be his. How could she have ever doubted?

He pulled away gently, but it felt as though they were still connected. Maybe they were. On some deep level that went far beyond feeling, it felt like their souls intertwined. And she didn't think any power on earth could reverse that.

When his body tensed to move her from him, she pressed her mouth to his once more, needing to be sure she hadn't imagined the stir of her soul. All the energy that had gone into moving away from her melted away as they kissed. His hands wound into her hair, and she realized with awe he wouldn't break the kiss this time. There was a hunger there, an excitement, an urgency, and she knew she shouldn't have kissed him again.

But they'd worked so hard to stay at arm's length from one another. Worked so hard to do the right thing, though now it was impossible to resist what was right. She started to tip away, but his fingertips hardened at the base of her neck, a refusal to let her go.

Vegan's voice broke through the connection. "Nikki, you should get back to the hillside where it's safe."

Her eyes snapped open and she broke the kiss. She hadn't meant for such a strong challenge to appear in her gaze, but she knew it had.

"No," Mace said. He gave her a wink. "Nikki can help."

She hugged him hard. "I'll be careful, I promise."

"You better," he warned.

Vegan gave her a hand up. "She can stay with me."

Mace was doing what he'd been created to do: lead. Orders flew from his mouth as he pointed Halflings toward different railcars to do a final check. Everyone deferred to his instruction, and the rescue mission moved with precision. Injured passengers had been carried on makeshift gurneys—pieces of thin metal, strips of broken boards from inside the train, even a steam trunk lid had been fashioned to carry the injured. The wounded lined a section of grassy area parallel to the train wreck at the base of the hill. Those who were less injured had rallied to help. After what seemed like an eternity, they heard the sirens. The train track snaked between the only road in and the only road out of this section near the Rhine River, sometimes hovering near the thin incoming road, sometimes veering away from it. Thankfully, in the valley where the wreck sat, the road wasn't far.

Raven ran toward Mace, wiping sweat smeared with blood from his hands. "You hear 'em?" he asked. The whine of sirens filled the air, bouncing off hills and seeping gloriously into the valley.

Mace nodded, trying to catch his breath. "Yeah. Took them long enough."

"We're out in the middle of nowhere, dude." Raven's eyes suddenly darted toward the road to the north, then off to the right, and then back again.

Mace watched as horror filled his brother's features. "What is it? What's wrong?"

Raven pointed toward the road on one side, then the road on the other. And with his hand he made a perfect swooping motion demonstrating the bowl they were sitting in.

It dawned on Mace what he was suggesting. A gauntlet.

Mace turned and started screaming to the others, "Get them away from the hillside!" His arms flailed, motioning for everyone in the vicinity to move the wounded. And he prayed it wasn't too late.

***

Nikki heard the screams, the yelling, the uproar. Mace was hollering something about getting people away from the hillside. She left her task of searching for survivors and popped out of the train car. What had been a scene of relative order under Mace's command had become chaos as people dragged, carried, and tugged the wounded back toward the train.

As she neared Mace and Raven, she heard the first explosion, a ground-rumbling boom that reverberated through her system. Behind her, the hill collapsed onto the road like a great brown avalanche. A massive dust cloud rose and engulfed them. If the people hadn't been moved, they would be buried under the dirt.

She drew in a breath, but sucked only dust that caked her throat and caused her to cough. The second boom threw her a few feet, and she fell forward into Mace and Raven, who'd each run toward her after the first blast. They caught her weight together, but the reality of the situation made all three less than solid. They'd barely gained their footing when on both the north and south ends of the mountain, the road disappeared beneath a hill of fresh earth.

"They've closed us in. It will take hours for the emergency vehicles to get through," Mace said, tearing off one of the sleeves of his T-shirt and wrapping it around his mouth.

Nikki watched him for a moment, then did the same. Raven's grip tightened on her arm. She protested and tried to pull away, but he looked as if he didn't even hear her.

Her eyes flew to Mace, who grabbed Raven by the wrist and twisted his grip from Nikki. "Dude, what's wrong with you?"

But Raven's eyes were focused on the top of the mountain. Nikki squinted to see what had drawn his attention and caused him to hurt her, but all she saw was a large white van and four men piling into it. She rubbed her arm.

"Raven, I'm going to need you to take charge of the wounded. I'll organize a group to start digging from this—"

But Raven wasn't listening. He stared at the mountainside, his breaths coming in short puffs. Raven snapped his wings open and leapt.

130

Nikki blinked.

Mace sighed, a long, sad sound.

"*He ... left?*" Her eyes found Mace, pleading for him to tell her she hadn't just watched Raven abandon them. But he wouldn't meet her gaze, and she knew he was fighting his own disgust.

Nikki looked at the pitiful scene around her. Women and children and a good number of men were crying, digging through the debris and dust, searching for loved ones they hoped escaped the earth slide. Stunned and bleeding, those who could walk were carrying wounded.

And Raven left.

She noticed a little girl clinging to a teddy bear. The girl's eyes were saucers and her nose was bleeding. She sat on a rock, covered in a layer of dirt, and stared into the distance.

And Raven left.

An old man was yelling for help, hollering about his wife going back into the train car to get her purse right before the earthquake. He used his cane to try to pry open the sheet of metal encasing her in the railcar. When he realized his efforts were futile, he crumpled to the ground.

And Raven left.

The shock melted into anger and she ran from Mace to try to help the old man.

"She went back in. We thought it was safe," he said through tears. "Then the ... the ... earthquake ..."

Earthquakes weren't accompanied by air-splitting blasts. She'd lived in Missouri long enough, had watched demolition crews blast through mountains to build roads often enough, to know that. This was intentional. Nikki grabbed the cane and tried to pry at the opening of a passenger car. From inside, she heard a whimper. It fueled her fight. She searched the surrounding area and found a piece of steel. Anchoring it, she pulled and heard the metal prison creak. Suddenly, tiny wrinkled hands appeared in the crack she'd made. They were bloody and quivering, but alive. The old man grabbed the hands and kissed them, and the whimper inside became a howl of despair and joy.

"Mace!" Nikki screamed.

Before she could fill her lungs to yell for him again, he was there, throwing his weight against the metal and prying it open around her. Blood began to run beneath his fingertips and Nikki knew the jagged sharp pieces of metal were cutting him. "Wait," she said, and ripped the remaining sleeve from her top. But the old man stripped his shirt from his back and forced it under Mace's fingers. The opening was large enough now for a child to pass through, and Nikki caught a glimpse of the terrified woman.

"We have to get her out," Nikki said and wedged her foot between the opening and the train track. She clamped her hands around the woman's arms and pulled with all her strength. Just as the woman was freed and falling into her husband's waiting embrace, Nikki felt the train shift. A deep rumble rose from the ground as the train car began to slide and settle. Her foot became trapped, but Mace's hands were there at her ankle trying to pull her free. His fingers were slick, and when she heard the second whine of settling metal, something in her died. Her eyes found Mace, whose face read everything she felt. The train was going to crush her.

Chapter
12

Nikki drifted in and out of consciousness for days. She knew it had been days because darkness turned to daylight and daylight to darkness. Over and over. She was so tired. But in the sweet euphoria that was one part sleep and one part wakefulness, she'd pieced the pieces together.

Raven appeared in the last moment before the train car came down. He must have taken most of the brunt of the falling car that would have squished her into the ground like a bug under a shoe. She gathered from the conversations around her, when everyone presumed she was asleep, that Raven had given Mace time to get her out and then disappeared completely.

Disappearance was impossible for a Halfling. Sure, they could leap out of this realm into the other if there was room for their wings to snap open, but disappearing from beneath a train, as if vaporized?

She heard Mace's voice often. Sometimes soothing her, sometimes talking in a soft whisper to one of the others. From what she could tell they were at Viennesse, one of the Halflings' ancestral homes in Europe.

A part of her wanted to stay in this state of consciousness where Mace watched over her and nothing bad happened, but the continual healing of her body disallowed that. She loved Mace. And watching him in action, saving lives and leading the entire operation, reminded her why she loved him. But it was the kiss that swept her away. They'd never kissed like that. It was a pure, sweet, honest promise. No walls between them, placed by either of them. Nothing in their way. And that was as treacherous as it was wonderful.

And then Raven had saved her. But, she tried to tell herself, he'd also left hundreds of people in order to chase after a mysterious van. Even if she were to decide his actions were right, that he'd done a noble thing, he'd disappeared without any explanation. And she had no idea what that meant. The Halflings seemed to think he was okay, based on the conversations she'd overheard. Some were even angry; another "Raven antic," Vegan called it. But when days passed and Raven didn't appear at Viennesse, their bitterness had softened. In fact, some were wondering if he'd even perished beneath the train, though they claimed he couldn't have. They'd done a thorough search for him. He'd left, then returned to save her, then disappeared. He'd reappear eventually.

With all that was swirling around her, Nikki knew it was time for her to join the world of the living. Even though it meant dealing with unsettling things like terrorists who blow up trains and demons who try to steal your soul to intimidate you, and most of all half-angel boys.

Mace left the room before she could open her eyes. Nikki

turned to the window and stared at a cloudless blue sky. "Come back, Raven," she whispered. "You weren't created to be alone."

There were a million reasons for Raven to stay dead and only one reason to be alive. Nikki. But the fact remained, Nikki was with Mace. Which made dead a whole lot more appealing.

It was the kiss that sealed it. Its power reached out toward anyone who happened to be standing nearby. It was what he'd always wanted her to feel when she kissed him.

He'd said he'd give her time. Against his better judgment, but hey, what did he know about this love thing? Now he was left with that day playing out over and over in his head. As if intent on making the anguish last, his mind forced him to watch Nikki rush to Mace even though all three of them could have been killed by the speeding train.

Her concern, her fear, her attention had been Mace-centered. And if anything, if anything at all, Raven had been a brief afterthought.

Women were nothing but trouble. Hadn't he known that before? The thing that really got to him was that he'd left the van of goons to go back and save Nikki when he heard Mace scream her name. By the time he changed course and got to her, other Halflings were there helping Mace hold the train car off the ground. They could have gotten her out. But he'd dived inside, tugged her ankle free, and took the weight of the car while she scampered into the sunlight.

And the van full of bombers drove away as the train met the ground. The screeching of metal still hung in his ears.

So, after the narrow opening closed and he knew she was

free and, oh yeah, in Mace's arms again, he'd scooted into the back of the train. When no one was looking, he'd shimmied out the back and leapt. They were probably crying over his death. Oh well. It was better this way. For all of them.

His first stop had been Dr. Richmond's house. The doc was glad to see him, and they'd even formed a bit of a bond since Raven visited him each evening. In fact, Raven had become an almost constant shadow of Dr. Richmond, helping him in the basement lab. Raven explained to the doc he was homeschooling now, and Richmond bought it. Or so he said. The mad-scientist-gone-high-school-teacher tried to broach the subject of Nikki leaving town and Raven and his "cousins" leaving school all in the same weekend, but Raven always redirected the conversation. Seriously, what could he say? *Yeah, well, we don't like Vessler, her godfather, because we think he's connected to an ancient being so evil he's actually seeking to destroy the human population. Did Nikki leave town with us? Why, yes she did. We all piled onto a yacht and headed to Europe. But I had to leave when I realized the girl I love is in love with someone else. So, here I am. Surprise. Did I mention I really need information on the laboratory you used to work for because they are also tied to that ancient being I mentioned earlier? Sorry to tell ya, but you were helping a group who is trying to destroy your race. But hey, don't let it ruin your dinner or anything.*

What Raven hadn't expected was that his plan to discover what Richmond knew had spawned a shocking revelation. One that caused the back of his neck to sweat.

He'd found unconditional approval.

Though there remained specific reasons for their time together, Raven couldn't discount the acceptance he received from the older man. Round and partially bald, Richmond

136

personified the weakness of man, his inability to control even his appearance. But deeper than the surface, the doctor gazed upon Raven as if he admired and … appreciated him. As if he respected and cared for—

Whoa! Enough with the sappy crap. Richmond had answers and Raven needed them. End of story.

Tonight, the good doctor seemed unusually excited.

"Can I trust you with a secret?" Dr. Richmond asked over reading glasses that magnified his cheeks and made the clogged pores even more visible.

Finally. "Sure." Raven shrugged, acting interested in the bubbling contents of the beaker. But inside he perked up. *This was it.*

"Do you like horses?"

Raven turned off the Bunsen burner. "Yeah. My uncle has a stretch of land in Europe where he kept horses years ago. It was sort of a remote area, so he'd sell them to people in the village— horses were an easy way to get around, especially in the winter. I always thought they were powerful animals. Pretty cool."

Richmond's face lit. "My boy, I could show you the most magnificent horses alive."

Raven slid the beaker aside and gazed at the doctor through slashes of long bangs. "Really?"

"Yes." Richmond tugged his glasses off, brow furrowed. He feverishly rubbed them along his shirttail. "I shouldn't," he argued with himself. "Then again." He stepped closer to Raven, halting inches away. "There is something quite unique and … special about you, son." Richmond searched his face.

Raven shrunk from the exposure. *Special.* Not the word most used to describe him.

"Something within me begs to trust you." He offered a quick nod. "Yes. That's what we'll do."

Raven's brows rose. "What?"

"Oh, yes. Sorry, sorry." Dr. Richmond moved briskly around the room gathering a flashlight, an umbrella, a notebook, and binoculars, balancing them all against his chest until he procured a backpack. "I'll go. Tonight. You'll accompany me. But you must swear—*swear*—never to utter a word of what you see." He pressed a free hand firmly on Raven's chest. The muscle mass he encountered seemed to shock him. Richmond patted around for several seconds, and Raven could almost see the gears whirring in the guy's head. Eyes fanned to Raven's shirt. Patted again. "You are unique indeed. And I think I was meant to share this with you."

Yep. You were. And right after we're done, maybe we'll take a nice stroll to the special place where everyone gets their own rubber room.

Mace spread a blanket and held Nikki's hand while she sat down. The foothills of Germany's Black Forest anchored their picnic area and the palatial spread of Viennesse rested on a mountaintop just behind them. "It's really beautiful, isn't it?" she murmured.

Mace followed her gaze, taking in the panorama of darkly colored vegetation. "You should see it from above."

Nikki lifted a brow. "Is that an offer?"

That devastating smile appeared on his face. "Just an observation."

"Well, either way, you have to show me now." Nikki scooted

around on the blanket, refusing to cringe. Her muscles were still sore from the train incident, but she didn't want Mace to know. Whenever she groaned, winced, or flinched, his face grew somber and his expression fell into worry. Worst of all, he'd search her with those cerulean eyes. It made her feel guilty for being such a wimp. The Halflings had all been more seriously injured than her; deep cuts and bruises on their hands, arms, and legs while she barely had a scrape, though her body felt like it'd been hit by a truck.

"What's wrong?" Mace said, moving closer to her. He slid the contents of the picnic basket to the edge of the blanket. "Here, lean on me."

He scooted behind her, and she tilted to rest her back against his chest. Her legs stretched in front of her and his to the side. This time he didn't see her wince. A gentle breeze feathered over them and Nikki sighed. His chest was warm, and his breath and heartbeat mirrored her own. She released the tension she'd been carrying for days.

"That's better," he whispered, as she let her muscles melt even more.

But pressures tugged at the edge of her mind and Nikki knew time was running out. "Things are bad, aren't they?"

Mace wrapped his arms around her. "I'd say things are pretty good."

She chuckled. "I'm not talking about us, Mace. I'm talking about ..." She couldn't believe she was about to say this. "About the world."

"It's a delicate balance between good and evil, a tightrope we all have to walk. But yes, things are getting bad. Titanium shipments meant for wingcuffs can only mean one thing."

"What's that?"

"The enemy feels like he has enough power on the earth to take over. Stopping Halflings would certainly help his cause. We're sent by the Throne, and the enemy hates the Throne."

"The enemy? You mean—"

"Yes, Nikki. The hater of men's souls. The despiser of all that is holy."

"Is he after me as well? Is this all part of the reason you were sent to protect me?" She shivered.

"You don't need to be afraid. We're good at what we do. And everyone here seems equally taken with you, so I don't think any of us will let our guard down."

"What do you mean?"

"Everyone likes you. The females, Dash, Sky, and Ocean. Even Will."

"Will won't be happy when he realizes we are ... well, we're ..."

"A couple?"

She nodded.

"Will isn't stupid. He can see how I feel about you. How I've felt about you since the very beginning, when you were running through the woods with hell hounds at your feet. Even when you and Krissy went shopping that day—"

She sucked a breath. "You were there?"

"Just to keep an eye on you," he said, smiling down at her.

"I bet." She tried to ignore the flush of embarrassment. She'd bought *underwear* that day.

"I knew you weren't safe."

"Nothing happened though."

"Not until later on your motorcycle, when the weird guy started chasing you in that beat-up SUV."

"I still don't know what he was so mad about."

"He was an evil man, Nikki. Evil is drawn to you for some reason."

She tilted her head, tucking it beneath his. Securely cradled against him, Nikki closed her eyes.

"But you're safe now."

Safe. But at what cost? "Mace, if all the Halflings here are busy protecting me, doesn't that mean there are a lot of other people who *aren't* being protected?"

His muscles tensed.

"I mean, so much attention for one person? It doesn't make sense."

"That's the nature of the Kingdom—remember, we were sent to watch over you. It rarely makes sense to the natural mind. But trust me, it's perfect."

"This situation doesn't seem perfect."

"That's because we're flawed. The plan, as well as the Creator and Executer of the plan, is perfect, but we aren't."

"Like a broken vase."

"What?"

"Nothing. It's just that a broken pot can still grow flowers if it's not too badly damaged. It just leaks more than other pots."

"Okay, I can live with that logic. We leak."

"Mace, do you think Raven is okay?"

Mace became silent for several minutes, finally releasing a long sigh tinged with sadness. "He's out there, but I worry about him being alone. It's really hard to resist evil on your own. You need a support system. And some need it more than others."

"I'm so sorry for breaking up your friendship."

He leaned away and looked at her through half-closed lids. "What do you mean?"

"You and Raven. Since I came along, the two of you have acted like enemies."

"Yeah, well, that's pretty much how we acted before. You just brought it to the surface."

"You mean you guys weren't close?"

"No. We're like brothers. Or maybe not brothers, more like brothers-in-arms. You don't have to like the guy in the foxhole with you as long as you're still willing to die for him."

"I don't get it." The breeze lifted the edge of the blanket, where a line of ants marched toward the basket.

"It's the nature of being in a war, I guess. Raven knows I'd lay down my life for him, and he'd do the same for me. But that doesn't mean we have to like each other's ethics. I've never agreed with how Raven operates. And I'm pretty sure I never will, because it's destructive."

She thought back to the train wreck. "I still can't believe he left."

"Yeah, well, that's Raven. Not much of a team player." Mace cupped an arm on her shoulder. "But you, you were quite the team player, Miss I-Can-Open-a-Railcar-Like-a-Can-of-Peas."

"I hope that's not my new nickname. It's a mouthful."

"I'm just saying you were really gutsy."

"Yeah, right up to the moment I nearly got myself killed." She shuddered. Or maybe that had been him; she couldn't tell. Either way, Mace drew her closer.

"I've never been as scared as I was then, Nikki. I knew I couldn't hold up the train car myself."

"I don't know how the other Halflings got there so fast. And Raven, he just appeared from out of nowhere."

"That's very Raven as well."

She didn't want to talk about it anymore. It had been one

of the most horrible days of her life … and she'd had a few bad ones recently.

"What do we do from here, Mace?" Almost the entire time she'd known him, she'd been aware it was an act of rebellion for a Halfling to fall in love with a human. And that their mutual feelings put Mace on very dangerous ground where eternity was concerned. In a strange twist, practically losing each other had sealed their fate. Or doomed it.

"Nikki, I don't know what the future holds."

She swallowed past the dry lump in her throat. "You could be taken away, couldn't you, when this journey ends?"

"Yes."

"Gone. As quickly as you appeared?"

He nodded. But that gesture said something else too. She realized Mace had finally stopped pushing her into some role he wanted her to fill. On the boat he'd been almost unbearable. Now, he practically couldn't get enough of her just the way she was. Almost like … like he knew their time was running out.

It hurt already, thinking of him leaving one day. "Then we need to make every moment count."

Mace dropped his chin to the top of her head. "Exactly."

She nuzzled deeper, resting her ear against his beating heart, tuning in to his breathing. If she could capture those rhythms, she would. If for no other reason than to remember him for all eternity, to remember what they shared, because she feared one day it would all seem like a dream.

Chapter 13

No mortal words could describe the magnificent animals before them. Lying on his stomach in a field with Dr. Richmond stretched beside him, Raven stared in awe while the scent of grass and wild horses filled his nostrils. And the animals were not hard to take in. Like a spotlight poised on a superstar, one large beam of brightness illuminated the night-darkened corral that sat adjacent to Omega Corporation's laboratory.

Raven and Dr. Richmond inched closer to the thick fence caging twenty-some horses. Belly-crawling like a couple of military snipers, they carefully observed the massive animals. "They *are* bigger than Clydesdales," Raven whispered. "I thought Glimmer and Vegan were exaggerating."

"Who?"

"Oh, some girls I know. They told me there were horses like this around here. I didn't really believe them."

"Most folks don't know about this place." Richmond's head

turned, and Raven could sense the man was studying him. "I'm surprised you'd heard about them before."

Raven shrugged, pivoting away from the scrutiny.

"Look at that one." Richmond pointed, excitedly. "I call her Debra."

Dragging his eyes from the other giants, Raven cocked a brow. "Debra? You named a beast like that Debra?"

Richmond nodded, rocked on his round belly for a more comfortable position, then pointed again. "She's something of a pack leader." He tilted closer to Raven, squinting as if to make out his face more clearly. "If you've ever read the Bible, you know that Debra was an Old Testament—"

"Prophetess and judge," Raven finished.

"My boy, you know the Scripture?" In the disappearing light, Richmond's teeth glowed.

"A little." Raven wasn't interested in a theological discussion. Especially while blades of dry grass poked into his forearms.

"Are you familiar with Revelation?" Richmond asked.

Don't remind me. When the end of days arrived, it would signal judgment. Like humans, on that great and terrible day, Halflings would be measured by the Throne, their deeds exposed. But while humans were allowed a safety net called salvation—and only those humans who refused the gift would end up in hell—half-angel, half-human beings had nothing to fall back on. With no written word, no contract, no covenant, the eternal fate of all Halflings—living and dead—remained unclear, and there would be no arguing with the heavenly decision. *That's what you get for being an unwilling freak of nature.*

When Raven didn't speak, Richmond continued. "I was not a spiritual man until nineteen and a half years ago when I left Omega's lab. I'm a man of science. A seeker of fact. But fact and truth are brothers, and the deeper I sought, the more I could see. In Revelation, it speaks of a great battle."

"Yes." A cold breeze swept Raven's body, and the blades of stiff grass brushed against him as if their purpose was to punctuate Richmond's words.

"There's a verse that tells us in the battle to end all battles, the blood will run bridle-high to the horses." Richmond's face radiated a faint but unnatural yellow hue as he spoke. "Isn't it strange that with all the technology we've acquired, we're told the blood runs *bridle*-high? It suggests, of course, that *horses* will carry the end of days' army."

"Maybe the writer of Revelation was just using what he knew to describe something he was seeing in the future. I mean, how could he describe Humvees or tanks?"

Richmond's mouth pursed. "The same way he described helicopters."

"What?" But Raven knew.

"In one area, John the Revelator describes giant locusts filling the sky."

Raven nodded. "Giant locusts. Helicopters."

"But horses carry the army to the great battle."

Raven's gaze slowly left Richmond. "Horses like these." Magnificent power was manifested in the animals before him. Moments ago he wanted Richmond to shut up so he could enjoy the moment; now he wished he'd never seen the animals, hadn't been sent on this journey, and didn't have a working knowledge of Scripture and the implication of giant horses and how they fit into biblical prophecy. It made the future too close, too real.

Too bleak.

"Once they've perfected these animals, they'll breed hundreds of thousands of them. An army, Raven. A literal army."

146

Trust me, I get it. Raven's jaw clenched.

Richmond chatted on about Debra the horse, her ill temperament, how she'd seemed to calm in weeks past, and numerous other details Raven tried to focus on, instead of the doomsday direction his thoughts veered toward.

"Why would she suddenly be calmer?" Raven asked. *Might as well keep up the pretense I'm listening.*

"Part of the beauty of the project before it went sideways was that personality traits from calm animals could be introduced into violent animals, controlling their temperament."

"The same way you were splicing DNA in your basement to make the snake able to reproduce at cooler temperatures?"

"Nothing escapes you, my boy. Once the gene sequences are altered, the animals can be controlled by simple injection."

For some reason Raven thought of Will and Zero arguing on the boat about human DNA. Both had different opinions on what would happen if that DNA was introduced into a Halfling specimen, how the angelic nature could eclipse certain human qualities. But Raven couldn't yet see how the two issues were related. *Best to keep digging.* "So, it's like flipping a switch?"

"Precisely," Richmond confirmed. "I created the technology nearly twenty years ago, but it was primitive at best. You had to inject the subject daily to obtain the desired effect. Now, they inject to calm the animals, so the subject remains in that dormant state until a new injection is administered. Days, weeks, even months."

"Aren't you a sneaky professor, spying on their every move?" Raven turned to focus on the doctor. "Basically, you're telling me they are Jekyll and Hyding them?"

"I never would have thought to put it in those terms, but yes."

Raven shook his head. "That's some scary stuff, Dr. Richmond."

The man lowered his eyes. "I'm so ashamed of my part in this."

Raven forced a smile. "You couldn't have known."

The reassurance clearly fell on deaf ears. "I just wish I could undo it all."

"Wait," Raven said. "Back up. Did you say Debra is the *pack* leader?"

Richmond scooted his elbows closer together and reached for the binoculars. "Yes."

"Horses aren't pack animals. Dogs, wolves, hyenas, even large felines, yes. But horses? Sorry, Dr. Richmond."

"My dear boy, have you ever seen horses like these? Listen to me. They are capable of more than I ever imagined. They think intelligently, they process information, and I'm telling you ..." He shook the binoculars at the animal. "Debra is the pack leader."

Muscles knotted along Raven's spine as his wings went on alert, tingling like goose bumps after a cold swim.

The dark, massive animal looked more like a bronze statue than a living creature. Her upper body rippled with the thick muscle of a work horse, one used to pulling a plow through untamed ground. But her rear half was sleek and slim as if bred for distance running.

The wind changed, lifting Raven's bangs.

Debra dragged her massive head from the ground, then she stood in the center of the field while a thick layer of fog curled around her hooves. Tipping back slightly, she sniffed the air. Her chest expanded. A heartbeat later, her gaze leveled on them.

Raven held his breath. "She knows we're here," he whispered, awe seeping through him.

Every muscle of her body tensed. She whinnied a warning in their direction.

"Look, look." Now it was Raven who pointed toward her.

Richmond lifted the binoculars.

"She looks like a predator." Ears up, nose to the air, head tilted, her tail swished a couple times as if releasing her aggravation.

"Yes, yes she does." Richmond stood from the ground and waved a clear, plastic zipper bag at the animal.

Raven grabbed Richmond's shirt and tugged. "What are you doing?" he hissed, eyes shooting from the horse to the doctor who refused to be bullied.

Giant hooves pounded the ground as Debra drew near. Richmond waved a dismissive hand. "It's fine, son. She loves a treat." He shook the bag again. "And who brings you treats?" he cooed. "That's right, come on." He slipped his hand into the bag and withdrew a handful of sugar cubes and pieces of hard candy. "The way to a horse's heart is with sugar."

Apparently Debra and Vine have a lot in common. Far beyond the fence was the entrance to the lab. Raven stood and shot a quick glance, sensed no threat, and relaxed enough to enjoy the creature's approach. When a giant head reached around him to get the sugar, Raven's mouth curved. He hadn't meant to plaster the goofy grin across his face, but he couldn't help himself. Few things in this world stopped him cold. Few things offered this kind of excitement: snowboarding, scuba diving, and apparently having a giant horse nibble sugar cubes inches from his face. Yep, that was one he'd keep to himself.

When the candy disappeared, so did Debra. "Cool," Raven said.

"They are *cool*." Dr. Richmond sampled the word, trying it on for size. It didn't fit.

"What is this place?" Raven asked. He'd let Richmond talk in riddles, but now it was time to ascertain what he knew about Omega. Stars twinkled above, sending distant SOS messages, or maybe warning messages not to push the doctor too far. Raven had never been much for heaven's subtlety.

"This is a laboratory, Raven. Much of it's underground, and I sometimes wish the earth would swallow the entire thing."

"Genetic alterations, obviously," Raven said. When headlights flashed on a distant hillside, both men dropped to the ground.

"True and worse." Richmond's face troubled. Suddenly, he looked old, worn out from too many regrets and too many questions.

"What did they do to these horses exactly?" *What did they do to you*?

"The short version is they mutated them." His face wrinkled under the stress of admission. "But they were hardly normal to begin with."

"What do you mean?"

Richmond tilted away. "I can't say. But this"—he waved to the corral—"is all my fault."

A rock was digging into Raven's ribs. He ignored it. "How is it your fault?"

"I uncovered the gene sequence that allowed us to introduce mega-steroids without the harmful effects that usually accompany them." He pressed his hands to his face for a moment. "You must understand my intentions were good. Honorable. If the genes could be manipulated, and specific chemical treatments introduced, we could literally obliterate many terminal diseases. Cancer, for one. The body fights to protect the cancer, mutating its own cells."

"So you suppress that, introduce chemo treatments, and end the cycle."

"Yes. When I discovered the lab's intention, I ran. Literally, I ran."

Raven shrugged. "You went sixty miles, doc."

He nodded. "I admit, fear overtook me. I couldn't look guilty, or they'd come after me."

"Guilty of what?"

"Destroying what I'd poured my life into creating."

"You did that?"

"Yes. Unfortunately, I didn't retrieve everything." He pointed to the lab. "Information was autosaved to a main computer system. I had no way to breach the security. But I removed what I could, and with a small, contained fire, slowed their progress and covered my tracks. The, uh, explosion wasn't intentional." He winced. "You wouldn't believe me if I told you the specimen they planned on testing next."

"I'd believe anything at this point."

"No, and I won't utter it. It still makes me ill to think about." He rubbed a hand across his nearly bald head. "It nearly killed us, my wife and me. We feared for our very lives. She was pregnant at the time but she lost the baby. It happened almost twenty years ago, and my wife still has nightmares. We thought they'd kill us in our sleep."

"No, doc. Men with this much power don't wait until you're asleep. They do it in broad daylight." When one of the horses reared back on powerful legs, Raven shook his head. "Why did you share all this with me?"

"Because my heart tells me you're the key."

Raven frowned. "The key to what?"

"Their salvation."

When a far-off gate slid open, the horses galloped for the fence line, creating enough dust to cloak their movements. The ground shook at the thundering of solid hooves. "I don't know what I can do," Raven said.

"Just do what you can."

"One condition." Raven met his gaze squarely.

"Anything."

"Draw me a layout of that lab."

<hr />

In eight days Raven had fallen into a routine. Visit Richmond in the evenings, eavesdrop on scientists' conversations during the day, and stay in the barn at night. He and Debra had even become friends.

But this night was anything but routine.

When Raven heard human footsteps approaching the stall, he rose to his feet from where he'd been sitting on a mound of hay. His hand slipped into his front pocket and seized the pocketknife. He liked the feel of metal in his hand, warmed by his own body heat and ready to strike. He rarely carried a knife. Metal objects didn't travel well in the midplane, which was one reason Glimmer was the only Halfling who carried a weapon. Raven liked to think of her as Tinkerbelle with claws.

But Glimmer wasn't there. Neither were Mace, Vine, or Nikki. He was alone. No other Halflings and no obligation to return home. They all thought he was dead, smashed in the train car. Even if he died tonight, no one would care.

With a smooth movement, his thumb slid the blade open. It was one of those expensive pocketknives carried by true knife enthusiasts and lawyers with more money than sense. *If you don't know what you're doin', you could end up with the stiletto blade stuck through your own flesh.*

But Raven knew his way around most—if not all—weapons. Just because Halflings didn't usually carry weapons didn't mean they couldn't wield them. Being a half-angel also had its perks. Stealth, for one. Raven silently slipped behind the barn intruder.

Hmm. Funny I'd think the guard was an intruder, seeing as I'm the one who isn't supposed to be here. But hiding out and gathering intel on Omega by splitting his time between Richmond, the laboratory, and the barn of mutant horses had made him a bit territorial. The barn was his domain now, and uninvited guests would be terminated upon contact.

He leapt forward and grabbed the guard, placing the blade carefully at his throat. "I could have had you, Cordelle," Raven whispered into the guard's ear.

Adam Cordelle released the air he'd sucked up. "Don't scare me like that, Raven. It's not funny."

Sweat from the guard's face dripped onto Raven's arm. The guy was shaking. Good.

Raven released the thirtyish man. Cordelle promptly spun around off balance to face his opponent. Unsteady and perspiring, he dragged a breath, probably trying to slow his racing heart.

Raven chuckled and examined the knife.

"Where'd you get that? You didn't have it when I found you sleeping in here." Cordelle's voice rang like an angry parent who'd caught their kid with a hand in the cookie jar.

Raven cringed. He'd *let* Cordelle find him because he needed an ally. No one, absolutely *no one* snuck up on him. Well, he supposed Winter had on the boat. But that didn't count. He'd been distracted by Nikki.

Cordelle pointed a surprisingly chubby finger. With such a wiry build, the fat fingers didn't fit. "Stealing is wrong, Raven. I'm not helping you get back on your feet so that you can return to a life of crime." Cordelle had presumed Raven was a dropout living on the streets, and Raven was happy to keep up the act. "When I found you eight days ago, I told you I'd keep quiet about your being here if you promised to choose a better path for your life." Daddy Cordelle turned away from Raven and straightened some papers on the desk, where surveillance cameras offered various snapshots of the corral and the barn interior. "Everybody needs a hand up sometimes. I'll help you all I can, but not so you can go back to being a vagrant."

Raven put his hand to his heart. "A vagrant? Man, that hurts."

Cordelle's chubby hands fisted and landed on his thin waist. "That's what you are," he said with a nod and a sad flash in his eyes. "If you continue on the path you're on, at least. Wouldn't you like to change things?"

Raven's thoughts flew to Nikki. He remembered closing her in the circle of his wings, holding her while she fed the dolphin. Her smile, her long hair floating behind them ... He swallowed the bitter memory. "Yeah. I'd like to change a lot of things."

"Good, because I talked to my cousin down at Fort Smith. He thinks he can get you a job at the chicken plant. It's not a pretty job, but it pays good and it's a lot better than hitchhiking your way to California." Another assumption Cordelle had made. Another one Raven didn't bother to correct. Seriously, what was he supposed to tell the guy? *I'm no transient; I'm here gathering information about your employer and trying to figure out a way to rescue these horses.* No, that admission probably wouldn't fly. What he couldn't figure out was how a mild-mannered guy like Cordelle had wound up working for scum like the Omega types. Must be somebody's brother-in-law.

Cordelle continued his monologue with excitement. "I'd have taken a job there myself, but my brother-in-law insisted I come to work for this company—he's been here a couple years and they treat him good. This is a state-of-the-art facility, you know? Doing big important things here, we are."

Right. So big and so important. He could tell Cordelle was oblivious to what Omega did or didn't do. Just another monkey swallowing propaganda about the infamous all-important work.

"And the wife didn't want to move away from the fam."

Uh-huh. Raven's powers of intuition scared even him sometimes. He faded out of the conversation as Cordelle droned on about being an active member of society. Blah, blah, blah. Who cared?

Raven cared about the society of one: himself. At least he had until Nikki. She'd changed him—both destroyed and remade him. There *was* a soul beneath his flesh. It had been a cold and shriveled empty place until she ignited it. Now it burned, and the awakened fire might kill him—if, of course, he wasn't already dead.

"Did you just say you're already dead?" Cordelle leaned forward and examined him with round little eyes that resembled two chunks of coal stuck in a snowman. Hands to the hips, again. "Raven, never ever say that. You aren't dead."

He really had to stop mumbling his thoughts. Of course,

Cordelle was right. Raven was very much physically alive. For now. But spiritually, he didn't know how long he'd last without the support of the other Halflings—a difficult thing for him to admit, even to himself, but facts were facts. Raven had always teetered between the light and the dark side, but he'd had Will to help keep his head above the proverbial drowning pool. How long would he last on his own? Did it matter?

He'd died a hero's death as far as they knew. Saving Nikki. Giving Mace time to pull her from under the train car. He'd always thought he'd go out in a blaze of glory. And so he had.

Besides, he didn't have to stay alone. There were other Halflings he could hook up with. The problem was they weren't in the same place as Nikki.

And so the questioned remained. Live or die? The more he considered it, the better dead sounded.

Chapter
14

Nikki stood on a patch of grass by a creek in the Rhine Valley, deciding how to best destroy the hell hound facing her. All around, vineyards stretched in zigzag patterns crossing the hilly terrain. It was beautiful. Later, she'd take time to examine the intricate details that reminded her of the cornrow braids she'd seen women wearing on a beach in Mexico. Back when life was simple and she had parents and was a normal teenager instead of a Seer who couldn't seem to master her vocation.

"You gonna daydream the day away? We are here for a purpose, or did you forget?" Dash said. He leaned his weight against a tree by the river, one foot cocked in front of the other and arms crossed casually.

Nikki knew why she was there. Will had said her martial arts skills could use a little improvement, since fighting hounds from the pit, as well as demons, was a tad different than human opponents at karate tournaments. She'd killed a hound before.

But that was in a fit of rage, and she'd almost fallen apart in the aftermath of the deed. Now she needed to understand the hounds' attack and her best defense. After all, evil was drawn to her.

Focus. Her muscles still ached, but her body had healed from the train accident. But as she took her fighter's pose, her thoughts went to Raven, the training he'd done with her. And that only reminded her of his recent sacrifice. While he probably wasn't dead, he hadn't returned, so it was a sacrifice all the same. She considered the strange turn of events that led to his disappearance, how she drove him away with her knee-jerk reaction when she thought Mace had been smashed by the careening train. She wouldn't forget the hurt that settled in Raven's midnight eyes. Ever.

And yet … he'd returned to save her.

"You sure you're up to this?" Vine asked. He stood opposite Dash.

She looked over at Vine's kind smile, which lit a face surrounded by yards of silky hair any girl would kill for. His body language hinted his readiness to fight. Dash's read cool confidence, almost boredom. His hair, unruly clumps of sun-bleached blond over darker brown, contrasted Vine's. Messy freedom versus silky-smooth control.

Freedom. The name Raven had given her.

The hound snarled, exposing fangs and demanding her attention. "I'm good," Nikki assured Vine with a nod, and was instantly glad that Ocean, Sky, and especially Dash had decided to stay at Viennesse. Who else but Dash and Vine could she have convinced to do this? She may not be the sharpest tool in the drawer—who lures a hell hound for practice?—but she knew when she could win a fight and when it was time to cut

158

and run. *Maybe Raven knew when it was time to cut and run too.*

Vine stayed in a ready stance. Dash rolled his eyes and slid down the tree trunk to sit. His nonchalance made Nikki that much more alert. If she did get into trouble, she hoped Dash could get to her in time.

When the hell hound took a step closer, Nikki lunged, trying to gain the edge. She caught it by the throat and clamped her arm around its neck. Growls rumbled against her skin and jaws snapped, slinging spit as it tried to sink its teeth into her. With a grunt, she slung the thing to the ground. Her foot slipped on her discarded sketchpad, and pain from the train wreck wound jolted from her ankle to her knee. She ignored it. "I'd forgotten how strong they are."

"They have a way of reminding you." Dash stood now that the fight had begun.

"How about the smell?" Vine asked, laughter in his voice. "Did you forget that?"

"No," Nikki said, brushing a hand across her forehead. "I remember that vividly."

"Road kill in a locker room," Vine added.

"Worse." Much worse. Hell hounds oozed the stench of death. Understandable since they came from the pit and carried the remnant smells of their home, a disgusting potpourri of rotten potatoes, rancid meat, and the copper bite of blood. She'd be fine to never smell one again. As the hound jumped toward her, she knew that was a hopeless prayer.

Black matted fur filled her vision. From the corner of her eye she saw Vine ready for a rescue. "No," she hollered at him. "I can do it." But just as the words escaped her mouth, the pinching pain of razor teeth clamped onto her arm. The canine fangs sank deep into her flesh, and she screamed, though she tried to channel the pain into a defensive escape. She punched the creature's neck, but it held firm to her arm, tearing the flesh further. She positioned her other hand to strike its windpipe, and was about to attack when something flashed from above. An instant later the hound was catapulted from her in such a rush that for a moment she thought her arm might rip from the socket and go with the sailing creature. The beast landed in a heap. And Mace landed on top of it.

As soon as the hound stopped kicking, he spun to face her, fire in his eyes. "What's going on here?"

"Lesson's over," Dash mumbled. He stiffened when Mace began moving toward him, fists rising to chest level. Dash held up a hand to stop Mace's advance. "We had her back."

Mace shoved Dash's hand aside with enough power that the boy's body jolted from his arm to his head. "Really? When were you going to step in? When the hound ripped her arm off?"

"I didn't *need* anyone to step in!" Nikki took a few steps toward Mace but sank to the ground, suddenly dizzy.

Mace's eyes widened, prompting Nikki to glance down. Her sleeve was wet, red, and shiny. Blood ran between her fingers where she'd clamped her hand over the wound.

He ran to her and dropped to his knees to examine the injury.

"I'm fine, Mace," she said, but guilt careened into her system when she saw the fear in his expression. It mirrored the look at the train, when he'd thought she'd be crushed. She knew how that felt, and it was awful to purposely put anyone through it. "I'm sorry."

His blue eyes scanned every inch of the bite marks and flashed only once to meet her gaze. A volume of words rested inside those blue orbs. A world of hurt hovered on the surface. "Why?" He tore off his shirt and ripped a length of cotton from it to staunch the wound.

Before she could answer, Mace looked first at Vine, who dropped his head in shame, then at Dash, who merely shrugged.

"Mace, I have to learn to fight." Nikki tried to sound gentle, but urgency stained her words. "Hounds and demons are after me. I can't expect Halflings to babysit me my entire life."

"You're barely well. And why would you have Dash bring you out here?"

She attempted a smile. "Because you wouldn't have done it."

"*I'll* help you learn to fight when the time is right. But there's no rush. This was a really stupid thing to do, Nikki. You purposely drew a hound into this realm. I thought you were smarter than that."

Nikki jerked her arm from him. "In case you didn't notice, there's a war going on around us. And I've been drafted. So I'm sorry you don't like the idea of your girl fighting, but you better get used to it. Because I'm not backing down."

The muscle in his jaw flexed. "Neither am I." His chest puffed a little, and she thought he might snap his wings open as a show of alpha-male prowess.

Those wings were intimidating, but so was her determination. "Then we have a serious problem." Her voice cracked. *Stupid voice, abandoning me in my moment of need.*

"I guess we do," Mace said through clenched teeth. His words were as forceful as Niagara Falls.

Dash began to inch a little farther from the two of them. "I am *so* not getting into this fight."

Mace rose from the ground and fisted his hands into Dash's shirt. "Don't ever bring her out again."

161

Dash clamped his hands on Mace's wrist, found the meaty flesh of Mace's thumb, and twisted. Mace's grip loosened and gave way. "I don't care if you are dating her. Don't ever grab me like that again."

Nikki stood and stepped between the two towering half-angels. "Mace, it wasn't his fault. I told him I was coming whether he tagged along or not. Vine too. Don't blame them."

"Nikki, you're not ready."

A slow burn slid down her body, pooling at her feet and fueling her anger. "And what makes you think you're the one who should tell me what I am and am not ready for?"

Mace was obviously incapable of thinking clearly where it involved her, but it was on the verge of becoming a very destructive tendency. He wanted to protect her, which was admirable. Even appreciated. It would be a great quality, in fact, if they lived in a perfect world. But this place was far from perfect, and there were things Mace wouldn't be able to protect her from. Unspeakable things. Things that were on their way. She didn't know how she knew, but she did, just like she'd known on the boat something evil was stirring. That premonition had culminated with a train wreck. The thing that scared her now was a sign her biggest battle loomed just beyond the horizon. And as long as she remained with the Halflings, the horizon was never more than a blink away.

Raven had the computer thing down to a science. Get bits of information about Omega, bounce it around in the ether for a few hours, then send it—untraceable—to Zero. But trying to learn anything from the few scientists roaming the lab was lamer than watching grass grow. They clicked away on their keyboards and stared into their microscopes and discussed everything in some infuriating code, using words like *specimen* and *centrifuge*. The code wasn't intentional—it's not like they thought someone might be listening—it was simply their jargon. Like Zero, who had his own techie lyrics to a song only other computer geeks could sing. Raven was pretty sharp in the science department, but these clowns took scientific communication to a whole new level. He half expected them to start beeping and making robotic noises. At least that would be entertaining.

Over the last few days, he had noticed something interesting, at least—there were very few people actually in the lab. If Omega had called in more genetic scientists, where were they?

He put the thought aside and sent out another installment of Omega information that he'd liberated. It was easy enough to move around the laboratory because the scientists had no reason to be cautious right now, or assume someone was hiding in the vents and exploring the rooms. That said, there was one room Raven wished he'd never discovered; the farthest exam room in the back of the long, narrow building made his blood run cold. It held a cage. A human-sized cage. Empty, but no less freaky.

Raven erased his fingerprints from the keyboard and returned to the barn in time to meet Cordelle at the beginning of his shift and keep up the homeless teen act. Ah. Life was easy. Boring, but easy.

He was actually beginning to like Cordelle. A sucker, but a likeable one. Raven lay on a stack of hay, hands behind his head, ankles crossed. Staring up at the barn's slat roof, he thought about Nikki. *What to do? What to do?*

Debra wandered into the barn and blew a puff of hot breath in his face. Yeah, they'd bonded.

She whinnied in assent.

"What do you know about love, Debra?" Raven stood and rubbed an open palm over her velvet nose. The horse leaned in closer, shifting her weight from one hoof to the other. She neighed and watched him with those big, round eyes rimmed with feathery lashes.

Cordelle came around the corner. "If you love someone, you should tell them."

Raven stiffened.

Fat fingers filled Raven's vision. What was it with this guy and waving those clubbed Mickey Mouse hands around? Put some white gloves on him and he'd be ready to give guided theme park tours. "It's not that simple, Cordelle."

"Love never is, but if it were simple it wouldn't be worth much."

Raven cocked a brow. Philosophies of Love by Adam Cordelle, horse guard extraordinaire. *How far can one Halfling sink?*

Okay, one thing was obvious—he had some thinking to do. He'd need peace and quiet to do it, which was not likely to happen here in the barn with Cordelle in one of his "let's talk about our feelings" moods. *So* not happening.

Raven sighed. "I found the knife in the top drawer of the tack room."

"The knife from the other night?"

Raven nodded.

A wide smile appeared on Cordelle's face. "You didn't steal it?"

"No."

Cordelle grabbed Raven's hand and pumped it up and down. "That's good. I didn't want to think all this time and energy I've put into you was for nothing."

"Well, there's still plenty of time for me to disappoint you." Raven took the knife from his pocket, gave it one last long look, then held it out for Cordelle to take.

"You say you found it in the drawer?"

"Yeah. Buried under some twine and horse liniment. It was all dusty, but it cleaned up pretty well."

"I'll tell you what. You keep it for a while. But when you're ready to leave here, for good, promise me you'll put it back where you found it."

Raven's hand closed on the knife. "I promise." Something passed between the two of them that Raven couldn't quite understand. He felt it though. Trust, maybe. Friendship? A bond?

He needed to get out of there. He needed to think. There was only one place where Raven could think, and it was ten hours away by airplane or two hours away by midplane. And days away by ship. "I'm gonna go for a walk. I probably won't be back before your shift is over, so I'll see you tomorrow night."

"Be careful, Raven."

Geez. Do I need to wear a sweater so I don't catch a cold? Raven tossed the hair out of his eyes. "See ya."

As soon as he stepped outside, he knew something was happening. Dark and elusive, it waited just beyond reach, something with the power to change the course of this journey, of … Well, life as he knew it. He'd tried not to think of Nikki. But she was tied to this new evil hovering in the distance like smoke from a forest fire. Her purpose was drawing closer at the same time he'd decided that one of the best ways to protect her was to stay away. Anxious to get to the castle ruins, the one place he could actually reflect, Raven sped his steps. He cleared the corner of the barn, then, with one last look to make sure he was alone, spread his wings and leapt.

"You seem to know him pretty well, Nikki. Would Raven do this?"

Nikki stared at Zero, then at the computer screen, then at Zero.

Vegan paced in the corner, her long, flowing hair blanketing her shoulders. "It's a trap. Set by someone at Omega."

"Why would Omega be feeding us information about their business?"

Vegan stopped. "It's only bits of information. And you can't trace where it's coming from."

Zero mashed some keys and pointed to the screen, his silver eyes framed with a frown. "We know next to nothing about Omega's EMP program. We *think* they could be working on a weapon of mass destruction, but we don't know for sure. Why would they give us any information about that? It doesn't make any sense."

"You've got information about what they're doing with electromagnetic pulses?" Nikki asked.

"It's somehow tied to these." Zero's long, slender fingers clicked away at the keyboard. "Look. The partial EMP file was sent with this."

Nikki and Vegan stepped closer and gazed over his shoulder.

"Those are military bases," Vegan mumbled.

"Yeah. There's no way Omega would compromise sensitive information like that. Not even if they thought they could somehow trap us—and I don't really see how they could."

"They could be planning anything. Please be careful, Zero." Vegan slipped a hand onto his shoulder.

Nikki couldn't help the eye roll. Not that either of them saw it. They were busy making googly eyes at each other. Why Zero and Vegan didn't just admit they were a couple, Nikki didn't know.

She cleared her throat. "Why wouldn't Raven just let you know it's him?"

"Raven—if he's alive—wants us to think he's dead," Zero said. "He's never coming back."

Nikki's knees suddenly felt too weak to hold her. While she'd thought the same thing, those words made it too final. The world started to go black.

"I think she's going to faint," Vegan said, but the words were far away, dreamlike.

Zero's tone sharpened. "Are you kidding me? Females are pathetic."

Immediately, there was a chair behind her knees, and Vegan's hands were guiding her to sit. Nikki tried to pull in deep breaths, but her lungs weren't able to accept the fresh air. "If. You said if." She hadn't allowed herself to accept that Raven may have actually died in the train car. She simply believed him alive.

"If he's snooping around Omega, he's as good as dead anyway," Zero grumbled, and Vegan punched him in the shoulder—the same shoulder she'd caressed moments before.

Nikki shook her head back and forth. "Either way, I killed him, Zero." Her eyes found his. Saw the flash of understanding that faded as quickly as it appeared.

"You didn't kill him, Nikki. Stop with the drama, okay? It's giving me a headache." Zero was great with sympathy.

But this threw a whole new set of problems into her life. She figured Raven had gone because he'd seen her with Mace at the train wreck. Raven knew they were … inseparable.

She'd thought Raven would eventually return with stories about a multitude of hearts he'd broken in a monthlong binge. But she'd never thought he'd fly right into the lion's mouth. Alone. If he was at Omega, it seemed he wanted to die.

Vegan broke the silence. "Where is Raven, if he's the one sending information?"

"I don't know. Not at the castle ruins, that's for sure. He'd have to be somewhere near one of Omega's labs. We know of places Omega's linked to in Arkansas, Nashville—although I don't know what's at that one—Chicago, and a really small town in Texas that I haven't had time to research yet. It only makes sense that he'd be at the lab in Arkansas. I almost guarantee he's there and sending whatever he can find."

"But why would he try to hide from us?" Vegan asked.

Zero's gaze fell on Nikki, and it burrowed under her skin. "Maybe he's tired of games."

Chapter
15

Viennesse was a stone giant. Nikki had always thought castles would be cold, due to all that rock from floor to ceiling, but for the most part it was surprisingly cozy. Decorated with Old World charm, with massive rooms allowing for numerous people. Not that the place was full right now with only nine Halflings, Will, and her sharing the space with a handful of other Halfling males who seemed to live at Viennesse fulltime. Most of them she'd already met.

On the boat she'd had no privacy. Here, she had plenty. Maybe too much, because she felt strangely alone. The only light she encountered each day was Mace. Nikki went to bed early but, like most nights lately, couldn't sleep. She tossed and turned for an hour then rose, dressed, and slipped from her room to the garage. It was after ten, but Gearhead was still working. She'd met him only a day before, when she'd decided to explore as a way to fill the hours. "Hey, Gearhead."

He stretched up from beneath an SUV's hood and she heard

169

his back pop. Light brown hair dusted with grease splatters framed a surprisingly boyish face. His eyes, as pale blue and vibrant as a summer sky, lit up when he saw her. "Nikki."

She frowned. "Was that your back?"

A half smile sent an endearing slash across his cheek. Under all that grease, Gearhead was a strikingly good-looking guy. Even by Halfling standards—on a scale of one to Abercrombie model, he'd rank pretty high. "I'm not as young as I used to be."

And how old might you be? she wanted to ask. Halflings didn't really talk about age much. It was sort of irrelevant. From what she could gather, the human side aged at a very slow pace for them, and the angel side didn't age at all. Basically, on a bad day, one might feel his or her years to some small degree, but still look young forever. Gearhead must have been having one of those bad days. According to Mace, trips through the midplane renewed their youth. Maybe Gearhead was overdue. What was it Mace had told her? Something about youth being renewed like the eagles. Whatever that meant.

She paused to lean against the Land Rover he'd been swallowed by.

"Your car?"

"They all belong to everyone. We have our favorites, though," he said, brushing at a grease spot on his chin.

"I'm into bikes more than cars," Nikki said.

He inclined his head and motioned for her to follow him. "Come on. I'll show you the bikes."

As they entered a side room he flipped a switch, illuminating the tarp-covered motorcycles. Gearhead vigorously rubbed his hands on a shop towel then grabbed the first tarp and tugged it off. It was a gleaming Harley Davidson. "Wow," Nikki said, inspecting the custom paint. "Is it brand new?"

"Nah, it's about fifteen years old," he said as he pulled other tarps to reveal their offerings.

Huh. Apparently, Halflings weren't the only things that didn't age here.

When Nikki noticed a black bird on the side of one of the Harleys, she crossed the garage to examine it. She knelt to inspect the paint.

"That's Raven's."

She spied Gearhead over the gas tank. "I thought you said they belonged to everyone."

"Yeah." He scrubbed the back of his head. "I did."

"Can I take it for a ride?"

"No. It's Raven's."

Okaaaay. "Where are the castle ruins?"

Gearhead's gaze faltered for a moment, but it was enough that she noticed.

She threw a leg over the bike. He flinched.

"I'm just wondering because I'd like to know where they are." *That was the biggest nonexplanation on the planet.*

"Raven's ruins?"

She hoped her own eyes didn't falter as she nodded, grasped the handlebars, and tilted the bike up. "It's comfortable," she said, gesturing to the seat.

"Yeah. Get off it."

"If Raven was here, he'd let me take it."

Gearhead turned from her. "He's not here. When he gets back, you can ask him."

Nikki tilted the bike back onto its kickstand. "You do believe he's coming back, right?" Hope that entered her voice and drifted through the cavernous garage. Glancing around, the remaining tarp-covered mounds suddenly looked like freshly dug graves. Each one shaped slightly different, each one representing a life that was no more.

Gearhead brought her the cover for Raven's bike. "He's coming back." A tiny flicker of a smile soothed her.

Reverently, she blanketed the bike while Gearhead watched in silence.

"So, which one can I take?"

"How about the Kawasaki Ninja?" Gearhead led her to a wall where a row of keys sat at the ready.

"Yippee. That'll be a treat," she deadpanned.

He scrutinized the key rings until he found one that read KN–05. "Here ya go."

She didn't take the keys he offered, and instead studied the display. "Your secret code? K for Kawasaki, N for Ninja, and the year it was made?"

"Not much of a secret code. Why are you going to the ruins?"

She kept her eyes on the various key rings. "I want to help Raven, and I thought if I go there, maybe it'll give me some inspiration about *how* to help him."

"That's stupid."

She nodded. "I know. So is your secret code."

Gearhead busied himself pulling the tarp from the Ninja while Nikki stood by, and told her how to get to the ruins. It was about a forty-five minute ride to the bottom of the hill. At the hilltop were the remnants of a long-dilapidated and abandoned castle. "You'll have to walk up the mountain to the ruins. It's too rough for a bike. The road will crumble beneath the tires. Trust me, don't drive up."

"I got it."

He tossed her a helmet. "Here, see how that fits." He hit a button on the wall and the garage door opened.

"It's too big. Are there others?"

He sighed. "Be right back. They're on the wall in the other room."

As soon as he left, Nikki snagged the keys, ripped off the tarp, jumped onto Raven's bike, and tore out of the garage.

***

Yes, this is definitely Raven's domain, Nikki decided as she scrutinized the monstrous formation of ruins. It was a little creepy at night, but the moon's bright glow helped ease her apprehension. Walls stretched to the sky, but crumbled into uneven mountains of stone; too weak to fulfill their destiny, too proud to give up their place. It had taken her awhile to find the stairway, but as soon as she made her way to the top, the remnants of the castle that once was became visible. The flat terrace, where she now stood, could have been a stone courtyard in Viennesse or in any other palace, if not for the eroding walls and columns.

She stopped in the center, her eyes examining the moonlit structure.

A sound behind her made her jump. She spun but saw nothing. The wind coaxed her to the terrace edge. She tested the crumbling ground, found it sturdy enough, and stepped into an open space along the palace wall, stopping when her toes dangled over the side.

A tilt of the head revealed a star-confetti sky hovered above. From this vantage point, she could view the Rhine River off to the right, which snaked through the land and shimmered from the moon's rays.

Nikki captured the night air in her lungs and spread her

arms. If only she had wings. She'd dive off this edge and let the wind take her. In answer to her request, the cool night breeze surged.

"You gonna jump?"

She turned without thinking. One foot slipped off the edge while the other tried unsuccessfully to clamber for better traction. Her arms, already spread, began a series of swirls and jerks as she slipped, and she lurched to grab the stone wall.

But rather than cold, hard rock, they found warm, strong flesh. Arms encircled her, materializing from nowhere. They held her, hands flattening on her back, pulling her closer.

Nikki sucked a breath of panic until she recognized his scent.

Raven.

Instinctively, she buried her head in his neck and dug her hands into the back of his shirt. She tried to breathe, tried to speak, but all that came from her tightened throat was a choked sob. As she trembled against him, he shuddered and drew her even closer.

So many emotions bombarded her, Nikki couldn't form words. *Raven. Alive. And safe.*

When the first shades of propriety revisited her, she unfisted her hands and tried to push away from him.

"Don't," he whispered against her ear, burrowing deeply into the waves of her hair. With his head tilted down, his long, slow exhale scorched her neck, and for a moment she wondered if her body might combust. His hands and arms finally loosened, and she thought she'd be able to step away, but when her muscles tightened in response, he pulled her back into an embrace so tight it felt impossible to distinguish where one body stopped and the other began.

For a moment Nikki allowed herself to dissolve against him. He was alive. He was okay. And he'd finally come home. Involuntarily, her mouth whispered his name.

In response, he adjusted his stance to accommodate her. A breeze swirled up the side of the castle wall and lifted her hair. She cast a glance downward. "Raven, we're right on the edge."

More than you know, he wanted to say.

But rather than follow her gaze, he tugged her to one side, where a castle wall waited to support them.

Pinning her to the wall, he loosened his arms just enough to look into her eyes. In those golden depths, he was home. She'd wrecked him. Wrecked him with her fierce desire to fight and her strength to stand when her whole world crumbled, had wrecked him with her eyes that beckoned him—even when her head told her not to allow it.

Her breathing was a series of short, hot puffs. Partially because of nearly falling off the wall, partially because of him. Her body had warmed as soon as he grabbed her, and her muscles gave way, thawing beneath his touch when she'd realized it was him. Him. Not Mace. Not anyone else. And even now as she tried to rationalize her reaction, he could see it—the love in her eyes and the absolute uncertainty of what to do with that emotion and what it meant for both of them.

When she sighed, he pulled the breath she released into his own being. Intoxicating, it entered his lungs, burning out all doubt.

Unsteady hands flattened against his chest. "Raven," she said. Her voice held an apologetic tone that he would have ignored had it not felt like an ice-cold splash of water. "Raven, please." She squirmed against the wall, still breathy, but her voice regaining its strength.

"You can't deny this," he said.

"What?" More force in her words now, a sign her head was finding control over her emotions. No matter; he knew how to fix that.

He pressed closer. "This." His hands slid along her side.

But she shook her head, ignoring her body's response to him. "I don't even know what *this* is!"

"I told you a long time ago you are in love with me."

She released such a long sigh, it was painful for him to listen. "Raven, I'm with Mace. He's right for me. I know that now." He could hear the doubt in her voice, every word ringing with uncertainty. *Still trying to convince herself.*

"And I know you're right for me."

"No," she said as her smooth forehead crinkled and her eyes glistening with tiny droplets of moisture. "I'm not."

His hands stopped moving.

As she blinked, the tears slid onto her lashes, where they sat like diamonds waiting to be sifted from the silt.

He worked to keep his voice even. "How do you know?"

One of the larger tears dropped below the outer corner of her eye. "Because I love Mace."

When Raven bent toward it, her eyes closed. His lips found the tear and kissed it away. "You love me too."

For a moment, he knew she was trapped. Her body stiffened, but her soul reached for him, a struggle so strong he tangibly felt the war. Finally, she said, "It's not the same."

"It is. You know it is or you wouldn't have come here." Still holding her captive with his body position, he dropped his hands away from her. "Why are you here, Nikki?"

When her hands fidgeted to reach for him, she clamped her teeth together. "I thought … I thought …" But no more words came.

"You knew I'd be here."

"No." Her cheeks flushed red with embarrassment. *Perfect.*

"You knew I'd be here or you wouldn't have brought my bike." When a confused frown betrayed her, he nodded toward the winding stairway leading to the road below. "I heard the motor when you stopped at the bottom of the hill. Only one Harley sounds like that." He took her hands in his, cradled them against his chest. "You knew I'd be here. You may not have known with your head. But you knew with your heart. Remember what I taught you on the boat? There's a difference between head knowledge and heart knowledge."

More confusion skated across her features as plainly as if a movie ran before her eyes.

"Tell me this doesn't feel right and I'll leave."

"Raven, it's not right because …" A little panic entered her voice. "Because it's not right."

"Does it *feel* right when we're together?" Then he went for the kill. "Who helped you master the faith ball? Who soothed you until you read the sign that told us where to find the train?" He could sense the victory approaching. "Mace couldn't do that, Nikki. I'm the one you were meant to love. You know that."

She closed her eyes, trying to shut him out.

"Just say it," he coaxed her. "Does it feel right when we're together?"

Her tense little gusts full of excitement and surrender were back. On the tail of one, she whispered almost painfully, "Yes."

Triumph bathed over him. His head dipped closer to her scent, to the source of those words. The admission not only clarified everything, it devoured every obstacle in the way.

His arms found their way around her again. She didn't fight. As if weakened, she clung to him and pressed against the wall at her back like an unstable child on a slippery slope, waiting for the moment when gravity won and dragged her down.

And though he held her—the only thing he'd wanted for a long time—Raven couldn't mistake the sensation that surged within him. Expecting to feel at peace, he felt unsettled. For the briefest moment, he pondered this new alarm.

Nikki was always strong. Except now. He'd beat her down. And weakness was one thing Nikki couldn't afford.

But conquest breached the warning. "Come on, Nikki, let's go for a ride."

"What do you think of Nikki?" Mace asked Gearhead as he stepped into the garage.

"Man, doesn't anyone sleep around here?" Gearhead exchanged the ratchet in his hand for a pair of pliers.

"Sorry. I'm worried about her."

"With good reason," Gearhead mumbled.

Mace toyed with a distributor cap lying on the Land Rover's manifold. "What?"

"Nothing. Hand me that," he said, pointing to a wrench in the tool box.

"This one?" Mace held one in the air.

A grease-smeared face popped up from under the Land Rover's hood. "No. Half inch."

Metal clinked against metal as Mace rummaged through the tool box. The scent of fresh grease and motor oil rose with each movement.

Gearhead murmured a thank you when Mace handed him the tool. "What do I think of Nikki? She's stubborn, certainly irritating. But it's sort of hot that she's so into bikes."

Mace swallowed.

"I don't really know her. But I feel bad for her." Gearhead's eyes saddened a little.

"Why?"

"Growing up, thinking you're this normal girl in a normal world. Then, *wham!*" He smacked a shop towel on the fender. "Wake up one day and you're a Seer, dragged into a war between angels and demons."

"It didn't happen quite that fast."

Gearhead usually kept his head stuck beneath various car hoods, but he gave his full attention as he stared at Mace. "Just saying. How do you deal with that?" He thought a moment. "And what about her parents?"

"They were killed in a robbery."

"Yeah, that's what I heard. As well as the fact Zero found her name on a computer you lifted from that fire you both just *happened* to be at."

"Will sent us to that fire, we didn't just happen to be there." Frustration burrowed into his gut. Mace didn't like where this visit was headed. "What are you getting at?"

"The obvious. Maybe she's a plant."

Mace's hands fisted, causing the blood surging from his heart to fill every vein with adrenaline-laced anger. "Are you serious?"

"Sorry, man. It's just that when she was down here earlier—"

179

Mace cut him off. "Nikki was down here? Why?"

"She came to steal a bike."

Mace's blood chilled.

The change was not lost on Gearhead. "Calm down. She just wanted to go for a ride."

"And you *let* her?"

"I'm not the warden," Gearhead said as he followed Mace, who'd brushed past him and headed for the bikes.

The last thing in the world Nikki needed was to be out alone. If she wanted to leave, why hadn't she come to get him? Why hadn't she asked him to take her? He found his answer as he flipped the light switch on the garage wall.

His eyes settled on the empty hole where the one bike he'd hoped would be there belonged. As he turned away, Mace felt a new kind of pain leech onto his heart.

Chapter
16

Nikki crisscrossed the night-darkened countryside on the back of Raven's Harley for more than an hour. Germany's Black Forest disappeared around them as they meandered along tree-trimmed paths and pebble-stone streets. In Baden-Baden, they stopped for a break at one of the town's numerous fountains. Nikki sat on the edge of the concrete structure and watched water spill over a stone statue illuminated by an underwater light. After a long silence, she spoke. "How long do you think this fountain's been here?"

Raven sat beside her and dipped his hand into the cool mineral water. "Hundreds of years." He gave a half-laugh. "Well, not the light kit. I'm pretty sure that was added later."

She gave him a sidelong glance. "Hundreds of years?"

"Yeah, there are even ruins of the Turkish bath houses beneath some of the mineral spas. The ancient Romans used to come here to soak in the mineral water because they thought it would heal their illnesses and make them immortal."

"Why did they think that?" Nikki's finger trailed through the water, carefully maneuvering around the hand Raven had thrust into the fountain.

With a water-drenched finger, he pointed behind them to Viennesse. "Well, for those of us who've been around awhile, we think it's probably because Halflings began dwelling at Viennesse centuries ago, and they didn't seem to age. The ancient Romans believed the mineral water was an eternal spring that flowed from Viennesse's hilltop."

"Did they try to uncover the Halflings?" When he didn't answer and instead ignored her by rummaging that hand through the water, she grabbed his shirt and shook him. "What happened to the ancient Romans?"

"They're all dead—hence the word *ancient*." He chuckled and she released his shirt with a playful shove. "Their goal for immortality didn't exactly work. But they did build a tunnel through the mountainside to Viennesse. They believed the top of the hill, beneath the castle, was the mouth of the eternal spring."

"So they were digging to reroute the water?"

"Maybe. No one knows. The Halflings had to leave the area when they became conspicuous. Not much activity at Viennesse for the next few hundred years, and once the legends died, the Halflings came back."

"Where did they go in the meantime?"

"There's another castle here in Germany and one in France." He shrugged while water ran in silvery rivulets off his fingertips. "A few others scattered around the globe. My favorite place is in Switzerland. Great snow skiing. You'd love it there."

She shook her head sadly. "But you can't ever rest, can you? Can't ever let your guard down or just wake up and say, 'Hey, it's another normal morning.'" She thought a moment. "Me too, I guess. Since I've been drafted."

"What's so good about normal?" he challenged, shifting on the concrete seat to face her more fully.

"I don't know. I can't remember. It seems like my old life is a lifetime away from me."

"We're in a war, Nikki, one that's been going on for thousands of lifetimes. And the responsibility to protect our generation falls on our shoulders. Welcome to the new *normal*."

"Thanks for putting it so gently."

"You want gentle, go find Mace. You want truth, I'm your guy."

"Raven, we need to talk about him."

One side of his face creaked into a humorless smile. "I'd rather not."

"No matter what you think of him, I love Mace."

"I thought we covered this," he said, rising from the seat and brushing his hands on his jeans. He walked a few steps away, staring down a deserted street lit only by the occasional cone-shaped glow of a street lamp.

"And I want to be with him." She looked away from Raven. She had to. Framed by the lonely street and the surrounding darkness, she thought about what his life had been since leaving the train wreck. Alone. Choosing to appear dead rather than face her with the knowledge that she'd chosen someone else. Nikki's gaze dropped to the fountain, hoping to find the strength to say what she had to say, but no words or encouragement materialized. The single light shone. It was designed to illuminate the stone statue. It was alone. It fulfilled its purpose. Just like Raven.

"Mace keeps me stable," she blurted, and turned toward

Raven. His powerful shoulders dropped a few inches and she knew he was trying to reject her words.

Her foot took a step in his direction, but she stopped, forcing her body to slide her feet back until they bumped against the fountain's edge. And there she'd be stone strong. Statue stiff. "With everything that's happened to me in the last few months, I need someone who can keep my feet on the ground."

He said nothing.

"Raven, I love being with you. When we're together," she said, shaking her head, "I feel free. I feel like I *can* fly. But that's not what I need right now. I need a stabilizer, not a jetpack."

"And you think Mace can give you that?" he said, without turning to face her. There was no emotion, no feeling in his voice, just dead words floating toward her over the emptiness.

If he'd only turn around, she could see what was going on inside him. Raven might be able to camouflage his voice, but he could never lie with his eyes. "I don't know how to explain it, but there's something …" Her voice trailed and a bitter wind swirled through her jeans. The night was getting colder as the day's warmth drained from the mountains and valleys around Baden-Baden. And with the chill air came an evil promise. Something desperate to get to her was slipping closer. She could almost feel the icy hands closing on her throat.

Nikki tried to focus her thoughts on Raven. "Like I said, I can't explain it, but there's something—"

He must have heard the fear in her voice. Raven turned, closed the distance, and seized her. His brows slashed into a worried frown. "Nikki, what is it?"

How could she explain the sensation? "I don't know. I just feel like something is going to happen."

"Then let's go. Let's get away from here, away from the Halflings."

She stiffened. "You mean away from Mace." Did he really expect her to just run away? Maybe running was what Raven did best. In the amount of time it took lightning to flash, Nikki's emotion toward Raven shifted. "I'd never walk away. I owe them." The pain materialized in his gaze, and she could almost hear his thoughts. She squeezed her eyes shut, hoping he wouldn't give those words voice. But of course he did. This was Raven, after all.

"What about the guy who was willing to die for you?"

It sounded like such a self-serving comment, the kind of bargain small children make. *You do this for me and I'll do that for you.* "Don't do this, Raven, please."

"You say you want a stabilizer, Nikki. But I know you. You don't want safe ground. You want castle ruins where you can stand on the edge, where maybe it will stay firm and maybe it will crumble." He let his hands roam over her arms, her back. "How long will it take before you're bored out of your mind? How long until Mace's firm foundation closes around you like a cage?"

Part of her wanted to shut him out completely, but part wanted to agree. If there was one thing Nikki'd always feared, it was being trapped. So much so she'd dreamed about it as a child: the cold, unforgiving floor, the bars where she pressed her face, the desperation to feel the air beyond the stifling confines of the prison. She shook her head against the memory, but the gilded cage would not dissipate. "I don't know. Okay? I. Don't. Know. Can we please just give this more time?"

He dropped his hands from her with chilling reserve. "Why? You've made your choice. And as I recall, giving you time didn't work out so well for us." Raven took a few steps back.

This is for the best. She pulled a shaky breath, released it slowly. "Yes, I have made my choice."

185

"You know I'm not going to sit around and watch. You don't expect me to, right?"

Fresh waves of panic unfurled in her chest. "What do you mean?"

He shrugged. "It doesn't matter. Come on, I'll take you home."

***

The garage door was open, but Raven stopped a distance away from it and got off the bike.

Nikki stared at him, questions glistening in her night-darkened eyes. Lights from Viennesse illuminated the grounds, giving it a homey glow. He wouldn't let the image take root in his psyche. It was hard enough leaving already.

Off the motorcycle and standing beside him, she tilted her head. "Why didn't you ride on into the garage?" Apprehension captured her voice.

"I'm not staying." *His* voice was solid. Solid as a rock.

"What? Where will you go?" She started to reach out.

Raven stepped back, erecting an invisible wall between them. It's what he had to do to survive this. "I still have work to do at the lab in Arkansas."

"So you *were* the one sending information to Zero."

"Yeah." Raven ran a hand over the smooth gas tank. A lone bird in flight. Just like him. Nowhere to rest, nowhere to call home. And no one along for the ride. Nikki would drive the motorcycle in and cover it with the lifeless tan tarp. There his bike would wait in lonely silence and fading hope, perhaps forever like some of the others.

"Have you been in the lab this whole time?" Concern filled

her words, along with a little bit of … urgency. Yes, she was eager to keep him talking, keep him engaged in conversation. Keep him there. But that didn't matter. His course was set.

"In and out. The air vents there are safe enough to hide in during the day, and nights I've stayed in the barn."

"Isn't there a guard?"

"Yeah, I guess you could call him that. Anyway, there's more information to obtain and now is the perfect time. There's hardly anyone in the lab. It's like there's been a mass exodus or something. I think they routed everyone to another facility when they hired the new geneticists."

"When you're done there, then you'll come back here?" Was that hope blooming in her? He almost couldn't wait to squish it. Until her eyes found his. There, trapped in the soft rays of moonlight, was his Nikki—hands clasped innocently in front of her, teeth nibbling on her bottom lip. The girl he'd rescued on countless occasions, the one who threw her arms around his neck and squealed at the chance to feed a dolphin, the one who loved him. And the one who was just too scared to accept the truth attached to those feelings.

Her eyes swam in fresh pools of tears. It made leaving that much harder. "No. I'm not coming back." *Harder. Not impossible.*

"Raven, please. Stay here. Don't go back to the lab." She grabbed his arms in a vice grip. "Something awful is going to happen."

He cocked his head like the defiant bird on his Harley. "If I stay here, it's with you."

The moisture in her eyes shrank back into the ducts. He sensed her resignation rise slowly as she accepted his plan and his fierce inflexibility. Nikki shook her head and let her hands fall to her sides—she was stubborn too.

"Then I'll see ya around. When you're ready to fly, let me know."

She choked on a sob. "Raven—"

He cut her off. "Do me a favor?"

She nodded. "Anything."

"Don't tell anyone I was here."

"What?" Confusion scrunched her face, adding a new dimension. It was better than the pain so evident a moment before.

"If I'm going, I'd just as soon they continue thinking I'm dead."

"Raven, I can't lie." The wind caught Nikki's hair, and he tried not to notice the strands dancing around her shoulders, playing against her upper arms.

"You don't have to. It's what they already think."

"No, it's not. They all think you're alive and just playing the loner."

That shouldn't hurt, but it did. "There's just no loyalty at all, is there?" he mumbled.

"Please stay." He knew it was her last-ditch plea.

So he countered with one of his own. "With you?"

"No," she whispered.

"Like I said, when you're ready, you know how to find me."

She frowned. "No, I don't."

"You found me tonight. Follow your heart, Nikki. No matter where it roams, it'll always lead you back to me, because my heart is always calling to yours. You can choose not to listen for a while, but eventually you'll go where it's leading you." And then he stepped close and kissed her.

Raven's lips roamed lightly over hers until she responded. Again, her body reacted without her mind's consent. A moment later she was lost in a spinning, sinking whirlpool of wonder and magic. His lips were alive against hers and a million butterflies seemed to take flight everywhere their skin touched. Gentle electricity tickled over her flesh, causing the strangest sensation. *A roller coaster submerged in honey.* Utterly trapped by the world below, then careening over hills and into valleys as if free, every motion thick and sweet. His hands were flattened against her back, just as he always did whenever … whenever she needed him. Fear lit a fire in Nikki's veins, and it burned like a match that ignited her blood. With it, a realization she couldn't bear to face.

She needed him.

The press of her mouth intensified against Raven's. A tiny cry escaped.

I need him. And he's leaving.

Nikki wound her arms around his neck in a useless attempt to keep him, but a violent conflict raged within. She could have him and lose Mace. Or she could let him go. As if he heard the battle, understood her struggle, Raven broke the kiss.

When he did, her fingertips flew to her mouth, desperately ashamed of her actions and desperately trying to retain the feel of his lips on hers—both emotions wove together as he took a step back. Her hand stretched to stop him, but her legs were still stuck in the rich honey that had poured from his kiss.

Through his long bangs, one eye winked. And for the first time ever, Nikki couldn't read the story swimming in his midnight-blue eyes. He'd masked what he'd always shown her—his truest feelings, deepest emotions. Gone. Hidden from her.

He shot a look up to the sky, gaze flittering from star to star. "When you're ready to fly …"

Then he took one more step back, snapped his wings open, and leapt.

Nikki stood for a long time gazing at the night he'd disappeared into. Over and over his words echoed in her head. *When you're ready to fly …*

<hr>

"I'm sorry, man," Gearhead mumbled as they watched Nikki.

Mace's jaw ached; this was the third time he'd seen Nikki and Raven kiss. *Doesn't get any easier.*

"I thought you and Nikki were—" Gearhead glanced at him in the garage's dim light.

Mace hardened. "We were."

Gearhead wiped his hands on the shop towel he kept tucked in his waistband. "Look, I'll give you two some space."

Mace thrust out a hand as the mechanic passed. "Don't bother."

"You couldn't hear what they were saying, and things aren't always the way they look."

Mace glared.

"Yeah, okay, that *was* pretty obvious."

"Ya think?" Without another word, Mace crossed the garage and headed back into the main house, wondering if he'd already lost the girl he'd recently reclaimed.

Chapter
17

"Hi," Nikki said, peeking her head into Mace's room.

Back to her, he shoved something into a bag with so much force it made her jump. He didn't answer her greeting.

"Can I come in?"

"Sure, but I'm on my way out," he said, words clipped.

Nikki frowned while he manhandled the zipper of the backpack, as if he had some personal vendetta against it. "Where are you going?"

He finally relented when the zipper stuck. He huffed out an angry breath and left it half open. "Some of the guys are going to a friend's house to hang out for a few hours."

Okay, everything was wrong with that statement. First of all, Halflings didn't just go to friend's houses to hang out. So where was he *really* going, and why was Mace acting like he'd eaten nails for breakfast? "Who's the friend?"

"You don't know him."

She chewed her lip. "Is it close?"

"Across the Rhine Valley, in France."

When she dropped her gaze to the floor, he exhaled. "It's at another ancestral home. A group of Halflings lives there. We won't be gone that long."

"Is it similar to the one here?" She wanted him to keep talking. Maybe if he did, she'd break through that tough shell of … well, of whatever it was.

"Yup."

"Is it the only one in France?"

"That I know of. But I don't know where the females hang out when they aren't infiltrating our domain." On Will's instructions, Winter, Vegan, and Glimmer were staying at Viennesse in case something happened.

Nikki thought back to the first conversation she and Mace had about Halflings. They'd sat on the back porch of the two-story house Will and the boys had rented in her hometown. "That's right. Until this journey, you hadn't met any female Halflings." Raven, on the other hand, seemed to know them and know them well. Of course, Raven had been on more journeys than Mace, and was the kind of guy who had no problem chatting up girls.

A muscle in Mace's cheek twitched. "So, I'll see you later," he said, and started to step past her.

Nikki glanced outside at the bright morning sun spilling through the window. "But it's supposed to be really nice out today, and I thought maybe we could take one of the cars and see the countryside."

He spun on his heel just as he reached the door. "Haven't you seen enough of it?"

What did that mean? She hadn't been outside the castle walls other than their picnic and her trip last night.

192

Fear filled her system.

Could he know about that? "Mace, I need to talk to you about something."

The only acknowledgement he'd even heard her was the quirking of his brows. Those cerulean-blue eyes she usually found comfort in were brimmed with tension and bore into her. At last he looked away, focusing on the wall by the window. She could almost feel his pain reaching its hungry fingers toward her.

"I did something last night."

His head tipped back a degree as if readying for a punch he'd seen in advance. "What?"

Nikki rubbed her hands together, nervous energy seeking escape from her body. "I took Raven's motorcycle."

His mouth hardened. "What happened?"

She forced a steadying breath and leaned her weight against the wall alongside the open door for support. "Well, I thought if I went to the castle ruins, maybe I could help him. Zero thought Raven was sending information, but then Zero also said he thought Raven could be dead, and—" She shook her head. "I don't know. I was really confused. So I went."

He crossed his arms over his chest. "And?"

She blinked, frowned. "And I shouldn't have done it."

The muscle in Mace's jaw tightened, highlighting the usually smooth lines of his face. He stood there, unwavering. Very Mace-like. But he had an edge as well. An unfriendly, almost mean edge that was most *un*-Mace-like. "That's all you have to tell me?"

A battle was laid out before them, but neither seemed ready to fire the first shot. If she told him Raven had been there, she'd be breaking a promise. Maybe the last promise she'd ever make to Raven. After all he'd done for her, it didn't seem right to divulge his secret. Even to Mace.

The uneasy nod of her head broke their stalemate.

Suddenly, the backpack's stubborn zipper was forced to absorb the full impact of his frustration. He launched into a furious fight with it while she watched, mouth gaping.

After a few awkward moments, she stepped to him and took the backpack into her own hands. "A bit of the material is stuck," she whispered so as not to disturb any more of the hornets needling his flesh. Using soft back-and-forth motions, she worked the zipper until the cloth was freed.

"Thanks," he muttered.

She held the bag out to him. When he reached for it, his hand fell against hers, but he snatched it away from her touch. "Mace, what's wrong?"

He became deathly calm as he fingered the now-functioning zipper. "You've got some things you need to figure out, Nikki. Being in a relationship with someone means there are certain boundaries. I'm not really sure how you feel about Raven or about me. But you can't feel the same for both of us, so you're either lying to yourself about me or you're lying to yourself about him. Either way, you're intentionally fooling yourself. You need to make a choice. Then you need to stick with the rules, because I'm sick of feeling like this." Before she could answer, he stepped past her and left the room.

Nikki blinked when the door closed. "I have made a choice," she whispered to the empty space. It felt like tiny needles pierced her heart. But with that sensation an unsettling irritation formed. *Stick to the rules? Was he kidding? What rules are there anymore?* She didn't want to hurt Mace, ever. But she'd stared death in the face over and over, and had been spared by either him or Raven. *A person can't just flip a switch and expect to be able to sort through the emotions that causes.*

What did she know about love, anyway? All she knew was how she felt, and that was an untrustworthy measuring device to be sure. The girl who'd never had a boyfriend was now surrounded by tall, beautiful angelic beings compelled to protect her.

Unsteady legs carried Nikki to the window. The wall clock ticked. A bird sailed past the stone opening, pausing in mid-flight. She watched its effortless movements as it gathered speed for a nosedive toward the courtyard. A smaller bird followed, unsteady, less fluid than the first. "Learning to fly?" she uttered, but as the question left her mouth, the reference to Raven's last words to her rushed fresh and blistering in her mind. She stepped away from the window ... and saw the opening resembled a cage. Nikki ran out of the room, rejecting the notion that her stone palace was quickly becoming her prison. And that maybe Raven really was the only one with a key.

After Mace left to go "hang out at a friend's house," Nikki made her way to the girls' room. Glimmer and Vegan shared a room, while Winter had her own. But more likely than not, the three were together in their own little clique. If not gathered in Winter's domain, than in the other room. Nikki wasn't used to searching out camaraderie, but after her argument with Mace, she needed a friend, maybe three.

Winter's room was empty, so she traversed the hall, walking slowly and thinking how out of character it was for her to search out support from other girls. A huge part of her wondered who she'd become. When she made it to the door, she could hear the females talking on the other side. Even through the thick mahogany, their words rang clear. She lifted her hand to knock, until she heard Glimmer say her name.

Nikki's hand froze in midair.

"I can see her messing around with Raven—I mean, he's always got one foot in the dark side, but I'm surprised she and Mace are taking such a risk. It's not like him. He knows better, and to throw away your eternity for a human—it's beyond stupid. That's not the kind of thing Mace does. And I can't believe she's letting him! They're walking around here like teenagers in love. Please. Happy today, eternity in hell tomorrow. Like she's worth it. Like *any* human is worth it."

"Relax, Glimmer," Vegan's voice soothed. "We haven't really known Mace that long, certainly not long enough to make judgments about him."

"I think his eyes have gotten darker. We all know what *that* means.'"

Nikki's hand fisted. When Halflings' eyes darkened, it meant they were giving in to evil. Was Mace slipping into darkness because of her? She hadn't noticed any changes …

Glimmer continued. "Mace is awesome, and there are plenty of Halfling girls who would love to have him fawning over them like that. Girls who understand him and his life, girls who can fight shoulder to shoulder with him."

"Are you volunteering?"

"No. I've actually got my eye on Raven right now. Provided he gets back here soon. I'm not going to wait forever."

"You change crushes like Zero changes flash drives," Vegan said.

"And who is Raven crushing on? *Nikki*. It's pathetic. What

do they see in her?" Glimmer's voice cut like a stiletto blade, each word stabbing harder and deeper into the same wound.

"She's a bit of a warrior herself. If I was a guy, I'd like her." Vegan again.

"Right up until Satan ushered you into hell. This infatuation with humans is all wrong."

"Glimmer's right." That one was Winter's voice, and hearing it made Nikki sink a little deeper into despair. "What Mace is engaging in is dangerous. Deadly dangerous."

Nikki thought she heard Vegan sigh. "Maybe Nikki doesn't know. Maybe she doesn't realize ..." But the girl—Nikki's supposed friend—held zero conviction in her words.

"If she loved him, she'd leave."

"Glimmer!" Vegan gasped.

"Well, if he's too stupid to leave her alone, she should take matters into her own hands."

"Winter, surely you don't agree with this."

Long pause. "I don't know."

"I can't believe you two. We've been commissioned by the Throne to protect Nikki. And you would have her leave?"

"Protect her from what?" Glimmer spat. "Nothing man or demon has made any kind of attempt on her since we all left Missouri. Nothing. Not even a sideways glance from an angry human. Nikki is fine. She just needs to go away for a while."

Nikki waited for Vegan to come to her defense again, but no words followed. In Nikki's heart she knew the other girls agreed. They may not have voiced it, but they thought the things Glimmer dared say. Sorrow wound around her and squeezed.

She needed to find Will. He'd make sense of all this. He'd remind her in that booming voice filled with years of authority that her safety was vital. Even key to protecting the plan handed down throughout the ages by the Throne. Will put things in perspective by reminding her that what the Halflings were doing was about more than a girl. It was destiny, and it was ordained by a power she could only hope to one day understand. Will made things better … by making her smaller. And right now, that's exactly what she needed, because the females had made her feel like a giant problem able to wreck both lives and eternities.

Nikki tiptoed away from the door and headed down the stairs, her heart feeling like a twenty-pound anchor. At the end of the long hall she noticed Ocean just as he entered Will's room. He hadn't seen her, so she took her time, putting one measured foot in front of the other. Like a prisoner on death row, each step felt like it was taking her to something she didn't want to face.

She started to go inside, but paused. What would she say? *Sorry to interrupt you, but I could use a pep talk right now.* No. She squared her shoulders while trying to force Glimmer's harsh words from her head. *Ugh. Why do things hurt so much when you aren't expecting them?* She hadn't planned on being chucked under the bus by the trendy Halfling with the curly bob. A few weeks ago? Sure, Glimmer would have gladly hacked her to pieces with her sharp tongue. But now, they'd become close—a huge mistake on Nikki's part. Because now there was no defensive shield, no armor, allowing the words to cut right through her.

Deeper in Will's room, she heard voices. They must be on the balcony.

"You can't sit around like a lifeless rock, Will." Ocean was standing beside the angel as they both stared out at the sky.

"I am not equipped with fear, and yet it grips my heart."

"It's Mace, isn't it?" At Ocean's words, Nikki sank to the floor.

Silence.

She squeezed her eyes shut. *No, no, no. Please, no.*

"My apprehension about this journey grows exponentially. As time careens toward its conclusion, I know the training of my Lost Boys was inadequate in the most elemental of areas."

Ocean shifted his weight. "Will, God was the perfect father, yet Adam still chose sin."

"Yes. For a woman."

"Mace is strong. In the end, he'll make the right choice."

"It is foolishness to question the Throne's judgment. But in my heart of hearts, I wish we'd never met Nikki Youngblood."

Icy-cold talons seized Nikki. Her mind blackened and the rope around her heart released slowly, leaving her chest empty and hollow.

Movement was difficult, but she managed to stand and trace her steps back to the staircase. Fingers closed on the railing while she paused. There was nothing else for her to hold on to—no thoughts, no words, no anything. Just emptiness like she'd only felt once before; when a police officer arrived to tell her of her parents' death.

Somehow, she made it to her room and locked the door. But the rock walls and high ceiling offered no sanctuary. They loomed, staring at her with accusing eyes.

Sensei Coble's voice echoed in her head. "Always find an ally." But there were none here. Not the females, not Will, certainly not Mace. "And when there is no ally, embrace the universe's decision to move you. For you will never be left without a companion."

Was that it? Was the "universe" moving her? Nikki'd never bought into the spiritualism Sensei Coble subscribed to. She crossed the room and dragged open her top drawer. There, in the corner, her cell phone rested against the clothing she'd purchased with the females. She didn't want to look at the garments she'd once associated with happiness. She'd allowed the girls to suck her in with the promise of friendship when, really, they wanted her gone. Nikki shoved the clothes away from her cell.

The slam of the drawer rocked the whole chest, no easy feat for the mammoth block of carved wood. Frustration flew from her fingers as she turned on her cell and stared down at the screen. It blurred. *Gah. Stupid, stupid tears.* She scraped at her eyes with the palm of her hand while the cell powered up.

Sixty-six missed calls. All the same number: Damon Vessler. Nikki found the open window and looked out on the rolling landscape. What was she doing here, in this dream turned nightmare? How could she go downstairs and sit at dinner and chat about the day when she knew what they were all thinking? She hit the button to listen to her messages, hoping the phone would work so far from home.

They were all the same; Damon pleading with her to come home. Hot tears scorched her cheeks as she listened to him speak of her parents' things. He kept reassuring her everything was safe and sound and in the lower level of his home. Waiting for her.

He'd set up an art studio for her in one corner. And if she chose, they'd keep everything that belonged to her mom and dad. Each message ended with "Nikki, come home. Please, come home."

Four hours later she'd nicked the keys to the Kawasaki, purchased a phone card with some of the "Throne funds" she'd been given, and punched the numbers into a phone in a hotel lobby somewhere in France. She felt slightly guilty for leaving everyone behind, but knew she couldn't call Damon from her cell. The Halflings didn't trust him, and to divulge their location would be wrong. If he pressed, she'd tell Damon she was in Europe. But she needed to hear his voice. Needed to see if he still wanted her back, because Glimmer was right about everything. Even about the lack of threats. In the four hours Nikki'd been gone, nothing had happened. No hell hounds, no crazed hate-filled humans. Maybe she wasn't even in danger anymore.

Yet that far-off voice beckoned to her. Something evil would find her. Very, very soon.

Chapter
18

"Damon?" She cradled the phone for support. "It's me, Nikki."

His words rushed out after a relieved exhale. "Oh, Nikki. I'm so glad you're all right. Please come home."

"I— I don't know that I should." What was wrong with her? This was what she wanted, right? But everything in her screamed against it.

"I have some new information about your parents. If you come back, I'll go after the guy who killed them. But it's somewhat costly. I have to know you're invested. I have to know it matters to you."

She hadn't expected this, and had to shake her head to sort it out. "You think it wouldn't matter to me?" Through the hotel lobby window, Nikki watched a young man sit down at an outside café. It was an inviting kind of place with streams of vines and flowers flowing from the transom above the doorway.

"Sweetheart, you ran away. How important could it be?"

"Damon, I didn't run away. I was—" What could she say?

"It doesn't matter, Nikki. Just come home. We can start fresh."

It sounded good, but impossible for her; the wounds she'd suffered were too deep for new starts.

"I've got everything organized downstairs. We need to go through your dad's things. My whole basement smells like them, you know. I walk down there and expect to see their faces."

Her eyes closed in an attempt to remember the scent of her parents. But only unfamiliar smells filled her nose. "I may not be safe."

"You're safe with me, Nikki. I have the best security men in the world. Nothing will hurt you. There's no demon in hell that can get to you if you're with me."

Was that a hypothetical statement? His voice suggested not. "What do you mean?"

"I mean there are forces around us that aren't human. And they can't be allowed to run rampant. I have in my employ some of the best monster hunters on the planet. You probably think that's silly, but I've traveled the world and I can tell you there are beasts, creatures unlike anything you've ever seen. Straight out of the pit and ready to kill. But I know their secrets, Nikki." He laughed. "I'm only divulging this to you so you understand the depth of my commitment to your safety. *This* is where you belong. Can't you feel that?"

She squeezed the phone tighter. She did feel it. She belonged somewhere, surrounded by her parent's things. Those items were all she had left of them. Didn't she owe it to them to go back?

Could Damon really protect her? He certainly sounded

like he could. "I guess I could come back long enough to sort through Mom and Dad's things. But I can't make any promises after that. And I really have to know I'm safe there." If today's journey out alone was any indication, there was nothing to worry about. As long as she didn't draw, she was fine. Ever since Will had taught her how to recognize when she was tapping into the realm of the spirit and how to avoid it, she'd been strong. She'd learned. What harm could there be in going home for a time? Vessler's house was safe. And maybe she'd even have time for the wounds—the ones inflicted by Glimmer, Will, and especially Mace—to heal.

"Where are you, Nikki? I'll come get you."

"Uh." She couldn't divulge where she was. No way. Too close to the Rhine Valley, the location of an ancestral home. As angry as she was, she couldn't rat out the Halflings. But Europe was small, and public transportation could take her anywhere. "I'm in Paris." She'd hop the train and leave the bike. Later, much later, after she was long gone, she'd get a message to Viennesse about the motorcycle.

"Uh-huh." He didn't believe her, she could tell. "How on earth did you get there?" Other questions drifted in the silence around his words.

"I climbed aboard a ship." Not a lie.

"I'll charter a jet to get you home. I'll text you information on which airport. We'll have to see what's available on such short notice."

Nikki pulled the cell phone from her pocket. "Damon, I'm using a phone card. My cell doesn't work here."

"Yes it does, my lady. I've already activated international service on it."

Trepidation gnawed in her gut. She ignored it. "Why did you do that? What made you think I'd leave the country?"

"A hunch. Nikki, promise you won't run away again."

"I didn't … and I promise."

The following day she was home. Or as close to a home she had. She'd gone to sleep on a bed of silk after Damon met her at the door and held her for so long it seemed he'd never let go.

She'd wanted to go straight to her mom and dad's things, but he said no. "Sleep, Nikki. Tomorrow morning, we'll go downstairs together."

She woke to the smell of freshly toasted bread and the realization someone had entered her room. She heard their whispered steps and the sound of their breathing, and she sensed them as well. Through her barely opened eyes, Nikki watched Anya, Vessler's housekeeper, pour a cup of coffee from the silver carafe, dump in a bit of cream and sugar, and stir the concoction vigorously. She breezed out of the room and the door clicked behind her.

Nikki leaned onto her elbows and stared at the tray of breakfast like it was a snake. Her mouth watered, but something in her begged not to trust what was in front of her. Not to trust any of this.

She threw the covers back. "That's ridiculous," she mumbled and sailed to the tray, taking a bite so big the bread barely fit into her mouth.

A knock caused her to jump.

"Come in," she said in a muffled voice, tongue maneuvering around the half-macerated bread.

Damon slid the door open. His dark eyes widened, brows raised high. "Glad to see you have your appetite."

She swallowed, wished there'd been a little more butter on the toast, and reached for the coffee.

With a mega-smile, he moved with the fluid motions of a man with years of martial arts training. He paused at the table, reached for the delicate pat of butter, and smeared it on her bread. Another devastating smile as he held it out for her to take a bite.

She froze. Did he actually expect to feed her? *Okay, that ranks pretty high on the creepy, possible-pedophile scale.* Her eyes cut from him to the butter-gooed bread, and noticed a stream of spread ran along the edge of the toast. She grabbed it from him and took another bite, making sure she caught the buttery river while stepping a good foot away.

The air kicked on and Damon's scent of clean linen and expensive cologne surrounded her. He always smelled so good. She took in the room, the *bedroom*, and again everything felt wrong. Very, very wrong.

Damon lifted his hands and bowed. "Forgive me. I know this must seem strange to you, Nicole, but it feels perfectly natural to me. In many ways I feel like you're my own daughter." His gold chain twinkled, catching the light in the hollow of his throat where the V of his designer shirt framed his tan neckline.

His own daughter? Well, that leveled the freak flag, but raised the *alarm* flag to full mast. "I barely know you," she uttered. Oops. She'd only meant to think that, not say it.

"But I know you, my dear. Through your parents, I shared every moment of your life. I know about your first bicycle wreck, your first B on a math assignment." He led her to the window and opened the curtains wide. Below, on a smaller hill-side, her house sat nestled inside the neighborhood of smallish homes where she grew up. "I've kept a watch over you. And as long as you'll let me, I promise to do so forever."

Great. Just what she needed right now: another guardian. But this one wasn't trying to toss her into an epic war, this one wasn't trying to dictate her life; this one cared simply because he cared.

"You got a lovely tan on the, uh, *ship*, was it?"

She focused on the windowsill. *Here it comes. The third degree about where I was and why, and I don't have a clue how to answer any of it.* She steeled herself. "Yes, it was a ship."

"The sun agrees with you. I wouldn't have thought it possible to make you any more beautiful, and yet you are."

Uh-huh. "Thanks," she said, more of a question than an answer. "I guess I should explain." She pivoted to face him.

"No, you shouldn't."

"Wha—what?"

"You've nothing to explain to me. You're an adult now, Nikki. You don't have to answer to anyone anymore."

Huh. She hadn't thought of that.

"In fact," Damon continued, "I forbid it. No talk of where you were and what you were doing."

Her eyes narrowed playfully. "If I've no one to answer to, then how can you forbid it?"

His smile was slow, alarmingly so, and it caused the blacks of his eyes to twinkle like quartz dazzled by sunlight. "Exactly." He rested his hands on her shoulders, and with a gentle press urged her to gaze out at the world beyond the window.

A few houses over, a small boy helped his dad rake leaves while a lady rocked in a porch swing. If Nikki really tried,

207

maybe she could forget all about demons and angels. Maybe, just maybe, Damon Vessler was her one shot at a normal life.

"Okay," she agreed, and felt the tips of his fingers throb where they rested lightly against the T-shirt she'd slept in. Why her awareness of his reaction caused alarm, she couldn't say. She pushed the sensation aside. If Will and Mace and Raven had taught her one thing, it was that she had no right to trust her feelings.

Tears kept her company as she journeyed through her parents' life. It seemed so strange that her mom and dad could be reduced to a basement full of quiet, lonely objects. What had once brought her joy—seeing the counter filled with a mix of Mom's baking dishes on a Saturday morning—now only added to her suffering. Those things sat patiently in a cardboard box waiting for her to choose one. But she never would. Nor would her mom ever tap her finger against her chin and say, "Hmm. I think a glass pan will work best for this." Each item was just an echo of the lives they represented. And echoes became quieter and quieter as time passed.

Damon had walked her to the foot of the stairs that first morning, but when he reached for the first box, one marked *Dale's Garage*, she'd gently placed a hand on his and shook her head.

He'd understood completely. Damon had nodded, taken a breath so deep she thought he'd pop the buttons on his expensive linen shirt, and given her a quick smile that conveyed more than words. And then he left. Simple as that. She'd once thought Mace understood her, then thought Raven better fit that role. Maybe *Damon* was the only one who understood her. The only one left, anyway.

In the days that followed, life became a solemn routine of working through her parents' things, practicing her karate, and spending evenings with Damon, who gave her space, who didn't coddle, who left her alone. And that's all Nikki really needed. To be left alone. She should have contacted Krissy, but even the guilt over not letting her best friend know she was back began to fade with time. It was like that part of her life died alongside her mom and dad.

But after a few weeks, the loneliness intensified, and a tiny part of her searched for something, anything, to replace the utter nothingness. Only a month ago she'd been so surrounded by life and noise and people. Now emptiness filled her, refusing to leave her unaccompanied for long.

Something was growing within her soul, something cold and black and deadly. She found it easier and easier to get rid of items her parents once cherished. Some things she kept, for one reason or another, but the reality of sorting had hardened her. People who are dead have no use for items. People who are dead don't come back.

Damon said the lead he'd had on the killer had gone cold. "Maybe if you'd been here ..." But he'd stopped himself. He hadn't needed to say more. She understood, and it fed the black thing growing in her stomach.

She sat before a box of old books, some of which her dad had purchased as research. *A robbery. My parents died in a robbery.* A handful of antique swords, possessions they'd gained by chance, led to the forfeit of their lives. She'd give the world to have them back, yet they died over a bundle of inanimate objects. Irony was an angry witch, a witch with sharpened claws.

It didn't matter anyway. Nikki'd reached a decision. Once she was finished with her parents' things, she'd go after the guy herself. And she'd do to him every horrible thing he'd done to her parents before he stole their lives.

Chapter
19

She'd stopped doing her classwork somewhere along the way. When she told Damon it was probably time for her to get back to school, he'd shaken his head. No need. He'd done some checking and learned she had enough credits to graduate two years early. Principal Schmidt apparently hadn't liked it, but had agreed under the circumstances. After all, Damon could be quite persuasive. Nikki'd tried to voice her concerns about the credits, about going from a junior to a high school graduate, but Damon shut her down.

No more chemistry tests, no more sweaty locker rooms, no more friends. Guilt over Krissy slinked back into her mind. She hadn't even called her best friend once since she'd returned from Germany, mostly because Krissy represented everything that no longer was. And Krissy—best friend extraordinaire— would be full of questions Nikki couldn't answer now or ever. When Mace, Raven, and Vine started attending her school— oh, so many innocent days ago—it was Krissy who first encouraged Nikki to get to know them. She was something of a bridge between Nikki's two worlds. And Nikki didn't need a bridge—she needed dynamite to blast the whole thing to dust.

So when Damon informed her she'd graduated, Nikki accepted it like she had everything else in her new world. He held an intimate ceremony in her honor and gave her the title to the Ducati concept bike he'd purchased from a doctor in Florida. Life should be good. But the walls, though soaring and palatial, were closing in around her.

"I've arranged for us to spend a few days at my beach house. And I have a surprise for you when we get there," Damon said. He handed her a fresh bottle of water. He was always doing that. Encouraging her to eat, making sure she had coffee in the morning and water throughout the rest of the day.

She turned from the library window. She didn't open the window in her room anymore, as she'd lost all interest in looking over to the house that had once been her home. But here in the library, she enjoyed the vivid view of a meandering garden. It reminded her of Viennesse. "Oh?"

"Yes, I thought a change of scenery would do you good."

Sunshine, beach, sand sifting between her toes. Too bad it sounded dead.

"Thought it would cheer you. And even if the setting doesn't, the surprise is sure to."

She didn't expect to experience cheer again. Even when he gave her the keys to the bike, a prize she'd once only been able to dream of, there'd been no delight. Waking, sleeping, she was a zombie. An undead. She felt nothing. Not pain, not joy. She couldn't remember what it was to smile, to laugh. She felt old, finished.

No. The beach held no appeal. She could just as well stay right here. "Do we have any news on the killer, Damon?"

"Ah," he said. "A spark of life."

True. The desire to see the monster brought to justice was the only thing that kept her heart beating. Black vines twisted in her chest and offered perverted comfort. She accepted their embrace. It was growing easier and easier to do so.

Damon maneuvered around a table and came to rest behind her. He placed his hands on her shoulders and kneaded with a gentle touch. "I *will* find him. I gave you my word. We even have a new lead." He leaned closer. "Nikki, what are your wishes when we locate the assassin?"

She spun to face him. "I want him to suffer like my parents suffered."

He seemed to fight a smile. "It's justice. An eye for an eye. It's the only way you'll ever be able to move on. To get closure."

Deep within her a still, small voice whispered revenge was not the answer. She smothered it and clung to her dream. Because revenge—right or wrong—had become her closest companion. Oftentimes, her only companion.

And Damon was going to help her accomplish it.

Nikki threw a punch into the heavy bag hard enough to double it. Damon had arranged for her karate instructor, Sensei Coble, to continue private classes at the mansion. "I want to learn KravMaga," Nikki said. "Are you familiar with it, Sensei?"

Damon had become her sparring partner, as her ability was quickly eclipsing her sensei's. Damon was a specialist in several fighting styles and the first to mention the style taught to the Israeli Special Forces.

Concern washed across Sensei Coble's usually calm veneer. "It's a brutal style, Nikki."

She punched again, embracing the sudden sting of the heavy bag against her fist. "Exactly." She downed half a bottle of water and felt the tightness of the tape around her hand. Nikki'd stopped wearing gloves while training, but Damon insisted she cover her knuckles to avoid cutting them.

"You'll be banned from tournaments. It's too deadly."

She turned on him. The anger gurgling in her belly boiled over in one quick gush. "Do you think I care about tournaments right now?"

He stood firm, but she thought she'd seen a flash of fear in his gaze. She tried not to enjoy it. "No, not now. But eventually you'll want to compete."

"My competing days are over."

It seemed to sadden him. He stepped from the bag then held a hand towel in her direction.

She snatched it from his fingers. Blotting her face, she pressed her taped hands to her cheeks, keeping her eyes trained on her sensei.

He frowned, probably noticing she'd continued to look at him.

Never take your eyes off your enemy, Damon had taught her.

As a show of trust, Sensei Coble turned his back to her and wiped down the heavy bag with another hand towel. When finished, he held the fabric out to her and nodded to the linen basket behind her. He was trying, with little success, to be passive about the whole thing, but it tasted like a lie. His motions were a little too drawn out, his brow a bit too furrowed, his eyes a bit too suspicious.

She understood. Master and student were close as father and child. She'd enjoyed a great relationship with her sensei for years, but she'd outgrown him. And one valuable lesson

Damon had taught her was to trust no one, especially those who know your weaknesses. Nikki challenged him with a look and snatched the towel from his hand. But rather than turn and walk to the laundry basket, she took two steps backward and half-turned. Gaze still locked with Sensei's, she tossed the first towel behind her.

His eyes widened and she knew she'd hit the target. That's another thing Damon was teaching her—how to shoot. She'd never known much about guns, but in going out to his firing range she'd discovered a fresh new appreciation for firepower. And aim. She wadded the second towel and tossed it into the basket. Of course, the wastebasket and the towel were far different from the Smith and Wesson she'd been firing, but aim was aim. And hers was dead-on.

"Good shot," Sensei said.

She didn't bother hiding the smug little smile.

"You're training so hard. I thought maybe you hoped to throw yourself into competing as a sort of therapy."

She laughed without humor. A corner of tape on one hand had lifted. She absently picked at it. "Only one thing will be therapy for me." She motioned for him to steady the bag again.

With a sigh, he pressed his shoulder to the canvas. "Do you remember when you were very small and I first began training you?"

Slowly, her hands dropped. It seemed a lifetime ago. Almost as if those memories belonged to someone else and she'd watched a movie of it. "Yes, I remember."

"I made you promise that you'd stay committed. You were too young to begin training, but I sat you down—"

"Yeah," she said, irritation edging her voice. "I remember. I told you I was a person of my word, and you had me promise to continue in training and tournaments."

"Exactly. You gave me your word."

Really? Was he *really* trying to do the whole psychology thing on her? Nikki challenged him with another hard look. His eyes softened on her, causing a spasm of guilt. Why was she being so mean to Sensei Coble? He'd always wanted the best for her. She loved him, sort of thought of him as the uncle she never had. She wasn't herself right now. That's all. But as she tried to reason away her attitude, she realized *why* she was angry at him. And both the thought and its implication made her sick, maybe a little more dead inside.

She was mad at Coble because he had nothing left to teach her. What was happening to her? She wasn't the type of person to use someone only to throw them out like yesterday's pizza box. She opened her mouth to apologize, but heard herself saying, "I'll never set foot in a karate tournament again. *I give you my word.*" Driving through, she doubled the heavy bag, jolting her sensei and erasing the hope that had moments ago lit his eyes.

Without ceremony, she turned, grabbed her water bottle, and left the exercise area to search for Damon.

Lying flat on his back atop his bed, Mace quieted his mind. He prayed for wisdom and thought about Nikki. "Where are you?" he whispered to the darkness. Will had moved the boys and females back to Missouri when Raven contacted Zero and informed him Nikki'd returned, and they'd spent the last three weeks reunited at the two-story house on Pine Boulevard. All except Nikki. Which meant the house was empty as far as Mace was concerned.

Every night he'd sat at the gate to Vessler's mansion. It was all he could do to keep from leaping inside the giant house to find her. But he knew that wouldn't work. He'd even gone to the door on several occasions to inquire about her, but the answer was always the same—she wasn't taking visitors. Nikki had things to sort through, he knew, and he'd pushed her away when she needed him the most. He'd accused her of having her loyalty in the wrong place when it was Mace who'd needed the lesson.

He'd watched her kiss Raven. Big deal. Raven had confirmed it was a good-bye kiss that meant she'd made her choice. But how had he responded? By pushing her away, giving her an ultimatum. Her whole world had crashed around her and he'd done nothing but throw dirt on the stones that had once been her life.

Help me.

He sat up, eyes fully focused in the dim light. Fear clamped its fingers around his throat. The words, *Nikki's* words, had been so real, so close, he thought she might be standing in the room. She wasn't, of course. But that didn't stop his eyes from roaming the empty space. Mace mopped sweat from his forehead. The perspiration had appeared as quickly as the plea. Dread pressed as the words dissipated into the air, and he had to wonder if he'd imagined her voice.

No. He hadn't. Mace closed his eyes and drew on the strength of the One he served. Waves of peace crashed over him. "Where are you?" he asked.

Drawing deeply on the presence of all power, he lay back, tuning in to his own breathing. For a few moments there was nothing. And his very being pressed him to get up. Do something. Instead he quieted his heart and listened with his spirit.

There. Eyes closed, he saw it. An airplane turning into the setting sun, golden rays glinting off the tilted wing. A shoreline. A concrete palace sitting on the beach. A green sign. Casey Key.

Mace bolted from the bed.

He ran down the steps and flipped on the kitchen light as he entered. Will sat over a cup of coffee, reading a book. He smiled as Mace approached.

"You shouldn't read in the dark." Mace took the cup from Will's massive hand and drained the lukewarm liquid. "Yuck. You know microwaves were invented for stuff like this."

Will turned to the stove clock. "It's three in the morning. Can't sleep?"

"No. In the weeks since Nikki left, I've discovered how little sleep we actually need."

"Have you seen her at all?"

"I met her best friend Krissy for lunch a week ago. She didn't even know Nikki was back here." He shook his head and sank onto the barstool beside Will. "I've gone to the door of the mausoleum that freak Vessler calls a house, but each time I inquire someone makes an excuse. I can't seem to permeate the atmosphere around Vessler's house. It's like there's this ..."

"Evil?"

Mace nodded. "Yes. She refuses to see me. But if she'd go outside into the gardens or something, I could see her, talk to her."

"Every man must choose his path. Light, dark. Forgiveness, revenge."

"But Will, she's like a pawn in this horrific chess game." That much was true. Zero had found another mention of Nikki in an encoded computer file from Omega. The word *surgery* was paired with her name.

Will's clear-blue eyes were troubled. "I wish she was simply caught in the middle. You can only help those who want it. I feel I owe you an apology."

"What? Why?"

"Words hold the power of life and death. It is what we speak that can rescue … or condemn us."

Mace felt for Will. So much wisdom confined in a being who's bound to the earth. "I'm not really following you, Will."

"I wished Nikki gone."

"You're not a genie, so I don't think that's possible."

"Mace." Will pivoted and dropped a giant hand onto Mace's shoulder. "I was concerned for you—about your feelings for her. And that concern caused my faith to falter. The Throne's judgment came into question and the seed of my fear grew."

Heart pounding, Mace tried to swallow. "Did you tell Nikki to leave?"

Will brushed a hand through the air. "No. Of course not. But in my heart I wished you'd never been called to this journey."

Mace tried to fight the anger now growing within him. "That's not your decision to make."

"I know. Believe me, I've been scolded for it." Will ran a hand through his curly hair. "So often I don't understand the Throne's decisions. His plan is perfect. It is only we who get in the way. And that's what I did. I just hope it can be repaired. The last time I got in the way of the plan, a human died. I was banished for it."

"Well, confession is good for the soul, right? Or as you like to put it, 'It ain't over 'til it's over.' Zero is still looking for a way to link Vessler to Omega. If he finds it, Nikki will know what her godfather really is."

"*If* that's what he is. We have no proof."

Mace nodded in reluctant agreement.

A slow smile formed on Will's face. "I should have warned you about … love. But I must admit, I don't understand attraction between sexes."

Mace slapped Will on the back. "Maybe I should have warned *you*."

Will sighed. "You said Nikki was a pawn. If that were true, this journey would be much less complicated."

Mace shook his head. "What role do you think she plays?" When Will failed to answer, Mace's voice rose. "What role do you think she plays, Will?"

"Not that of a pawn. Possibly that of the queen." He paused. "I see her slipping. You must reach her, Mace. So much rests on the edge of the blade."

Mace nodded. "And the blade is already tipped in the wrong direction?"

"Yes, thanks to my interference and lack of faith. This could have eternal consequences for countless people. But right now, my thoughts dwell with Nikki. Saving her."

"I'm working on that."

"What do you plan to do?" Will shoved back from the counter.

"Go to Casey Key. As soon as I figure out where it's located."

Will frowned. "I don't know." He thought a moment. "And why?"

"I think she's going there, or maybe she's already arrived. Wait a minute," Mace said with a flat stare. "You've lived for millennia and you don't know where Casey Key is located?"

He shrugged. "Sorry. Is it in Florida?"

Mace grabbed his laptop from the kitchen table. "Let's find out."

Within a few minutes, they discovered Casey Key was a five-mile stretch of beachfront on Florida's Gulf Coast. Mace read, "Pristine and exclusive, it's touted as one of the most beautiful in the country. If one so chose, they could purchase a one acre piece of beachfront for a mere $3.8 million."

"Pricey." Will whistled.

"Just the kind of place a snake like Vessler would hide."

"You have no love lost for the man, do you?" Will scratched his head. "I have to admit, I never understood that phrase. Just seems like a confusing way of saying, 'I don't like him.'"

Mace closed the laptop. "No love lost. I don't like him. I don't trust him. Take your pick. Each one fits Vessler."

"How does he play into this journey, Mace?"

"I'm not sure, but the longer I spend away from Nikki, the more danger I feel she's in."

"I've sensed no attacks from the supernatural realm," Will said.

"Exactly. Don't you think that's weird? When we first met Nikki, both humans and demons were after her. Then her parents died at the hands of a thief, not to mention her dog was killed by a hell hound. Now nothing."

"What are you suggesting?"

"That she's played right into the enemy's hands. If not, he'd be attacking her. What do you see, Will? Is she physically in danger, or is the danger actually worse than that?" Mace asked.

"Sometimes heaven whispers and I'm alerted to physical attacks. I'm not told everything, Mace. Just bits and pieces, scattered like salt across a table. And with my recent breach of faith in the One, my vision is dim."

"What about psychological attacks?" Mace said.

"What do you mean?"

"I think Vessler is poisoning her mind. At the police station—back after her parents were killed—I heard him whisper to her that he would find the killer. He'd make the man pay. I think the thought of avenging her parents could be blinding Nikki to everything else. Hate is a deadly enemy to fight."

Will nodded. "Hate has only one nemesis able to conquer it."

"What's that?"

"Love. Go to her, Mace. Bring her back into the light."

Chapter
20

S urprise!" Krissy screamed, jumping from behind the drapes and landing on the bed.

"What?" Nikki sat up, rubbing the sleep from her eyes. "Krissy? How—how'd you get here?"

"I snuck in with your breakfast."

Nikki had arrived on Casey Key late the night before, and Damon sent her directly to bed. Exhausted, she hadn't argued. Waking in a sundrenched room infused with the scent of coffee, warm blueberry muffins, and saltwater boosted her dismal outlook somewhat. A petite woman dressed in a black-and-white uniform had knocked gently a few minutes ago, deposited breakfast in the nook, and pulled the gigantic shade open. *But the best friend springing up and down like Tigger Junior on the corner of the bed must be ... a mirage?* Nikki stared at the door, the curtain where Krissy'd been hiding, and then at her friend.

"Don't look so befuddled. We're going to have so much fun!"

Krissy bounced, screamed, clapped, hugged her, and bounced some more.

Did she just say befuddled? Nikki reached to hug her again, since she'd missed the first one. Krissy *felt* real enough. And no self-respecting figment of one's imagination would use a word like befuddled. Yes, this *must* be her best friend. "What are you doing here?"

"Mr. Vessler didn't want you to be here alone, and he'll be gone for a couple of days. So, ta-da! Best-friend weekend. Yay! I've been here for three days."

"What?"

Krissy's eyes rounded. "Yeah, I know, right? Crazy. Mr. Vessler actually owns the company my mom works for. Isn't that bizarre? But I mean, not *that* weird, right? Seeing as he owns half the world."

Nikki rubbed her eyes again as if continuing to do so would clear things.

Krissy cocked her head. "Four days ago, he shows up at my house and says he wants to bring you and me here, and my parents are like, 'Sorry, no way are we sending our daughter, blah, blah, blah.'" Krissy hopped up and went to the breakfast tray, grabbed a strawberry from the selection of fruit, and popped it into her mouth. Talking between chews, she continued. "Within less than an hour, he'd arranged for my mom to have a few days off, *and* my dad is working on a real-estate deal for him. My dad is brokering the *very* property Mr. Vessler wants to purchase." She pumped her fist. "Oh, yeah, Dad will be the listing *and* selling agent for the half-million dollar property, so that doubles his commission. Do I look tan?" She did a pirouette.

"You look gorgeous," Nikki responded, but her heart thudded. Everything—abso-stinkin-lutely *every little thing*—worked out the way Damon orchestrated. The realization burned like a chili pepper, though she didn't know why. After all, this entire trip and everything that went into it was for her. At the same time, she knew the exact reason Damon's dealings rankled her. If he couldn't have something, he'd just manipulate things, people, and circumstances to his liking. He was a puppet master and the rest of the world his wooden dolls. Except her. He treated her like a queen. Even called her *my lady*. Well, Nikki knew Krissy's parents, and they'd never send her off with some strange guy, no matter how handsome, how charming, how irresistible, or how rich. She found a trace of comfort in that fact.

Nikki shrugged out of the covers and met her friend at the silver breakfast tray. She needed to sit Krissy Doll's folks down and have a chat with them. Find out what they thought of Damon, what they *really* thought. "Can your mom and dad meet us up here for breakfast? We can sit out on my balcony."

"Uh, that would be difficult, because they're on a plane right now headed home."

A slow molasses drip of alarm released into Nikki's body.

Krissy tipped out her bottom lip. "Don't be sad, Nikki. You're gonna love the beach house. This is the kind of place we've always dreamed about."

Was it? Nikki no longer remembered her dreams. She'd become more of a nightmare kind of girl lately.

Krissy was chatting on like one of those chipmunk characters that were supposed to be adorable, but who just gave Nikki a headache. "Remember when I had that ridiculous crush on Joe Jonas and you— Well, you really didn't ever crush on anybody except maybe Josh Nolens, but we'd talk about awesome houses in the Hills and throwing parties for celebrities."

"Those fantasies were all yours, Krissy. Not mine." And it irritated her that Krissy had suggested she'd sat around fantasizing about rock stars and living in California. She wanted to tell her to shut up. Just *shut up*. But that would hardly be a proper greeting. Warranted, maybe, but hardly proper.

As the one-sided conversation rambled on, Nikki just couldn't wrap her mind around the fact that Krissy's parents left. "Why didn't your mom and dad stay?" She took Krissy by the wrist just as her friend turned to pour coffee. She repeated a little louder, "Krissy, why didn't your parents stay?" She shook her arm.

"Ouch," Krissy yelled as hot coffee splashed onto both their hands.

"I— I'm sorry." Nikki sank her free hand into a goblet of ice water and grabbed a handful of cubes from the bottom. She pressed them to her friend's burn.

"The coffee got you too," Krissy said, pointing to the dark droplets on Nikki's other hand.

"Your hand's going to blister." Nikki moved the ice to a spot where bright-red skin began to pucker on Krissy's wrist.

"Not yours."

Nikki angled her hand. Where the coffee had splashed, there was nothing. Not even a tinge of discoloration. She didn't even remember feeling the hot liquid hit her skin.

Krissy shrugged. "No surprise. I've been in the sun for three days, so my skin is probably a little sensitive. And as far as my parents, Mr. Vessler thought it would make you sad because your parents are—"

"Dead," Nikki finished for her. "Because they were murdered."

Krissy's eyes widened. "So, well, he thought I should stay

and they should go. His assistant Betty is here with us as an adult chaperone and there's the, um, staff." Her smile returned in full force. "He's like the most *amazing* godfather."

"So it would seem," Nikki mumbled and split her alarm between Krissy's parents and her over-the-top godfather. A voice in her head whispered that cages came in all shapes and sizes.

The dark ocean churned beneath her balcony.

She and Krissy had spent the day catching up, since Nikki'd refused to see her in Missouri—a fact that mortified her now, but she reasoned she'd had to work through her parent's belongings. There'd only been time and energy for them, no one else. Except Damon. Strangely, Krissy hadn't complained or asked why; she just hugged Nikki over and over and told her she missed her. Now the two of them sat before the setting sun watching the waves cascade and roll onto the shore.

When he appeared, Nikki's breath caught. Without meaning to, she seized the railing and leaned toward where he stood like a Greek god highlighted against the glistening sea. Perhaps even Titus, emerging from the water to claim his bride. Fifty yards below, she felt his eyes on her. Mace looked so much like a wounded angel, her soul cried.

Restraining her emotions, Nikki turned to her friend. "What's he doing here?" She released her grip on the rail and took a few cautious steps back, crashing into the balcony door.

"I don't know, Nikki." Krissy said. "But I think it means Mace loves you."

"What do you know about it?" Nikki spat, and was instantly

troubled by her response. "I'm sorry. I don't know why I said that." Nikki searched her best friend's face for the unforgiving stare she was sure to find.

Instead, a wide smile enlivened her features. "It's okay, Nikki."

Come to me, Nikki.

The sound of his voice, though barely a whisper, crashed through all those barbed wire fences she'd been constructing. Bombarded with memories of him, her chest ached from the weight. Images danced through her mind like embers from a campfire, but each landed and burned. And that, *that right there*, was the problem. Burning holes in an already compromised nucleus, while she was courting more punctures to a damaged core. How stupid could she be? There was only a portion of her heart left. Did she really intend to ice-pick the rest into oblivion?

She started to turn toward her room.

No. Come to me. He must have sensed her intention. *Of course he did.*

He took a step toward her. *Don't run away, Nikki. You're too strong to run.*

Krissy grabbed her shoulders. "What's wrong with you?"

Nikki's eyes pleaded with her friend. How could she explain? With no ally, with no one to share her pain, her resolve started to crumble. If she hadn't left him at Viennesse, maybe things would be okay now. But *Mace* had been the one to walk away, not her. Maybe not physically, though hadn't he done just that when they argued in his room at the castle? She loved him. It barely mattered. "I can't be with him. Not the way my heart tells me to."

"But he cares for you. You need him right now, Nik."

The hard box that kept Nikki's fragmented heart safe began to shut. "It's easy for people to talk about *right now* when they have a future."

Krissy's innocent eyes clouded.

"You have a family, Krissy. People to love you. You have a *future!*" she screamed.

"Mr. Vessler is going to give you a great future. He told my mom and dad he'll see that you go to the best college. Have every opportunity. Work in whatever field you want."

At what cost? The certainty of more pain confronted her. Crossing her arms, she squeezed, hanging onto what warmth remained inside her body. Hanging on to her strength.

"Nikki, Mace *loves* you."

Everyone who loves me dies. She choked on the thought. It took her by surprise and, unguarded, slid into her being. She had to make Krissy understand. Nikki couldn't divulge the truth, so she opted for practicality. "But his family moves, Krissy. One day soon, they'll leave. And he'll have to go. One more thing I love will be stolen from me. How many losses can I survive? One more?" She dragged Krissy inside. "I can't take the chance." She threw one last look out the balcony's glass door, where Mace still stood waiting. "It would destroy both of us." Eyes still on his face—she could see it incredibly clearly, even from the distance—she locked the patio door.

I won't give up filtered to her through the glass.

Later, while she lay in bed, the voice returned. *I'm still here.*

She shoved the pillow onto her face and pressed. But the battle was over before it began. She'd go to him. She had to.

Once she'd known he'd arrived, he'd consumed her thoughts. And that realization only added to her confusion.

Rising from bed, she pulled a chenille robe around her body. Though dressed in sweats and a T-shirt, the robe offered an extra layer of cover. Cover she needed right now. She swung the doors open and stepped onto her private balcony overlooking the sparkling water.

The breeze tugged her hair, gently at first, then intensifying as she stepped out.

He wasn't at the water's edge. She panicked until she heard the rustle of feathers beside her. Nikki turned slowly, facing Mace just as he tucked his wings behind him. He'd touched down near the banister and waited.

She read no emotion on his face, which was good. For a moment, she just needed to take him in. No smiles, no frowns, no greetings. They understood each other that way. His face was smooth and the moon played in his eyes, sending sparks toward her. The muscle in his jaw tightened and his throat made a sound that was neither a cough nor a swallow but somehow both. Then she saw it—the tear in the corner of one of those beautiful cerulean eyes.

And it undid her. Nikki's emotions surged to meet his. Relief, sorrow, joy all crashed together. When he opened his arms, the feelings collided in a desperate release of all the tension and fear she'd harbored. She tumbled into his waiting embrace.

He kissed her hair, her cheeks, her jaw. His hands roamed across her back as if making sure she wasn't a figment of his imagination. Had his mind orchestrated this moment? Played it over and over so many times he couldn't trust if it was really happening or if it was just another of a thousand fantasies?

He pressed against her as if his forward momentum alone held the power to keep her forever. Step by step, he backed her to the balcony wall. Once there, he whispered, "Nikki," capturing her face. He paled as he searched her. She knew of the dark circles that hung beneath her eyes, making even her irises appear darker. And then he was confessing, words pouring forth in a rush of desperation. "I'm so sorry for what I put you through. I never should have talked to you like I did." Hands cradled her jaw. "You've been through so much, and I added to it with my stupid jealousy. I have a fallen nature, Nikki. One I'd like to forget, but it prods me sometimes, pushes me. Can you ever forgive me?"

She nodded, her cheeks rubbing against the smooth skin of his palms. "I didn't want to see you," she said, throat closing around each word. "I don't want to lose you. Isn't that horrible? Isn't that awful? Being with me would cost you eternity, and I'm worried about myself. Nothing makes sense anymore."

"This does." Cautiously, he tilted toward her lips.

She drowned in the Mediterranean-blue gaze she'd come to love. His eyes closed, dark lashes shadowing his cheeks. When his mouth lightly feathered against hers, she felt like her body could float away. He tasted sweet, like powdered sugar, her favorite ingredient when baking. Mace was her perfect ingredient, his mouth against hers conjuring warm thoughts of a home, a promise, a recipe for life.

But that was no more real than the hope of her ever having a normal life again. Desperation lit a fuse inside her. She broke the kiss. "Promise me something," she rasped.

"Anything." His fingers threaded into her hair, combing through methodically as if making up for the time they'd lost. When he reached the ends of the strands, his hands slipped to her temples and began the trek again, soothing her with each stroke.

Nikki sank into his touch. "Mace, I'm so perplexed about everything. Tonight, can we just *be*? Promise me we won't talk about tomorrow or what will happen to us." She squeezed her eyes shut. "I know it's wrong, but can we just forget all the horrible things we're involved in?" The words caught in a throat too hoarse to cry anymore.

"Nikki, I'll give you the moon if you ask. Tonight is yours. Where do you want to go? What do you want to see? I'll fly you to Europe so you can watch the sunrise, or we'll go to where it's setting. Whatever will make you happy, I'll make it happen."

To fly across the ocean on angel's wings. To watch the sunrise atop the Eiffel tower. "Anything? Anywhere?" she said.

"Anything you want."

She pressed into the rock-hard muscles of his chest. "I just want you, Mace."

And as the moon smiled down at the tumbling sea, Nikki and Mace held each other with the promise of right now the only dream they dared hope for. She felt like their emotions ignited the space around them, seeping into the wooden slats of the balcony, drifting on the ocean's constant rush, replacing the atmosphere of doubt with that of purest love. If she only lived another day, she'd die with the knowledge that she'd felt something this strong. Though every obstacle remained in their way, love had conquered. Sliding from his embrace, she slipped into her bedroom and emerged with her sketchbook and a charcoal pencil. "Do something for me?" she asked, words soft as a kitten's purr.

A slow smile spread across his face. "Yes?"

"Take off your shirt and show me your wings. You still owe me."

His brow arched, but he obeyed, drawing his shirt up and over his head to reveal the smooth muscled flesh beneath. With one great snap, his wings flew open, catching her by surprise.

White with tiny flecks of gray, they stretched out and into the air. Caught by the ocean wind, they danced, pushing against the current. Mace's body flexed to hold him on the balcony. The wind grabbed with persistence, causing the muscles in his chest and arms to strain and enlarge. He nodded to the sketchbook. "You sure that's safe?"

"Mm-hmm." Her cheeks were fire hot.

A grin toyed at his mouth.

"It's safe. Will taught me how to tell when I'm tapping into the other realm. As long as I work slowly and I'm careful, it'll be fine."

A rakish smile replaced the playful grin. "Work slowly, huh?"

"Yeah, you'll just have to stay like that for a while."

"An angel's work is never done."

"You'll survive."

Nikki forced her gaze to her sketchbook. Flipping past drawings, she stopped at a blank page. With warmth pooling in her stomach, she pulled a steadying breath and began to draw. He would be her masterpiece.

Chapter 21

W hat's it like when Halflings fall in love?" Nikki asked, snuggled up against Mace on a deck chair. Once she'd finished her drawing, they'd settled onto a cushioned seat by the water. Waves rolled toward them, pushed along by the current just like the two of them had been pushed. Together, apart, then back again.

Mace really did stabilize her world. He truly was the one who made everything make sense. With Raven, she wanted to run away. But Mace forced her to face the hard, unforgiving truth head-on. And there was a strength in that she couldn't deny.

Mace maneuvered his head to look at her face.

She smiled. "It must be amazing."

He kissed her forehead. "Do you know much about eagles?"

She shook her head.

He leaned back against the cushion. "Eagles mate for life. But before they do, they go through this elaborate ritual where the female soars to these amazing heights."

"She's showing off for him?" Nikki asked.

"No, she wants to make sure he's worthy. She carries a stick high into the air and drops it." His fingertips traced her arm.

She quivered. "And?"

"He has to catch it."

"Sounds simple enough." She moved just enough to press the length of her leg against his.

"That's just the beginning. She chooses another stick and another." Mace angled and kissed the side of her head. "Until finally she picks a tree branch that weighs the same as her."

"And she drops it?" Nikki asked.

"Yes."

"Why?"

He pivoted to look at her. "Because every female should know that the mate she chooses can catch her if she falls." Then his arms were there, all around her, holding her, protecting her. That's what Mace did. Always. And she'd not made his job easy. Over and over she'd fallen, and over and over he'd been there.

As if he heard her thoughts, he whispered, "I'll catch you, Nikki."

She nuzzled deeper into him, drawing his scent into her nose. "You already did."

Some horrible, irritating thing was pulling at her arm. She moaned before realizing it was Mace, and that she must have dozed off. She squeezed her eyes shut when he tried to rouse her.

"Come on," he said. "I want to show you something."

"Can't it wait until … oh, say, next year?" she teased.

"We've been out here on the deck for two hours."

For all she cared, time could stop.

"And, no, it can't wait until next year." He rose and tugged her dead weight.

"Fine," she said in a breathy whisper. "Where are you taking me?"

"To watch the eagles."

Her interest piqued, she lumbered off the chair.

Once standing, Mace caught her in a firm hold. A sexy smile crossed his face. "Hang on," he said, and unfurled his wings and leapt. From above she could perceive the earth below, but as if through a veil. A golden hue tinted everything. Other times she'd flown, they'd been moving at such a phenomenal speed her eyes hadn't adjusted in time to see anything.

But now they watched it through a dazzling fog. Cities came into view and disappeared as they passed.

Sometimes Mace beat his powerful wings, body tensing with each push. But most of their time was spent soaring on the thermal drafts. She spotted a city below. Gatherings of lights illuminated various portions until it appeared to be made up of miners with their oil lamps huddled together. "What is that?" she asked, awed by the light so beautiful she wanted to stare at it forever.

"Prayers," he said.

"What?"

He nodded below. "The youth groups in that city are holding an all-night prayer vigil."

Upon closer inspection, she realized the gatherings of lights were concentrated within buildings, many of which sported crosses on the rooftops. The golden lights were visible *through* the buildings.

"What you're seeing are their prayers rising to the Throne."

"Wow. Does it … you know, make a difference?"

He scanned the area beneath them. "It can change a city. If caught, it can change a state, even a nation."

She started to ask him what he meant by *caught*, but she noticed he'd slowed as he angled toward a distant mountaintop.

She didn't know how long they'd flown. She didn't care; time seemed so inconsequential now. They touched down on a flattened rock with a natural seat carved into the stone.

He snapped his wings shut and gestured for her to sit. "Do you need me to build you a fire? I realize it's a little cooler here."

"Not if you sit by me. Keep me warm?"

He sank into the seat and pulled her close. "Look." He nodded toward another rock face.

Two majestic eagles soared and dipped in the sky as the sun began to peek over a mountaintop near them.

Awestruck, Nikki gasped when the first bird climbed higher and higher. When the eagle dropped a stick, the other sailed on the wind to capture it. The dance continued as sticks became branches. As Mace had said, the final limb was so heavy, the female seemed barely able to lift it. Once in flight, she carried it to an incredibly high point.

Mace whispered against her hair. "Look closer, Nikki."

She flashed a frown, but concentrated.

"Closer," he encouraged.

She focused her attention on the eagles as the female dropped the tree limb. "Halflings," she whispered almost reverently. Her eyes widened, blinked, then widened again. "They're actually Halflings."

The branch plummeted toward the earth. Mace pointed. "The male must wait until the last possible moment before capturing this one."

But Nikki could barely listen, and couldn't move. The limb rolled and tumbled closer to the ground. Just behind it, a male Halfling with wings tucked in rocketed like a bullet. He gathered speed until he was only a blur, gaining on the branch as he dropped.

Her hands shot up to cover most of her face. "Will he make it?"

But Mace wouldn't let her hide. He grabbed her hands and dragged them from her eyes. "Watch and see."

After excruciating moments, and just before the branch crashed into the rocky ground, the male's wings cracked open as he snagged the limb.

Nikki released the breath she'd been holding.

Meeting in the air, the two Halflings tumbled into one another's arms, drifting, climbing, falling. "It's beautiful," she said. *It's something I can never give you.* But she forced the thought from her mind. Tonight was perfect, tomorrow seemed forever away, even if the sun was rising near them.

"I've never seen anything like it."

"Me either."

She pushed back to look at his face.

"Just heard the stories." His eyes followed a trail to the Halflings. "I didn't realize it would be so ..."

"Amazing," she finished for him.

"Yeah." But there was something there. Some irritating little worm boring into their perfect night. Nikki recognized it as reality and rejected it with fierce determination. Nothing would steal her perfect night. It might be the only one she got.

Mace touched down on her balcony and hugged her.

Nikki snagged her water from beside the lawn chair and chugged the whole thing. "So thirsty these days," she said.

Faking an English accent, he bowed. "Other than water, did the evening meet your expectations, my lady?"

She frowned. *My lady.* Damon's special nickname.

Damon. His name officially brought reality crashing down. What was she doing? What was she thinking? She'd reacted carelessly. Watching the Halflings only solidified the stupidity of her actions. She slid a hand through her hair. "Everything is so confusing right now." Nikki hugged the bottle like it was a lifeline.

Mace frowned.

The last month flashed like fireworks in her mind. She had a job to do. She had to find the man who killed her parents. Then, only then, could she move on to a life with … What? With Mace? No, certainly not that. She couldn't give him what he needed. Damon was the only hope of a real life, one separate from boys with wings, and eagles … and love.

Mace noticed the change in her. His eyes sharpened.

"I'm confused," she repeated, and placed her palm against her throbbing temple. "Everything is … wrong."

Mace placed a hand on her arm, and she could feel the panic coursing through him. "No, Nikki. It's not. We'll find a way to be together."

Was it possible? She didn't see how. Maybe once she settled the score for her parents, but not now. She wouldn't ask Mace to trek that path with her. It would definitely destroy him. Wasn't it destroying her bit by bit, wearing away her conscience like a poison corroding her emotions? "This was a mistake," she said.

"A mistake? How can you say that?" His fingers tightened. "Everything is right when we're together."

"No," she pulled from his grasp. "The only time I feel all right is when I'm with Damon. He makes everything better."

"Nikki, *don't* trust Damon Vessler."

She felt her eyes harden. "Damon protected me."

"I'm telling you, he's an evil man. And I'm the one who can protect you."

Her chin jutted forward. "We're about to find out who killed my parents. Once we've avenged their deaths—" Damon told her she'd never be able to move on without closure. That the mystery of their deaths would cripple her. She *had* to find the killer.

"Nikki, do you hear yourself? The path of revenge only leads to death. Revenge harbors hatred, and hate destroys everything. You're only hurting yourself by continuing this. You can't bring your parents back."

Resolve overrode the pain in her eyes while vengeance wrapped around her. If she spoke the words rising to the surface, they would destroy any hope of a relationship with Mace. Ever. But if he kept talking, he might convince her the risk was worth it. Clenching her teeth, she barreled on. "And you didn't protect them."

His hands dropped. As if physically pushed, he stumbled back. "What?"

She let her fury gush forth. "You could have protected them if you'd wanted to."

So much hurt wafted from him, she had to step back for fear of being caught in its orbit. "No," he shook his head. "I didn't know."

She swallowed. She had to, because if she didn't, she'd

vomit. *He'll survive*, she assured herself. *Mace is a survivor.* So she continued, pushing him to the absolute brink. "I'll never forgive you for it. You didn't save them, Mace." Piece by piece, her heart was cracking. "And I don't need you to save me. For the first time I realize I have to face things on my own. When I return home, I'm moving out of Damon's mansion and back into my own house, but I don't want you there. I need you to stay away."

His tone became a plea. "Nikki, listen to me. We can't cross a human's will. If you say I can't come onto your property, I won't be able to. No matter what." Everything in him pleaded. His eyes, his body language. "Take it back, baby."

"Why? It's what I want." Her head tilted defiantly. "And if you remember, you promised earlier to give me whatever I want." She pulled from his touch and disappeared into the room.

When she was sure he'd gone, Nikki collapsed onto the bed, trying to erase the picture of him from her mind. Lying there, she understood what it meant to be heartless.

Two days later, she settled in at the home she'd grown up in, but Damon had bought new furniture for the space. Good thing, because she'd gotten rid of most of her parents' belongings. "You don't need anyone to raise you, since you're grown," Damon had told her. She agreed. He'd said she was free to choose between living at the mansion with him or at her own house with a full staff. She'd almost laughed. How much of a staff could one teenager in a three-bedroom ranch house need?

Despite her wishes, Mace appeared every few hours and

stood at the edge of her property. She could feel his presence. When he drew near, her chest ached. Every. Single. Time. And she hated him for that. Or maybe she hated herself. Though she couldn't help it. She felt strangely disconnected to her past, like it wasn't her own. Again, her memories seemed more like a long, sad movie than reality.

The following morning, Damon arrived with a bouquet of fresh flowers. He handed them to the housekeeper and barked for her to put them in water. He'd also brought a case of the imported water she'd grown so fond of. Crossing the living room, he took Nikki's hands in his. "Are you settling in, my lady?"

"I am." But his grasp sent a cold chill through her.

Making sure the housekeeper had disappeared into the kitchen, he grinned. "We found him."

"What?" The whoosh of anxiety took her by surprise.

"The man responsible. He had your father's wallet, your mother's credit cards, and the case of swords. He'd sold one for three hundred dollars, and was attempting to sell the others on eBay when we found him."

Anguish and disgust fueled her hostility. *My parents' lives reduced to a few hundred dollars and a classified on the Internet.* "There's no justice."

"Worse than that, a police officer who's a friend of mine says the evidence is circumstantial. If turned over to the authorities, he'll likely go free."

"No!"

"We have to make our own justice, Nikki. I can order a kill on him, but—"

"But what?" she insisted.

His black eyes cooled. "Nikki, you need to make this kill."

"What?" She grabbed his arm for support and detested her reaction; so filled with weakness. Hadn't she wanted that very thing? Hadn't she invested the last month into training to do exactly what Damon proposed? But now that the opportunity arose, she couldn't imagine taking a life, even one that didn't deserve to continue.

Damon's suggesting it himself also seemed wrong. She'd kept quiet about her desire for revenge, fearing Damon would try to talk her out of it. Instead, he *suggested* it. Shouldn't he want to protect her? Seriously, what kind of man urges a seventeen-year-old to kill someone? Maybe she'd misunderstood. He couldn't have said what she thought.

Then he repeated it. "You need to make this kill—to set you free. Then you can move on. It'll all be over."

On the outside her emotions were raw and bleeding and eager, but far deeper she knew she couldn't murder. It just wasn't in her. She shook her head. "No," she mumbled. "I don't think I can."

His once-gentle touch became painful. "You can! Think about them, Nikki. Your mom and dad, robbed of the chance to see you graduate. Imagine your wedding day, with no father to walk you down the aisle. This man has taken everything from you."

Her teeth clenched while visions of a familyless life played in her head. Everything she loved, stolen from her by someone who deserved to die.

Damon slid her hands into his. "Come outside with me, Nikki," he purred. "Show me what you can do."

His words pounded in her head, a drumbeat growing in intensity. Joining the anger she already felt, her emotions coalesced into a frenzied desire to destroy the monster who'd shattered her world. She allowed him to lead her outside. With each step, blackness hovered at the edges of her vision, darkening the boundaries, but the center was in sharp focus.

Once on the lawn, Damon caressed her hair. "You know my ability as an opponent?"

She nodded, trying to separate his words—so soft, so caring—from the fury burning in his eyes. "There is none better."

"Try to kill me. You won't succeed, but you have to let it turn. Forget about my life. Only see the killer. Do it for your parents, Nikki. Do it for yourself."

She blindly obeyed by raising her hands and sliding into a fighting stance. An image of her parents' attacker emerged in her mind. Nikki jumped and landed a front kick to his chest.

Damon reeled back, but his quick reflexes made it appear as if she'd never made contact. "Good girl."

Something deep within churned. Her reason dimmed like a streetlamp that had outlived its life span, flickering before finally going out. Once it had, a tarlike loathing inched through her, suffocating every desire to preserve life.

The killer stood before her now. His smile a sickening gloss of hate. His smug posture, tilted head, his coaching her like she was a first-year karate student. She tuned in to the fury driving her, and it was glorious. More vivid than the most beautiful of paintings, sweeter than the choicest of fruit. She faked a punch, spun, and connected a ridge hand to his head. His skin compressed as she felt bone, then sliced as her fingernail slit his cheek.

Seeing the bright crimson beginning to leak, she dropped her hands, and the shadowy veil fell from her eyes. *What am I doing?*

When she retreated, Damon struck and pain exploded

across her face, then down her neck as her head snapped back violently.

"You gotta do better than that," he scoffed, his tone condescending. "Poor little fatherless girl," he continued to taunt, shoving her to the ground. She landed with a thud. He hovered above her and screamed, "Come on, Nikki. Try to kill me. Pretend I'm him. Because I did it. I killed them."

Calm descended on her, like the quiet assurance she'd experienced whenever jumping off the high dive. *Water is below, and soon it will swallow me.*

"And you know what?" He leaned within a breath of her face. "I loved it. The way your father pleaded for your mother's life. The way she cried and called out your name. She was calling for you, Nikki. You could have saved them if you'd been there."

Her bent fingers flew out and grabbed his pompous, gelled hair. She entwined her digits and jerked his head down while using her legs to fling him over her head.

He landed flat on his back, air hissing from his lungs.

Nikki jumped up and had to suppress a feeling of giddiness rising in her throat. *Do you want to see what else I can do, Mr. Vessler?*

He gasped for air as she pressed her foot into his chest. The toes of her tennis shoes dug into his throat. "The thing about having the air knocked from you is that if enough pressure is then applied, it will collapse your lungs," she said with soft, controlled words. "Eventually your respiratory system will shut down." She pressed harder. "I bet you didn't know that."

His arms flailed as he attempted to suck gasps of oxygen, but she made sure his efforts were in vain. Vessler's face reddened.

She pressed a little harder.

His eyes bulged.

Nikki fisted her hand. She had no intention of waiting until *eventually.* One blow to the throat—that was all it would take to stop the pathetic sucking and wheezing sounds. She drew back, ready to finish him. And she would have if she hadn't heard the voice.

Chapter 22

Nikki, no!" Mace yelled as he touched down at the edge of her yard. He started to step, but couldn't. She'd ordered him to stay off her property.

At least his interruption gave Vessler just enough time to squirm from under her grasp and lumber to his feet. As much as Mace hated to see the guy live, watching the girl he loved commit murder was far worse.

Nikki, tell me to come and save you, Mace pleaded.

She looked across the lawn to him but only shook her head. *I'm already dead.*

While her attention was on Mace, Vessler, who'd regained a bit of breath, seized the moment and punched her in the stomach.

She doubled over.

Nikki. Don't give in.

Vessler swept her leg, causing her to land on her knees.

Raven appeared beside Mace and started to step onto the

property. "No." Mace stopped him after a moment's shock. Raven must have seen him leave in a hurry and followed. "She's ordered us to stay back."

Raven's weight shifted from side to side. "You, maybe. She'll die." His foot moved onto the blades of grass.

Mace grabbed him and dragged him back. "If you cross her will, you'll disappear from this journey." He shook him. "Raven, you know that."

Turning their attention to the center of the bright-green lawn, they watched helplessly.

While Nikki was on her knees, Vessler grabbed a handful of hair along her hairline. As she started to writhe he punched her in the kidney then jerked her head back to examine her face.

Her eyes met Mace's across the lawn. He watched the gold in them darken, deepening almost to black. He staggered, grabbed Raven for support. *She can't be … Will said it would be impossible to hide.*

Damon slowly fisted his hand.

Nearly black eyes shone on Nikki's face.

Raven stammered, "She's a …"

"She's a Halfling."

Mace turned to Raven, and the expression on his face confirmed they were thinking the same thing. "That means she's not human, and we don't have to honor her free will." The Lost Boys charged onto the lawn.

Mace caught Nikki before she could hit the ground.

Leave it to Lover Boy to give me the dirty work. Raven dove on top of Vessler. Like an animal, he attacked him, sinking deep blows wherever he found an opening.

At one point it seemed Vessler may obtain the advantage. As Raven shifted in an attempt to regain the upper hand, he noticed Mace was laying Nikki softly in the grass and preparing to enter the fray.

One man should be no match for two Halflings. For that matter, one dozen men wouldn't be able to overcome *one* Halfling. Vessler's brute strength and fighting ability surprised them both. Still, he offered opposition only for a fleeting moment. Raven stood and took control once more, prompting Mace to return to Nikki and lift her into his arms. Not that she seemed to notice her pretty little boyfriend had trotted back: she was staring at the fight.

And that was all he needed to know. "You tried to turn her," Raven screamed, holding Vessler by the now-bloody lapels of his expensive Italian shirt.

Vessler's arms dangled lifelessly at his sides.

"What are you?" Spit flew from Raven's mouth as he shook the man. *How did one human almost take the advantage in a fight against me?*

Vessler's head bobbed forward, back, forward, back, but no words formed on his lips.

Raven searched his face for an answer.

Vessler licked his swollen, bloody mouth. "She belongs to me."

The choked words almost made Raven's vision go red. He grabbed the freak's throat and squeezed. "We belong to no one," he hissed.

"I ..." he gasped. "I made her."

The human throat could only sustain a limited amount of pressure before collapsing. Raven's fingers dug into the tender flesh, enjoying the feel of muscle, tendons. Within Vessler's

249

veins a ball of blood attempted to force its way beyond Raven's grip, but he denied it access.

"Wait," Vessler rasped, his eyes widened in fear. "I can offer you the world." His jittering gaze darted to Nikki, now in Mace's arms.

Reluctantly, Raven followed his trail for a moment.

"Please." Vessler's hand came to rest on Raven's, fingers trying to pry free, though his voice was getting weaker. "I can offer you ... her."

For an involuntary instant, Raven's fingers loosened.

Vessler's gaze softened. "That's all you really want, isn't it? Don't you deserve her? She loves you—she told me she did. I can make it so the two of you live a long life together."

Raven tried to keep his mind from traveling that road, but it wasn't a choice he could make. Him and Nikki. Together. Forever. But rather than loosen further, his grip tightened. He lifted Vessler off the ground. "Are you also offering thirty pieces of silver?" Straightening his arm, he flung the demented freak down. As he was ready to drive Vessler six feet under with one final blow, a hand landed on his shoulder.

Mace's grip was firm. Loving. "Come on, Brother."

Raven shook his head. One more blow, one more hit, and Nikki would never have to worry about Vessler again.

"Brother," Mace repeated, letting a dazed Nikki slide from his arms. "If you murder a human, your fate is sealed. Do not expect me to walk eternity without my brother at my side."

Raven's heart hammered.

Mace placed a protective arm around Nikki when she swayed. The other he placed around Raven.

Unwinding his fists, Raven attempted a smile and nodded toward Nikki.

She scratched her head, eyes clearing slowly.

Raven reached to her cheek and dragged his finger along the side of her face. He swallowed hard and gestured to Mace. "Carry her," he ordered. "She needs you."

Mace nodded, understanding. He swung Nikki into his arms.

As the three walked off the lawn, her eyes began to focus on Mace. She shook her head. "Damon's not what I thought he was."

Mace and Raven both laughed.

Mace kissed her forehead. "Neither are you, baby. Neither are you."

"You're telling us Nikki's a Halfling?" Will asked while sitting in the living room beside Zero and Vegan, who'd arrived a few minutes earlier. Feeling the rumblings of intrigue and munching on Sweet Tarts, Vine meandered down the stairs to join them and see what was up.

Zero nodded. "As best I can tell."

Vegan scooted closer to him, but he shot her a warning look.

When Vine realized the statement wasn't a joke, he nearly choked on the candy. *Nikki? A Halfling?*

"We're worried about her." Vegan dropped her hands to her lap and threaded them together. "Damon Vessler is capable of anything. He's literally orchestrated her entire life."

"But why?" Will asked.

"Isn't it obvious?" Zero stood. "Look, Vessler wants to build Halflings that are loyal to him. If he had a female specimen, fully under his control, he could use her DNA to create an entire race."

Will's face paled. "But female Halflings can only have one child."

"You're the one who told us there had been anomalies, remember?" Zero said. "Which may be why it's taken him so long to accomplish this."

"So Vessler's main interest is in genetics?"

"Electromagnetic studies are a cash cow for Vessler. I uncovered files from around the globe where his projects bring in billions. He must use it to fund the genetic research."

"Nikki's a Halfling and he planned to turn her?" Will said, repeating everything they already knew. But Vine saw the shock had yet to be erased from their guardian's face or voice. "Then use her to create an army ..."

Zero threw his hands into the air. "When a Halfling is fully given over to evil, the DNA changes. There's no good left within—only hate, pure darkness. And there's no going back. Maybe Vessler's tried to turn Halflings in the past without success. So he constructed one."

"Constructed?" Vine interrupted, sinking onto the couch.

"Yeah, I'm not sure if Nikki's an in vitro baby or a clone of some kind, but make no mistake, she was birthed in a laboratory. And she's important because she has the ability to birth more than one offspring."

"And how did you discover that?" Will said.

"When I found the report with her name and the word *surgery*, I did a search on every file we've obtained from Omega."

"Omega Corporation, aka Damon Vessler," Will said.

Zero shot him a *duh* look. "Anyway, they intend to stick her under the knife and remove some of her eggs."

"That's why you think she may have been an in vitro baby herself?" Will said. "A common practice these days, but cutting-edge seventeen years ago when Nikki would have been born. Besides, even if they removed hundreds of eggs, that's not an army and it would take the offspring twenty years to be battle ready."

Zero leaned forward. "It's the *beginning* of an army. They have the theoretical capability to use the DNA to clone the eggs, but some will surely die in the process. I'm pretty sure they are working with hormones and a cold-process to induce rapid aging."

Vegan nodded. "Hundreds would become thousands, and thousands can become millions. And that *is* an army. If he can do in five years what normally takes twenty ..."

"So why hasn't Vessler done it? Why hasn't he extracted the eggs from Nikki?" Will asked. Then he answered his own question. "She had to turn first, and I would assume she would need to tap into her angelic power as well. If she's fully given over to her fallen impulses, her DNA would ensure a race of dark Halflings. Otherwise, he could be birthing an army that could fight against him rather than for him. No wonder she was being chased and tormented, but never killed. It was all an attempt to turn her. Vessler wants her filled with hatred."

"Yeah, and that also gives a reason for all the titanium shipments. His work is unprecedented, so he'd want plenty of wingcuffs on the off chance that his plan failed and the dark Halflings turned against him," Zero said.

Vine grabbed a handful of candy and chewed anxiously.

Zero leveled his cold stare at Will. "Plus, he'd want plenty to trap the Halflings fighting on his enemy's side."

"And it all depends on Nikki." Will rubbed his hand over his face.

"She has to tap in *and* turn. Nikki's a Halfling, but since she hadn't unearthed her angelic side, none of us saw it. Even you, Will."

Will nodded. "Halflings who are untapped seem pretty much like everyone else."

Vegan shrugged. "She could tap in any day. And if Vessler's played it right, she'll become dark the instant she finds those powers. The entirety of Vessler's plan—whatever it encompasses—rests on her shoulders."

Vine set the rest of the package of Sweet Tarts on the table. They didn't really sound good anymore. "What about her parents?"

Zero shot a look to Vegan. A tiny smile and nod coaxed him onward. "We think Mary and Dale Youngblood were scientists."

Will slumped onto the couch.

Vine chewed his cheek as he thought about Zero's theory. *Poor Nikki.* "Do you think her *dog* was a real *dog*?" he blurted before he could stop himself. But it just seemed so unfair. So ... awful.

Zero's head dropped a degree. "Nothing would shock me now. But Dale and Mary aren't her real parents. Who knows if she even *has* parents? The point is, as Halflings we know who and what we are from the time we're born. It's what keeps us on the side of good. Imagine being a human, hitting the age of accountability, and suddenly having supernatural powers. And—"

"And having everything you love stripped from you." Will pressed his hands together in a prayer posture. "She was to be the queen after all," he mumbled.

Zero shared a confused glance with Vegan. "What?" he asked Will.

"Checkmate."

Another glance. Zero shrugged.

"I don't want Nikki hit with all this information," Will said. "Not yet. She needs time to absorb her unique origin and who she is. Understood?"

Three Halflings nodded. Vine still couldn't get over it. *Nikki a Halfling ...*

A question burst from Vine's mouth. "Where's Nikki now? It's not safe for her to be with Vessler."

Will looked weary as he answered. "Mace and Raven went to her house to talk with her."

"To Vessler's mansion?"

"No. Vessler let her move into her parents' home. She should be there now."

Zero pressed thin lips together, then spoke. "There's more."

Will's lightning-blue eyes met Zero's silver ones. A warning rested there—Vine figured Will had heard enough for one day. But that didn't stop Zero, who presented a plan so destructive, Vine's stomach churned. He stared down at the coffee table and wondered if Sweet Tarts would ever sound good again. *Maybe in a few years.*

After several minutes, Will interrupted. "What you're suggesting could alter the entire existence of humans in as little as a generation."

"It could alter it," Zero repeated. "Or worse."

"Worse?" Will asked.

"It could end it."

"It was a dangerous game, sir," the short, thin scientist said while sliding the needle through Vessler's skin. *If I wasn't in so much pain, he'd pay for that comment. But there's always later.*

Vessler gripped the edges of the examination table while the scientist tied the last knot. "She couldn't kill me."

"She's quite capable, Mr. Vessler."

"No. I am the world to her. She just has to be reminded of that."

"Well, it may have to wait. Your cargo arrives in a few days, and I'm certain you'll want to make decisions on where the shipment will go from here. With the last one lost …"

Vessler's eyes closed, a slow burn working through his system. Details. He didn't have time for details when the star of his plan had escaped. Not escaped—kidnapped. Nikki wouldn't leave. Not on her own, at least. She may stray a bit, like that ridiculous stunt to Europe, but he was her universe. He was her life.

He was her god.

All he had to do was find her. Especially now that she'd … What did they call it? Tapped in. He'd seen her eyes go dark, and that would only happen once she was in possession of her powers. Satisfaction took the place of frustrating disappointment. It had worked. All his difficult labor, everything he'd sacrificed to bring her to fruition, had not been in vain.

"I'm sorry for the pain," Dr. Shindler said.

Damon realized his eyes had become misty—the doctor must have thought he'd actually hurt him. Did this throwaway in a lab coat have any idea what he'd suffered to get to this point? Of course not. When he'd lost Project J, it nearly destroyed him. With the others, there hadn't been time to bond. But J … Well, Nikki had done well to take the place of the dead specimen. She'd been his last hope. And she'd excelled as she grew.

"I fear she may be gone for good, Mr. Vessler."

"No, she'll be back." He smiled. "And sooner than you think."

The white-haired man shook his head. "Turning her in the confines of a fight, you're lucky you escaped with your life."

He grabbed the scientist's wrist. "This *is* my life," he gritted. "*She's* my life. Everything rests on her."

The scientist's eyes fanned to the edge of Vessler's mouth, where Damon's stitches strained beneath his anger.

Vessler shoved the man's hand away.

"We've shown promise in Nashville," Shindler said hopefully. "Especially with the group of new scientists working around the clock."

"No. She's the one. Only her."

"But, sir, without the DNA change completed, there's no promise that the … offspring … would be Darklings."

"Even if it's not by her choice, I'll find another way to complete the change." Vessler rested his head against the cool table. No more Halflings. Just darkness. Just hate. A beautiful army of his Darklings. Light, golden skin and eyes as dark as the coldest night.

And all in allegiance to him. Their father. Their creator.

<hr/>

Will was huddled over her when she woke. Nikki sat up, her side screaming in protest. She put a hand over her right kidney and applied gentle pressure. About a million sets of eyes were on her when Will stepped back, unblocking the rest of the room. She was on the couch and *they* were all around her.

Mace and Raven were about a foot away, a little blood

257

splattered here and there on their T-shirts and jeans. Vine stayed in the corner, sitting on the floor with his legs crossed, and straight across from her, the females and Zero stared down, looking anything but confident.

Vegan spoke first. "Nikki, we're so glad you're okay."

The last time she'd heard Vegan's voice was when the females were bashing her and wishing her gone. When she should have heard Vegan, *her friend*, rally in her defense. But she hadn't. Now, she was suddenly glad Nikki was okay? *Really?*

"What were you thinking, running away from us in Europe and going to stay with—" Zero stopped midstream when Vegan elbowed him in the stomach so hard it disturbed his white hair.

She turned from Zero and happened on Mace. He studied her with the intensity one gives a freshly polished gemstone. She knew what he was thinking, that maybe Vessler pushed her beyond the point of no return. Could she ever come back to him out of that strange blackness she'd sunk into?

She ached for him, but it hadn't been her choice to leave Viennesse in the first place. He'd—they'd—*all* pushed her away. Even Will, the only one she thought she could count on to be objective. Her gaze narrowed slightly, and she was sure Mace noticed the change. He always reacted when she showed some sign of strength. She took a careful breath and tried to ignore the poker in her side. "Wow, you all seem so worried." She hadn't meant for her tone to be sardonic, but hearing her voice caused a spike of pride.

"Of course we were worried," Winter said. "We didn't know what Vessler would do to you. Nikki, there's something we need to tell you."

She froze for a moment, trying desperately to remember what had just happened beyond "something horrible." She and Damon were fighting. On the lawn. Mace and Raven were there. Her eyes fanned to the two of them for a moment—both still fresh from the fight—but neither offering any clue. What had happened? Her head was aching, make that pounding, out rhythmic blasts to her brain. She pressed her hands to her temples and squeezed her eyes shut.

"Nikki, I know this must be difficult, but—"

Movement around her. Tension in the air. Mace's voice. "That's enough." Then he was there, hovering and reaching around her to lift her into his arms like she was some broken china doll. "No more talk until she rests."

She didn't want to go with Mace. She'd pushed him away at the beach house, though now she couldn't remember why she'd been so angry. Everything was blurry, and she wondered if she'd been drugged.

A stiff voice, filled with irritation, ended her thought. "We need to know what happened. This can't wait, Mace. We need answers." *Well, whatever happened, it has Zero all worked up.*

"No!" Mace's words so abrupt, she squeezed her eyes tighter. "Not. Another. Word. Until. She. Rests."

And he swept her from the room and up the stairs. *Rescued. Again.*

Chapter 23

W elcome back," Mace said as Nikki turned and stretched. He looked like he'd been sitting in the chair by a window for some time. "How's your side?"

She yawned and looked down at the covers. "Okay, I guess. Not as bad."

"Going to be sore for a few days if your kidney is bruised."

She nodded and noticed the movement of her hair against the pillow. She chanced a quick peek to the right and to the left. Hair fanned around her. Had he done that as she slept? She remembered being angry with all of them—including Mace—but now she just felt relieved to be here. Safe.

He rose and stood with his back against the door. Her sentry, her guard. And she doubted any being—regardless of its origin—would be able to penetrate the wall of Mace. She watched his hands fist. Not angrily; this was a motion she'd seen many times. He'd contract, then flex his fingers, and then they were usually touching her somewhere. As if the digits had a will of their own and wouldn't resist, no matter what his mind said. She realized she was anticipating his touch. But Mace just smiled down at her and clamped his hands behind his back.

She hoped her disappointment wasn't too easy to read. But of course, it was. Mace seemed to have an instant translator where she was concerned. "Looks like I need a babysitter after all."

"Is that what you think of me?"

"You tend to order me around a lot." Where had that come from? Then again, she couldn't deny it.

He sank onto the bed. "Remember on the boat when I told you my judgment is all messed up where you're concerned?"

She nodded. "I do, but I don't want to be locked in a cage."

"Nikki, your life is more important than we ever imagined. From the beginning I've felt the urgency to protect you. But I don't want to lock you up in any way. If anything, I want to help you fly. But you're like a bull ..." He ran his hands through his hair.

"A bull?"

"Yeah. I'm sorry, but you're constantly taking on risks, trying to test the boundaries."

"That's who I am, Mace. And it's not going to change."

"I don't want it to change. That's what I love about you. But you're also called to be a leader. And a leader doesn't always get to do what he wants."

She was called to be a leader? Seriously? With pounding surety, his words rang true and scared her. "That's why it feels like you're constantly pushing me but at the same time holding me back?"

He shrugged. "I guess. I've never thought of it that way. Leading isn't easy. You have to make the hard choices. It's seldom the thing you want."

A new respect for Mace sifted into her system. With all his infuriating stop signs, he was really trying to prepare her to move forward.

She needed to change the subject. "You saved me, didn't you?"

The lines of his face contorted for a moment, then the tension smoothed. "You were doing all right on your own."

"I don't know what happened. There was this blind rage that just overtook me. Damon, he ... he ..." Her voice cracked and her throat closed.

With a sigh, Mace reached toward her and allowed his index finger to trail along her hairline, coercing stray strands from her face.

Instinctively, she knew he intended to discuss the obvious: her, Damon, what happened. She'd have to somehow guide the conversation into a different direction, because she needed to sort the vivid things she'd dreamed while he stood guard at her door.

She forced out the words. "Raven is downstairs. Is he staying here? Are things back to normal?"

The index finger slid to her chin and moved silently back and forth beneath her bottom lip. She really wished he'd stop that. It made it difficult to continue.

"He spends a lot of time with Dr. Richmond and at the lab these days."

"The lab?"

"Yeah, he's been watching Vess— He's watching Omega. Things are as back to normal with Raven as they can be. Before today we'd been taking turns sitting outside the gate of Vessler's mansion."

"For me," she said, voice so soft it could have been an echo.

"What kind of guardian would I be if I didn't?"

Nikki stared at the door for a long time. "You rescued me twice today."

The perfect face flashed a frown. "Twice?"

She nodded. "Downstairs."

His jaw tightened. "Yeah, about that—"

Nikki lifted her fingertips to his lips to stop his words. It worked. Mace was almost always leveled by her touch. The tightening of his lips beneath her fingers, the quickening of his breath as he exhaled puffs that landed on the back of her hand, the look in his brilliant-blue eyes …

With great force, Nikki pushed all that aside. Everything had changed. *Everything.* The weight of that pressed against her shoulders like the safety harness of a roller coaster that spun and tossed you from side to side then left you inverted.

His breathing slowed and remained steady—Mace was always steady—but somehow comfortable now, as if he'd eased into a warm pool. When her gaze touched his, she saw it—relief and awe and joy all rolled into one package. He tried hard to contain his emotions, but she'd studied him as much as he had her. The cadence of his voice, the soft sound of his breathing, the firm feel of his battle-toughened hands that could turn to silk against her skin. He was pulling her into that place of quiet safety that she only knew with Mace.

She looked away.

But that moment of eye contact told her everything she feared. Nothing stood in their way now.

What Mace couldn't understand was that at the same time a new wall stood in their path. One that rose higher than ever before. He couldn't know, and she couldn't blame him for that. But, oh, she wanted to. It would make this so much easier.

"We need to talk about … you." His lips brushed against her fingertips as he spoke.

Nikki's eyes drifted shut in an attempt to capture and seal the emotion he was giving off. What would it be like to simply *feel*? To be allowed a sensation separate from all the pain attached to it? She didn't know. And unfortunately, she was about to give up her one chance of learning, as she knew what Mace was talking about. They needed to discuss who and what she was. The day's adventure was a blur, but tiny portions flickered with crystal clarity in her mind. Nikki wasn't human. She'd heard Mace and Raven say it. And if her suspicion was correct, it was the worst kind of trick. Because it meant her actions in the next few days would ensure her ticket to hell.

* * *

"How is she?" Vegan asked as she handed a cup of coffee to Mace.

"Resting again."

Vegan motioned with a dip of her head to Zero, who widened his eyes in question. She dipped her head again, a little more forcefully.

"Sorry, dude, for pushing her earlier," he conceded on an exhale.

"It's all good, Zero." Mace stared into the depths of the coffee mug. *Things should be good. Should be better on every level, and yet …*

"What's wrong, Mace?" Winter asked. A blanket of her long, dark hair framed her face, and when combined with the way she sat arrow-straight on the couch she looked like a portrait from a different time. No, not just seemed; Winter belonged in

264

a different time. Her perfect posture, her manners, the frequent glints of wisdom in her golden eyes. How long had she lived? What had she endured?

Mace hadn't given much thought to the hundreds of years that stretched before him. That now stretched before him and Nikki.

Nikki was raised by humans. And the confines of human life rested within a hundred or so years. But that limit became meaningless when he watched her eyes change. Why wouldn't she talk about the fact that she was a Halfling? She'd deliberately shut him down, even though he'd seen in her eyes she knew.

When Winter repeated the question, he stared at her a moment before answering. "It's Nikki. She wouldn't talk about what happened on the lawn with Vessler."

Heads nodded. But they didn't understand. This went beyond a need to adjust. There was a fierce determination in Nikki's eyes, a resolution in the set of her jaw, and the hint of a departure in her touch. Nothing had been spoken. Words wouldn't have been as loud.

But one thing Mace knew for certain: he was no closer to claiming the female that was his match than he had been on the day they met.

"She just needs time, Mace," Winter said.

"Well, time's the one thing she's got plenty of now." He couldn't help the bitterness that crept into his voice. He should be laughing; instead, he felt like the girl he loved had been dealt one mammoth of an unfair hand. And to make matters worse, she was about to bluff the dealer.

Glimmer stood. "Let's go home. We girls have to at least keep up the illusion normal people live in that apartment downtown." She tilted her head toward the stairs. "Nikki will probably sleep the rest of the night, but we should be here for her in the morning … You know, for support."

Several sets of eyes turned to Glimmer and widened.

"What?" she barked. "She's one of us now."

"Let's do something nice for her," Vegan added. "Maybe a party."

Zero mumbled something about girls and rolled his eyes.

"Yeah," Glimmer agreed. "We'll think of something on the way home."

But Mace wasn't in a mood to enjoy any sort of get-together. Everything he'd dreamed of and never thought he could have was slipping away, before he even got a chance to enjoy it.

⁂

By the following morning, Nikki was rested and full of questions. She had to be careful though. She wanted answers, but only answers to the right inquiries. Maybe if she was careful that no one uttered what she was, it would sort of make a loophole big enough to slip her eternity through. Because of all the things she was uncertain of, one thing remained clear: she had to find—no, she had to hunt—the man responsible for killing her mom and dad. If her parents were alive today, they could explain this mess to her. Were they the same as she was? Could they have hidden their true identity for her entire life?

Nikki seized the railing and slipped down the stairs to find Will waiting for her in the living room. A sweet scent wafted from beneath the kitchen's swinging door, and male and female voices mingled together as well. It sounded as if they were arguing.

Will put down his paper. "Did you sleep?"

"Some," she said, rubbing her hands on her thighs. "Thanks for letting me crash here."

"Of course."

She dropped onto the couch beside the giant teddy bear of a man … er, angel. "How could I not know?" she asked, careful to avoid the word, and hoping Will would pick up on that little fact. "How could *you* not know?"

"Male Halflings reach the age of accountability in their teen years. For each it's different. Raven was barely seventeen when he tapped in. Mace was seventeen as well. Vine, my early bloomer, was fifteen. Halfling females tend to reach the age of accountability around eighteen, sometimes nineteen or even twenty."

"Vegan, Glimmer, and Winter. Do they live with a heavenly angel like the Lost Boys?"

"Females are raised to the age of accountability by Xians— do you know what a Xian is?"

She nodded. "Yes, Mace explained it to me once. They're humans who are tuned in to the supernatural realm, right?"

"Yes. Since females tap in later, they are raised by Xians with a heavenly angel overseeing their lives. They are usually grown—college-aged—when they tap in. So they live together, but a heavenly angel doesn't need to be there as well. Winter, Vegan, and Glimmer have their own apartment downtown. But there's still an overseeing angel."

"Why haven't I seen their angel?"

"The girls were placed in my care. I'm the overseeing angel now."

"Oh."

He studied her for a long time before launching deeper into

the discussion. "In your case, Vessler kept an eye on you, and when you began to show the signs, he threw his plan into high gear."

Vessler. She knew him as her godfather, her protector. *Some protector. He tried to kill me on my own front lawn.* "Show what signs?"

"First, it was fortunate for him that you'd become a Seer. It made tapping into the supernatural realm easy. He'd simply drop something before your eyes that would cause you to draw. You'd sketch what your mind saw, not realizing it was actually *in* the other realm."

"That's why the hell hounds showed up in the woods the first day I met Mace, Raven, and Vine?" It seemed like it had happened to another Nikki.

"Exactly. Hounds can kill you or torment you to the point of—"

She held up a hand to stop him. "Yes, I know." Mace had explained their capabilities on the night she first met Zero in his secret underground hideout. "So all that time Vessler was making me into a monster like him."

"Yes, with fear as his wingman. But you're not like him, Nikki. Not physically, emotionally, or genetically."

Not like him. Oh, but she was about to be. She forced her thoughts away. There was time, lots of time, to put her plan into motion. "What *am* I, Will?" It was not a question to be answered; Nikki made that clear by the tone of her voice. Her gaze drifted to the window, where the sun's rays warmed the yard beyond. But a bleak indifference closed around her. The same one she felt over and over at Vessler's house, like a dark veil shading her world. She actually detested the heat the sun offered. Even the green grass and gently swaying trees repulsed her. They were liars, acting as if the world was a beautiful place, when all the while they'd sat back and watched its ugliness time and again. This morning she hated the sun for shining. "I just don't understand how I couldn't know."

"You've told me time and again lately that you don't feel like yourself. Remember, on the boat? Mace and Raven said the same thing. You've been sensing something, something evil."

She laughed without humor. "Yeah, I didn't expect it to be me."

"You are not evil, Nikki. You have fallen blood streaming through your veins, yes. But it is your choices that determine what your soul reaps."

That fallen blood drained from her face and right to her feet.

Will must have sensed it was too much for her to take in, so he shifted the conversation. "Mace and Raven both shared instances where you said you could *feel* their emotions. You killed a hell hound with your bare hands. That's hardly human."

"That was a long time ago. And right before that, I got burned in the laboratory fire and Mace didn't," she argued. "So how could he and I be of the same species?"

"Having angelic abilities and being able to utilize them are two different things. A Halfling must tap into her angelic power."

She leaned forward. This could help her execute her plan.

"First, abilities arrive a little at a time. If you were to be burned now—"

She gasped softly. "I did get burned while at Damon's beach house. Except I didn't. Krissy's hand blistered instantly. Mine didn't even turn red."

"And I would venture to say your eyesight has improved drastically."

Nikki grabbed a throw pillow and hugged it. She thought of the clarity of Mace's face when he stood at the water's edge and she on the balcony. Every detail was in sharp focus. "It has." But even farther back, her eyesight had been strong. "When we first went to visit Zero in the underground, Mace said, 'I bet you need a light,' but my eyes had adjusted."

Will smiled. "No, they didn't."

She frowned. "They did. I could see everything. All I needed was that little bit of light."

"There was no light to adjust to. You were seeing in the dark. Once the door to the surface is closed, it's pitch-black in the tunnel."

So many disjointed things connected together, it made her dizzy. "That's why Zero examined my eyes. He first thought I was a Halfling female. And even after Mace assured him I wasn't, I could tell Zero didn't believe him. Wow." She sank back. "What about seeing things in slow motion?" *Oops, just broke my own rule about admitting what I am.* But her dark veil had lifted, and she couldn't help being drawn into the awe of what she was.

"What about it?" Will shrugged.

"Well, Raven said that the realm of the supernatural moves so fast humans are hardly ever aware of it. But in instances like car wrecks, sometimes everything slows down. For a brief moment of time, humans see what it's like in the other realm. But for Halflings, it's as if everything is always moving more slowly."

"Yes." Will reached to the coffee table behind him, picked up a coaster, and lobbed it at her.

Excruciatingly slow, it flipped end over end, rising first, then falling to shoulder height as it tumbled in her direction.

On one side of the coaster she read the words, 'My house shall be a house of prayer.' The phrase disappeared as it flipped, replaced by the cork-covered side of the coaster. Lifting her hand, she caught the disk with no effort. As soon as it landed in her grasp, she dropped it to the ground. "How'd I do that?"

"You've probably been doing a lot of that without realizing it." He leaned toward her. "Nikki, you are a Halfling. Half-angel. It's second nature to you. A child who's a prodigy doesn't realize he's anything special. He simply does what he knows to do. As you embrace who you are, you'll grow more and more at ease with your ability. And more aware of when you're utilizing it."

Unsure eyes scanned his face.

"Nikki, you *are* a Halfling." Will stretched back, placing a large hand to his forehead. "I can't believe I didn't see it. I should have known the moment the females first arrived. Standing by them, you could be their sister." He leaned toward her for emphasis. "You *are* their sister."

But she was no longer listening. She settled her mind comfortably around the words *you'll grow more and more at ease with your ability. And more aware of when you're utilizing it.* That, she could use.

Nikki blinked, and confusion fluttered around her. Her conscience and her thoughts were unequally divided, weighing far more heavily on the side of revenge. But the still, small voice that had become an almost constant companion beckoned, and before she could silence it, a question slipped quietly from her lips. "Will, what's going to happen to me?"

He placed a reassuring hand on her shoulder. "Heaven will tell us. But you're not safe on your own. Vessler won't give up so easily. He's going to hunt you, Nikki. He'll use humans and hell hounds and wraiths. Make no mistake, he will try to get to you."

Fingers tickled along her spine. "Will, I'm afraid."

"Don't be. We're on the winning team." He stood and pulled her to her feet. "Until we hear differently, you'll remain with me. We'll continue to protect you. And I will train you in the proper use of your angelic ability."

As if life hasn't been crazy enough in the last months, as if I'm not already enough of a freak, let's add more training and some wings.

Wings. Her blood pressure dropped, leaving a sluggish *whoosh, whoosh, whoosh* in her ears.

"Are you okay?" Will asked.

"Uh, do I have … I mean—" She pivoted to show Will her back and looked over her own shoulder. "Are there … you know …"

"Wings?" he finished for her.

"Yeah."

He grabbed her shoulders and spun her around. "Nope. Not that I can see." His fingertips roamed her shoulder blades before turning her to face him. His eyes twinkled. "Can you feel them?"

She concentrated. "Um." She shook her shoulders. "No, I don't feel anything."

"Well, I wouldn't worry. They'll be along soon enough."

His condescending tone irritated her. *They'll be along soon enough? What in the world did that mean?* It's not like they were talking about a litter of puppies here. But rather than argue, she answered, "Okay." She rolled her eyes. "This is so weird. Are yours heavy?"

He seemed to bite back a smile. "No. They're as much a part of me as my shadow."

Voices in the kitchen rose. She turned toward the door. "Is everything all right in there?"

"Probably not. Vegan, Glimmer, Zero, and Winter arrived an hour ago with the ingredients to bake you a birthday cake."

Her eyes rounded. "Really?"

Will placed his hands on his hips. "Yes, and Raven, Mace, and Vine are certain they're doing it wrong. They've been battling the better part of the hour. Though I don't know what they're fighting about now. The cake is in the oven."

"I can smell it. It's for me?"

"We're your family now, Nikki. We all want you to feel like you belong."

"But I don't, do I?" She pulled her bottom lip into her mouth and bit down. Something flashed in his eyes. Secrets, that's all she could think to call them. And it angered her that he wasn't telling her. "What are you hiding, Will? I have a right to know." Her hardened voice seemed to take the giant by surprise.

"I have no argument. In time, I promise you will know. But right now, you have enough to absorb. And you have a birthday cake to eat."

She conceded, for now. Besides, she'd actually won that battle, whether the angel knew it or not. "Birthday cake for breakfast." She paused at the kitchen door. "Oh, what kind is it?"

"Angel food, of course."

As he led her into the kitchen, seven Halflings yelled, "Surprise!"

Chapter 24

That night Nikki lay on her belly on the cool earth, staring through the French doors that opened to Vessler's office. He'd just left the room with another man trailing his steps. A friend? A late-night business meeting? Her godfather kept conspicuous hours.

A spider crawled onto her arm from a blade of grass and she flicked it away.

At that moment, she almost backed out. Was she nuts? No, not nuts, *desperate*. Although he hadn't come right out and told her, Vessler had information on her parents' deaths. She needed that information, and his office was the best place to start looking. She'd ceased to think of him as Damon, the man who "loved" her, the man who gave her a hundred-thousand-dollar concept bike and promised her the world. The man who'd bought her a dog as a child then sent the very hell hound that stole its life. No, she'd never call him Damon again, unless, of course, it was to gain the advantage. Because annihilating an opponent was all about having the advantage. *Vessler* had taught her that.

Now he was the enemy, the man with a plot to destroy her by turning her into a dark creature. But darkness had become shades of gray, and Nikki prepared to sink to a depth Vessler wouldn't believe her capable. When she was done, gray would be a welcomed if not unattainable gift. For where she intended to go, there was no color at all.

Learn your opponent's weakness, he'd taught her. Who knew him better than her, the person he'd trained? No one. If he had a weakness, she'd find it. Then she'd use it to annihilate him.

Because she was finally free to make her own choices.

The chilly earth made a comforting bed. Silent, still, she rested her cheek against the grass and closed her eyes. Something inside begged caution, and her eyes snapped open as if denying the sound, the conscience, the warning. Dark surrounded her, but she had no trouble seeing through it. She was a Halfling, after all.

Along the driveway, two black sedans sat at the ready, cars Vessler kept in the adjacent garage. Her eyes scanned the oversized building. Inside, her concept bike waited patiently. When she was done in Vessler's office, she'd go get her motorcycle. Even if she only drove it out of the garage and into the nearest lake on her way back to the room under Will's roof, she'd take one more ride on the awesome machine.

Because this trip was just a quick investigation, something her Halfling "siblings" could know nothing about. She couldn't afford to tip them off before her real mission began.

Yet her gaze trailed the walls of the garage. Something in her core pulled her toward the place, dimly lit by a security light and scrunched by a row of trees butted against its backside like chairs shoved against a table.

A half moon hung over the building, but something about it was off. Her eyes fanned the treetops. Yes, that was it. In the very center, a division in the trees on either side split the woods like a curving river. It was subtle, and if she shifted her body a few feet to the left or to the right, she'd not even notice the breach in the foliage. But there was no doubt it signaled a path that led into the woods from the back of the garage. As if looking at something for the very first time, Nikki tilted onto her elbows. She'd passed the garage a million times, parked inside it on numerous occasions. How could she have missed the trail?

Vessler's office held little interest for her now. The garage waited, ready to divulge its secrets, and Nikki was eager to listen.

She slipped along the back wall of the structure. Through a thicket of shrubs and overgrowth, she tried to keep her movement silent, though there was no one to hear but the bugs and spiders. She stepped onto the path leading from the back of the oversized building and inspected the wall, her hand running against the wood. No, not wood—metal. The framing, the blades of grass trampled and caught beneath the ground-level section—it all told her what she'd expected. This wasn't a wall, but another garage door. But there seemed to be no way to get in. She looked down the trail, newly scarred by car tires. The winding dirt road must lead to the main street beyond.

Counting off each step, Nikki returned to the front of the garage then tucked inside. From the door she started counting again, suspicions confirmed. The garage was much deeper than the inside wall suggested. With her knuckles she rapped on the structure and listened as the echo floated and disappeared. Hollow.

Within minutes she found tiny scrapings of paint on the floor beside a large tool closet. Point of entry? If there was a hidden garage behind the known one, maybe there was a way to get inside separate from the outside door.

Nikki shoved the tool closet, but it wouldn't budge. She went to the other side and inspected the scrapes. It definitely slid this way. *Think like Vessler.* She paced for a few minutes, avoiding the three sports cars and her Ducati. *What tricks would he use?* Nikki spun and returned to the side of the closet, but opened its door before pushing. The entire closet slid easily out of her way.

She entered a cavern of a room where a large vehicle took up much of the space. Should she risk leaving the door open? Someone could come in and catch her. Judging stealth was best, she reached through and closed the entryway, hoping there was a trigger from her side as well. Along a wall was another closet like the one she'd moved. She pulled it open and found a flashlight resting among three shelves of various handguns. *All Vessler's guns aren't locked in the gun room inside the house. Interesting.*

Vessler had taught her to shoot at his private firing range, offering her a mix of guns to practice with. When she spotted her favorite, she reached for it: a Smith and Wesson .357 Magnum, with a corresponding box of hollow-point ammo. Her hand had paused over the Ruger Blackhawk, but no, too heavy. Then the Colt 1911. She loved its accuracy, but the Smith and Wesson felt more comfortable in her hand. She'd spent more time practicing with it than the others. And since the shot she may need to make was an important one, comfort factored in.

Nikki turned her attention to the vehicle, and as she looked at it her blood began a slow drain from her head to her feet. Nikki hugged her upper arms, handgun dangling beneath an elbow.

A yellow Hummer.

Mace had told her a yellow Hummer had been parked nearby the night the lab was on fire, and the man beside it had shot and killed the scientist she'd just resuscitated, missing her by mere inches.

This was the car of a murderer. *And it sat in her godfather's garage.*

She should leave. Instead, she reached to the door handle and pulled open the driver's side. She smirked at the discovery the keys were dangling from the ignition. *Always so confident, so sure of yourself, aren't you, Vessler?* Had her godfather pulled the trigger on the scientist? She figured not. He had thugs to do his dirty work.

She slid into the driver's seat and closed her eyes.

She could smell the guy, could taste in the blend of sweat and precision that this man was a professional. Deodorant barely masked the scent of stale flesh and old coffee that lingered. Nikki glanced down to the cup holder splattered with the brown evidence of an uncareful drinker.

She got out and climbed into the backseat. Nothing unusual. Her hand trailed along the edge of the seat, but still felt nothing out of the ordinary. Then she saw it, a darkened stain in the puckered corner where fabric met fabric. She had to press with her fingers to see it, but in the bright dash light, it was unmistakable. Dried blood.

Why should she be surprised? She'd already established this as a murderer's car. But something about the blood cried out to her.

Nikki closed her eyes and pressed her fingers into the crease of the seat. *Talk to me,* she urged. All was still and quiet. When her father's face flashed in her mind, she jolted. Nikki's eyes flew open and she jerked her hand from the spot. The silence of the room closed in with fresh horror.

Pulse racing, she slowly reached toward the fabric again, hoping—*praying*—she'd imagined it. Her fingertips trembled as they approaching the stain. And again she saw her father's face.

Her fingers closed into a fist, trying to capture the life that was no more. "No," she whispered to the hollow room. It was a plea and a cry and a resolution. So this was it, proof they were truly gone. Dead. At the hands of the man who'd killed the scientist and who was parked in *Damon Vessler's* garage. Sorrow turned to rage, its slow transformation burning away any innocence that remained.

She didn't need to be told her eyes were darkening. She felt it. She was turning. Killing the killer would complete the change, she was sure, but she gave it little thought. If she'd been uncertain about what she'd do, now it was evident and the only thing she *could* do. Nikki would kill the man who'd killed her parents. Then she'd deal with Vessler.

She checked the gun's safety and tucked it into the back of her jeans, gangster-movie style, but that felt completely uncomfortable, so she returned to the gun closet and searched. On the bottom shelf were a variety of holsters. Vessler had taught her how to shoot, how to handle a gun, but how to use a holster? No. She pulled a smaller one out and gripped the largest section upside down so the straps dangled below and offered a clue how it worked. Then she flipped it over and slid the shoulder harness into place. The gun fit nicely and she adjusted the straps for comfort. She pulled the gun from the holster and held it in her hand.

Nikki settled in to wait.

⊱────── ⋆⋅☆⋅⋆ ──────⊰

She heard movement outside and slid into the back of the car to hide beneath a wadded-up tarp. She couldn't kill him here on Vessler's property—too obvious—so she'd tag along and discover where murderers go late at night.

The man's smell intensified as he got into the driver's seat. Movement of keys, the motor's rumbling, and soon they were bouncing along the hidden path. She wished she'd found something else to hide beneath or nothing at all. The tarp seemed to screech and moan every time she moved. Her leg and shoulder ached, but she didn't dare readjust. Her side was screaming in protest of every pothole until the driver finally pulled onto the smooth street.

When Nikki heard his voice, she nearly screamed, until she realized he must have called someone. "Almost to the park."

Then another voice filled the air. A familiar voice, muffled through the tarp and a phone speaker, but undoubtedly Vessler's.

"Leave it in the bin in the center."

"You sure you want me to follow through with this? This is a lot of cash. It'd be easy to just finish them."

"No, I may need them later." Vessler's tone was clipped.

"A lot of good that will do if they flee the country," the driver said.

"The money is marked. I'll know everywhere they go."

"So this is just insurance?"

"Exactly."

"Why now?"

"Because the bird has left the nest. Obviously, they've been watching." Vessler did nothing to disguise his frustration.

"But you weren't worried at all when they disappeared, so you must have expected this."

"What could they do without me? I'm their life."

"Will you need me tomorrow to start the search for her?" The driver was reaching for something, Nikki could tell by the change in his voice. "Hold on a sec, gotta plug in my cell."

Vessler released an aggravated sigh. "Tomorrow morning my shipment comes in at eight. I'll call you after."

"You need me to go along?"

"No. There's no threat."

"Okay. I just reached the park."

Nikki felt the motor slow to an idle as the car rolled to a stop. If only she could breathe more silently. She prayed he wouldn't shut the motor off completely, and someone up there must have been listening because the Hummer continued to rumble. Not that it was enough to allow her movement. Her left leg was asleep and stabbing her with tiny little needles. It masked the pain in her side. A glorious—albeit painful—reprieve.

"You're sure you need them alive? I've got a great vantage point above the trash bin. It'd be like shooting fish in a barrel."

"No."

"I've got a new scope too. Need to try it out."

She could feel the tension on the other end of the line as Vessler said, "No."

The man rustled something on the seat beside him. It sounded like a trash bag.

When he got out and she heard his footsteps become faint,

she felt relief. Now to get out of the car. Nikki peeked over the seats and carefully transferred the tarp to one side. He was almost halfway to the trash can and carrying a lumpy bag. She had to move fast and wasn't sure how loud opening the rear door might be, so instead she clambered over the seats and slipped out of the driver's door and into a patch of woods about fifty feet from the vehicle.

They hadn't driven far. Once she did what she had to do, she'd walk back to the house on Pine Boulevard. She wouldn't drive his car. You don't kill a man then drive away in his vehicle.

Nikki took her station in a row of trees near the Hummer. She was a good shot, but not a perfect one, so she stayed close. Probably too close, but what did it matter? There was no going back. With the gun in her hand and the safety off, she sat patiently.

Once he'd dropped the bag into the bin below, he started back up the incline to the Hummer, which was still running, lights shimmering on a row of trees across the park.

As he approached her position, he slowed his pace and stopped to face the trees, and her. Keen eyes, one with a tear-drop tattooed beneath, scanned the ground around her. Nikki closed one eye and took aim, hand shaking.

But the man did something unexpected. He reached to the ground and lifted a butterfly into his hands. Palm flat, he studied the insect. With a fingertip he nudged it to the edge of his hand until the butterfly tumbled downward. He caught it; this time its wings spread to show the injury that kept it from flight.

Nikki squeezed her eye shut, willing the man into motion. *Smash it*, her mind screamed. *Smear it on your pant leg or grind it into the dirt, anything to make me able to do this!*

But he didn't. Her eye opened when he carried the butterfly toward her and sat the wounded creature in the crook of a tree.

It was such a *human* thing to do, and it turned her inside out.

Her teeth clenched. She hated herself for not being able to get vengeance on the man who took her world. A stupid, *stupid* wounded butterfly was all that kept her from pulling the trigger. And not pulling the trigger was all that kept her from hell.

As the man got in his Hummer and drove away, Nikki sat down in the grass and cried until nerves that had been taut with adrenaline and fear melted into emptiness.

Several minutes passed, but she remained there with the sounds of the forest blanketing her. Strange that she felt no fear now that the man was gone. But the whine of a far-off engine triggered her attention, and she brushed the tears from her face as if an approaching vehicle meant she'd be caught in her moment of frailty.

The small white car approached slowly. She craned her neck and watched it entering the park from a different road. The vehicle doused its lights, and she had to chuckle. Like anyone wouldn't see the glowing white car on a surprisingly bright half-moon night. It slowed to a crawl, so excruciating she wanted to scream at the driver, *It's all clear, he's gone.*

This was no expert bad guy.

After an eternity, the man stopped the car and eased the door open. Dressed in a long coat and a misshapen hat, he approached the trash can like it would explode if he moved too suddenly.

He looked of average build. And something about his gait seemed familiar to her.

He dug in the bin like a hobo, then came up fast, eyes darting in all directions. Halfway back to the car he broke into a run, and the added momentum coupled with a bit of wind stripped the hat from him. His hand clamped onto his head, trying to grasp what had already escaped. The man spun around, ran a few steps toward the hat, then stopped, his feet doing a confused little dance as he turned and headed to the car again.

But Nikki felt as if her platelets congealed, stopping her systems and shutting them down. No oxygen entered her lungs, and she didn't feel strong enough to encourage any. Because from fifty yards above, Nikki stared down into the eyes—not the face, not the body, but certainly the eyes—of her father.

Chapter 25

It took several breaths before she could process what she'd seen. It *wasn't* her dad. Her dad was dead. And the man's body size and facial structure were all wrong. But he had her dad's eyes. Bile rose in her throat as her mind concocted gruesome scenarios inside Omega's laboratory, and all the horrific things that must go on there.

But this wasn't like that. The guy looked like a … relative … of her father's. A brother or a cousin, maybe. Which was impossible, because her parents didn't have any relatives. Or did they? Vessler knew her parents well enough to know every detail of her life. And he was tied to the man in the yellow Hummer, and the man in the Hummer killed the scientist as well as shot her mom and dad. Vessler had manipulated her life. And in doing so, maybe he'd forced her parents to deny her the rest of her family.

Every trail led back to Vessler. Nikki's hatred stirred. Seeing the man run to the trash bin like a mouse hoping for a few morsels of food made her despise Vessler even more. She hadn't been able to kill the man in the Hummer. But she was certain of one thing. It would be her pleasure to pull the trigger on Vessler. As soon as possible.

Nikki waited until the car was gone before she stood. She stretched, ignoring the pain in her body, and reached down to pick up the gun before starting the long walk back to town. When she took the first step, her eyes focused on something in the dirt. At the edge of her shoe, the butterfly lay dead.

She walked a lonely stretch of road with only the moon to guide her. A small green sign assured she'd gone in the right direction. Halfway back to Vessler's house, a pick-up pulled over.

A door opened and a young man stepped out. "Hey, are you all right?"

Nikki kept moving forward, closing the distance.

"Are you okay? Did you have an accident or something?" She watched him look beyond her, searching for a car. "Did you break down?"

Purposeful steps carried her onward, ignoring the tension in his tone.

"Nikki, is that you?" His words loosened with more than a little relief.

She recognized the voice from somewhere far away. Red taillights shined in her eyes, making his figure appear tall and broad, cartoonish. She didn't answer, but kept moving toward him. Her steps neither slowed nor sped.

He stopped a few yards away. "It's Michael, from school." He lifted his hands and dropped them. "What are you doing out here?"

She continued her approach and didn't stop until they were face-to-face. She searched his eyes, the curious bend of his mouth. Had Vessler sent him? Her gaze narrowed.

No. He'd approached weaponless, yet she had a handgun strapped to her shoulder. Besides, Vessler didn't know he was being hunted.

His eyes trailed to the holster. "Are you ... okay?"

Fear and concern laced his voice. Concern for her, or for himself now that he knew she was armed. Her hand covered the weapon. He'd asked a question. What was it?

"Nikki, are you okay?"

His gaze was split between her face and her hand, now petting the gun in the holster. The metal felt cool to her fingertips.

"Your car break down?" he asked.

Her mouth started to form the word no, but her voice had slipped away in the night. She shook her head.

He offered a nervous smile. "That thing loaded?"

Her eyes fanned down to it. Was it loaded? She couldn't remember loading it, but it was ready for Vessler's lackey, so it must have been. Then she remembered clicking the button to red. "Safety's on," she mumbled.

This seemed to satisfy him. He offered a hand. "Come on, I'll take you wherever you're headed."

She climbed into the cab of his pick-up.

"I was camping down on Bull Shoals," Michael said.

She glanced over her shoulder to the back of his truck: camping gear, a cooler, lanterns, and a stack of firewood. "That's good," she said.

He gave her a long look with brow raised. "Uh, yeah. It was good. Where to?"

"Damon Vessler's mansion at the edge of town."

"So, the girl *can* string an entire sentence together. I was starting to wonder." He'd relaxed. Heart rate slowed, breathing normal, scent of fear and confusion leaving him. *I really am a freak.*

"It wasn't a sentence."

"Huh?"

"No verb. It was a fragment."

Michael nodded.

"And stop looking at me like I'm crazy."

"Sorry, Nikki." He nodded toward the gun. "You just don't find a lot of hot teenage girls walking alone late at night with a handgun." He laughed. "Well, there was that dream I had once, but uh, I'm pretty sure stuff like that doesn't happen."

It settled into her bones how far she'd sunk, the depths of melancholy she'd disappeared into. After tonight, there was no going back to so many things. Least of all school and friends. Yes, she'd graduated early, but that didn't exempt her from football games, bowling nights, pizza and movies. Why hadn't she appreciated those opportunities when she possessed them? Nikki dropped her head to the dashboard. Why was she always so busy telling Krissy no, like all that stuff was beneath her, when right now she'd trade her Ducati for a night with friends and laughter and fun. And really, wasn't she trading much more for much less? Revenge wouldn't fill the hole in her heart. At best, it was a rotten patch filled with too many faults to be useful for long.

She was doing exactly what Vessler had taught her.

The truck seat squeaked as Michael reached over and patted her shoulder. She felt the closeness of his hand as it hovered above her back. But he didn't touch her again, must have decided against it.

As instructed, he dropped her off a block from Vessler's house. "Do you have any blankets in the back?" she asked as Michael opened the door for her.

"Sure. A sleeping bag and a quilt."

Without asking why, he fumbled around the bed of the truck and held them out to her.

She took the sleeping bag. "I can pay you for it."

He placed his hand over hers. "Don't worry about it." He grabbed a small pillow from the bed and rested it on top of the sleeping bag in her hands. The motion brought him close, and her eyes locked with his. "Nikki, I've always admired you. Wow, that sounded cheesy, didn't it?"

Admired her?

He nervously brushed a hand through his hair. "If you need some help …"

Her feet carried her a step back, head shaking, steamrolled by his words and the honest offer in them. She'd prefer to deny it, but there it was. Undeniable humanity in all its glory. She skittered farther away.

"Okay, okay." Michael held his hands out in surrender. "Just … Well, if you need anything, give me a call. Maybe my dad could do something to help."

Nikki's heart sank. His dad. The sheriff. She'd just had the sheriff's son drive her to her crime scene. "I don't need any help," she said, but her hands had tightened on the sleeping bag and pillow.

He nodded, studied her with sheriff's son's eyes, and finally gave a tiny smile. "Well, if you need me to do anything for you, my number's on the tag on the sleeping bag." He turned to walk around the truck.

"Michael, wait." Such a pathetically weak little voice.

He stopped and rested a hand on the bed liner.

"Promise me you'll do one thing."

"Okay."

"Tomorrow morning after ten o'clock, tell your dad you gave me a ride here and I took your sleeping bag, okay?"

He stared up the hill at Vessler's house for a long time. "Anything else?"

No. But she heard herself saying, "Then go to the Victorian house on Pine Boulevard and let them know ..." *Let them know what?* "Tell them everything is going to be okay. Tell Mace ..." But no more words came. Her throat squeezed and pinched them off. Besides, there were no words that could express what she felt, and nothing that could excuse her actions. She shook her head. "Scratch that last part."

"All right, Nikki."

"Promise you'll wait until morning, *late* morning."

He crossed his arms.

"Promise!"

"I promise." He headed to the driver's door. "Don't get into any trouble, Nikki."

Into trouble? Oh, she couldn't possibly get into more than she was already. She painted on a cheery smile. "I won't." As an afterthought. "I promise." And the lie didn't even taste bad on her lips.

She slept curled up in a corner of the garage, with the scent of tires and grease keeping her company. She wouldn't dare try to do anything to Vessler at his house. Too many bodyguards and servants, too much could go wrong. She'd have to follow him.

And this morning—with a shipment of whatever coming in— was the perfect opportunity. After all, he'd told the Hummer driver there was no threat.

She wouldn't be able to hide in his vehicle, because he had three different cars he could choose depending on his mood. She'd follow on her Ducati. Good thing she'd tossed that whole "drive it into a lake" thought. What had changed her course of action? Oh yes, finding the man who killed her parents while visiting her so-called godfather.

Vessler appeared in the garage, and her heart started kicking against her ribs. She was hidden from sight, and he seemed to be alone. He chose the red Porsche, and it was all she could do not to plug him right there.

She followed from a safe distance until they reached a small airfield about thirty miles from town. The shipment must have come in by plane. Near a white metal hanger, a tractor trailer rig sat at the ready. A dark cargo plane—looking like something that belonged to the army—sat at the base of a landing strip as if it were ready to take off again. Vessler was alone. No one had come with him, and from what she could tell, no one was meeting him.

He traversed the landing strip, but just before climbing aboard the aircraft through an open cargo door he turned and stared at the tree line where she watched. Her breath caught when she realized he looked right at her. Everything in her wanted to move, to shrink farther into the trees, but she held her ground. There was no way he could see her. Impossible.

But when a slow smile spread across his face, she had to wonder.

Chapter 26

I'm going after her, Will." Mace brushed past Vine and headed to the door, with Raven right behind him.

"Me too," Raven said.

Upon waking, they'd discovered Nikki missing. It wasn't until the females arrived a few minutes later and checked her room that they realized she'd been gone all night.

"We don't even know where she is," Glimmer said.

"All I know is that she's in trouble. We need to find her now." Mace's mind ran through scenarios, especially those where Vessler had somehow gotten to her, kidnapped her. Or maybe she'd gone back to him. Her behavior following the party yesterday had certainly been strange.

Will nodded. "Let's spread out. Glimmer and Winter, go to the lab. See if she's there."

The girls nodded and leapt from the living room.

"Vegan and Zero, check her parents' house. Vine, the Omega warehouse."

"I'll go with you two," Will said to Mace and Raven. "We'll go to Vessler's front door."

"What if they won't let us in?" Mace asked.

"Then we'll let ourselves in." Will's apprehension was evident. "She's at too vulnerable a place to be with Vessler. Even for a short time."

When the pick-up truck pulled into the driveway, Mace, Raven, and Will ran toward it. It had to carry news of Nikki. Maybe she was fine, and had only gone to Krissy's house or something. But as the guy stepped out—someone Mace remembered from Waterside High—his worst fear was confirmed. Nikki was in trouble.

Nikki peeked inside the open plane door, but couldn't see Vessler. Voices floated out to her. From the conversation, he must be talking to the pilot who'd landed the plane. Words like *fuel* and *landing gear* drifted from the discussion.

Off to the left, another truck rumbled down the gravel road headed toward the airfield. She had to move now. Nikki stepped onboard the plane and pulled the gun from the holster. She felt queasy instantly and hoped she had the nerve to finish the job.

He was facing the pilot and hadn't seen her yet. Vessler's crisp white shirt was tucked into designer jeans. His gold bracelet glinted where his hand was clasped around the pilot's chair. Nikki's heart had stopped hammering and settled into a sluggish rhythm, making her legs and arms weaker by the second.

She'd prefer to be alone with Vessler, but this was the best she could expect. Everything was right. She tucked behind a stack of large wooden boxes, a large number of which filled the cargo space. Nikki raised a hand and swept sweat from her brow. The night's restless sleep was playing against her. Her legs were jelly.

As if hearing her thoughts, Vessler answered, "It's titanium, my lady."

Nikki's eyes widened in horror, seeing the boxes for the first time as what they really were: stacks and rows of titanium. Which used to mean nothing to her personally. But now that she was a Halfling, it was her kryptonite.

Again he answered her thoughts. "You walked right into your weakness, my dear." Then he turned to face her and motioned for her to step out. "Come on, Nikki. You don't hide behind boxes. You're a warrior."

She swallowed and stepped out. "Yes, I am. You saw to that, didn't you?"

He sighed heavily, and she wanted to smack that condescending grin from his face. It made her feel small, like a disobedient child. "Training you has been my life's crowning achievement."

Nikki leveled the gun at him.

Vessler only smiled. "Really, dear? A handgun? That's the best, most creative thing you could come up with?"

"I'm not trying to be creative, Vessler, I'm trying to get a job done."

He angled a look over his shoulder at the pilot. "Take off," he barked.

Nikki panicked. *Take off? Was he kidding?* What would happen if she fired the gun while in the air and missed? But it was too late to wonder, because before she could protest, the plane was bounding along the runway. And she felt weaker with every leaden movement. She had to think. She'd had the advantage; now it was gone.

Think like Vessler.

Nikki braced herself against one of the boxes. "Toss me your gun."

Vessler always kept a small handgun in an ankle holster.

When he refused to comply, she screamed it at him, but he swatted the air like one swats a fly and shrugged. "Fine. We'll play your game. For a while. Though I warn you, Nikki, I make up my own rules."

He propped a foot on a box and removed the Robar nine-millimeter, then slid it halfway to her. It wasn't as far away from him as she'd like, but it would have to do.

"Do you really think you're going to shoot me?" he asked.

"No. I *know* I'm going to shoot you."

"Then what are you waiting for?" He took a step closer, tightening the twenty-some-foot gap between them.

Think like Vessler. Right now, they were pretty evenly matched. She had a gun, but he had a plane in the air. What happened if she missed? Would a bullet through the plane's fuselage cause it to crash?

"Drop altitude," he told the pilot. "Then rise high as she'll take us."

The engine noise changed, and Nikki felt her body being propelled toward Vessler. Instead of fighting the momentum, she threw herself forward and crashed into his chest. He hadn't braced for that. A desperate gasp of air left his lungs as he landed on the floor. She tumbled on top of him.

Putting the gun in his face, she pressed her free hand against his throat as she felt the plane begin to incline.

The rumble of a laugh surprised her. But not as much as the snap of a handgun to her right, cocked and ready. Vessler raised the Robar—which must have slid to him in the dive—inches from her nose.

"Here we are again, Nikki. Check." Vessler's training in the weeks spent at the mansion came back to her. *Never allow yourself to be in a fight that's evenly matched. Find the advantage. An opponent always has a weakness. Use it against him.*

Why didn't she pull the trigger? She wanted to, she just couldn't.

"You can't kill me, Nikki."

Tears stung her eyes and her gun trembled. "And you can't kill me. So we're at an impasse."

"You're wrong." He pressed the gun against her cheek. "I could pull this trigger easily." And in the depths of his eyes, she knew he could. But she also sensed he *wouldn't*. There was a lie hiding in his words.

"Then do it," she bluffed. "If I'm dead, so is your plan."

He snatched the barrel from her face. "Sadly, you're right. I suppose you think that gives you the advantage."

"Not really. What gives me the advantage is knowing that when I pull this trigger you die and your plan dies with you."

Vessler laughed. "Oh, Nikki. Sometimes you think too small. You can only destroy my flesh. You can't kill my soul or the essence of who and what I really am. It will live on to see all my dreams reach fruition. Killing me only solidifies your transformation into what you were born to be, what you've been trying so hard to deny."

Cold washed over her. "Killing me will complete you, Nikki. I win either way."

Panic crept at the edge of her conscience. She knew he was right. And when he raised the gun to her again, she almost hoped he'd pull the trigger.

The shot rang through the airplane, and Nikki felt the engine's drastic change. Her eyes followed Vessler's hand and the weapon. He'd shot the pilot through the back.

"What did you do?" Nikki jumped off Vessler and pressed her back to the wall of the plane that was holding steady, regardless of the loss of pilot.

"Taking the advantage, of course. You see, Nikki, you have two choices: Leap and take me with you, and we continue our chess match on the ground, or leap alone and leave me to die in the airplane that's headed straight for downtown St. Louis … and all those innocent people."

Nikki's mind raced. Leap? She couldn't leap; she didn't have wings. A thought struck her. "A Halfling can't leap with this much titanium."

His face flashed shock but he quickly recovered. "No problem." Vessler moved to the side door, unlocked its safety bar, and slid the door open. "We can jump. Your wings can open once you're away from the titanium."

Wings open. Ha. They were going to die. Both of them. And no matter what happened, the plane would crash into downtown St. Louis and kill hundreds of others. Hate built inside her.

Vessler, who'd snaked to the opposite side of the plane, had noticed her emotional shift, if his smug look was any indication. But what she couldn't understand was why he was so willing to give up his life.

"You're such an evil man."

"Oh, I'm not evil. You are, Nikki—bouncing from one side of the war to the other. You're the worst kind of evil, because you justify playing on both teams and never really choose a side. You know what that means? The rest of us have a purpose; we all serve a greater power. But you, selfish little spoiled Nikki, you only serve yourself. You're already on the way to being the general who will lead my dark army, and the best part is you don't even realize it because you're too busy manipulating people into doing what you want."

Out the front window, she could see land, the first signal that the plane was slowly going down.

Nikki's knees buckled and she dropped to sit on the floor. "If I'm so evil and destined to serve you, maybe it's best we both die. Right here, right now."

Shock replaced the calm on his face. Vessler leapt toward her, but Nikki raised the gun and fired. His hands clamped his leg as he crumbled.

"God, please forgive me," she cried, throat closing on the words.

Vessler jerked a cabinet open and dragged supplies from inside. He found a bungee cord and tied it around his wound to stop the bleeding. *Why would he do that? We'll both be dead in another five minutes.*

"Nikki, please. Leave me here, but you can jump."

She chanced a spiteful look at him.

"Go, Nikki. You deserve to live."

"A moment ago I deserved to die."

"Live, Nikki."

"With the fact that this plane will kill innocent people? No, Damon."

He didn't want to die. She could see it in his face, the way he struggled to stop the blood flow. But she wouldn't be bluffed this time.

Again, they were at a stalemate. *Think like Vessler.*

Vessler loved his life. Yes, if she jumped alone, it would ensure her turning into a dark creature, but he'd be dead, at least physically. No, there's no way he'd give up his life that easily. Nikki's eyes drifted to the pilot, now slumped over a board of controls with blood seeping from the wound to his back. Then her eyes found Vessler's.

"You want me to jump because you can fly the plane."

He tried to cover his reaction, but his nostrils flared. She'd found him out. "I'll survive, you'll land the plane, but my willingness to let you go down will be my ruin? That's what you're gambling on."

Fire burned in the depths of his inklike eyes.

But, being Vessler, his loss of composure was only temporary. "If you don't jump, we'll crash. And all those deaths will be your fault."

"It won't matter. I'll be dead too."

"No, you won't. You're a Halfling, Nikki. You'd be amazed at what you can survive."

Was he right? She couldn't be sure. Could she live with the deaths of innocent people, with innocent blood on her hands? With renewed vigor, she lifted the gun so it was aimed at his chest. "Land the plane." She had to find his weakness.

"That's an empty threat, my lady. If you shoot me, I can't land the plane."

She cocked the gun. "Land the plane, Vessler." Then she saw it. Hurt in his eyes when she called him Vessler. Nikki saw her opportunity and softened her voice. *She* was his weakness. "Land the plane, Damon. Please. Don't you want to watch me fulfill my destiny? Don't you want to be there? To be able to smell the scent of fresh kill on my flesh and taste the vengeance you've worked for?"

He was like a deer caught in the beam she was casting. It was working.

She angled a step closer and chanced a glance through the front window. The earth was moving closer, green blobs becoming individual trees. She had only another couple of minutes at the most. "Please, Damon."

But a fierce flash of resistance overtook him. "No. You're not as strong as I thought you were."

She frowned.

"You couldn't even shoot me—at least not to kill."

The flash of the gun surprised her, and she stared at her hand as if it belonged to someone else. She'd pulled the trigger. Her aim had dipped to his opposite leg, and now Vessler crumpled over to grab the new injury, his gun flying from his hand and landing behind a box.

She hadn't meant to shoot. Had she?

When his face came up to meet hers it was red with anger, and sweat poured from him like the blood pouring from his new wound. Hands slick with both, he reached for a strap to tie around his newly wounded leg.

"Land the plane, Damon." It was an order. A cold, solid order given by one in charge. His eyes trailed from her to the wound, still shocked, still uncertain.

Yes, she'd taken the advantage.

He hauled himself up and stumbled toward the cockpit, but stopped. "No!" he screamed in defiance.

Nikki angled the weapon toward his arm. Her eyes flashed back to his. "I'll take you apart one piece at a time if I have to, but you are going to land the plane."

He shook his head and braced for the shot.

But her adrenaline had seeped out through every pore, leaving her weak. She couldn't pull the trigger again. Nikki sank to the floor. It was over.

Vessler would bleed to death, and she'd go down in a cargo plane filled with titanium and kill a mass of innocent people.

She imagined the plane hitting a park. Children, families, all dying together in one giant fireball. Nikki pulled her thighs to her chest and, still holding the gun, wrapped her arms around her legs. Across from her, Damon worked to tighten the tourniquet around the fresher wound. His breathing was unsteady, and it seemed that all the blood in his face was escaping through the bullet holes in his legs.

"Checkmate," she mumbled, and put her head down. She pressed her eyes into her knees so hard, it hurt. She thought of her dog, Bo, her parents, the karate tournament where she won a national title. She wouldn't allow herself to think of Mace. That was too painful and it might be enough to change her mind.

Suddenly, his presence was there all around her. Warm hands closed gently on her shoulders and he uttered her name.

Chapter
27

Mace?

When Nikki looked up, he was standing between her and Vessler. *Have we crashed? Am I dead?*

Mace slid the gun from her hands. "Come on, Nikki. It's time to go home."

Confused, she let herself be lifted from the floor. *If this is death, it's quite nice.* But the smell of blood, the scream of the plane engine, and the wind from the open door proved she was still part of the world. She focused on Mace: he was life, he was hope, and she was safe. Her relief turned to fear as she scanned his arms, bloody and scraped.

"It's time to go," he said, and placed a steadying arm around her.

"How'd you get in here?" She looked from side to side, confirming they were still inside the plane.

"I wasn't able to get in until you opened the door. I'd tried to leap inside and kept hitting the side of the plane and bouncing off." He moved her gently toward the open door.

"The plane's filled with titanium," she said.

"I figured that out. We need to hurry. Raven can't hold the plane up, only slow its decent. The titanium is taking its toll."

The wounds on Mace's body were from trying unsuccessfully to leap inside the plane?

He tightened his grip on her. "We'll have to jump, and it'll be a bit bumpy until my wings can open."

Nikki grabbed the side of the door. "Wait." Her gaze traveled to the front window. "Mace, if Vessler doesn't land the plane, it will strike downtown St. Louis. People will die."

Mace gave a long, surrendering sigh. He released her reluctantly and moved to Vessler. Grabbing him by the shirt, he lifted and dragged him to the cockpit. After removing the dead pilot, he dropped Damon before the controls. Mace leaned down, leveling his face with Vessler's. "It's the people she's saving, not you," he growled.

Vessler grinned through a sweat-smeared face. "Keep telling yourself that, boy."

"And don't even think you'll get to keep the titanium." Mace returned to Nikki and together, they jumped.

They stayed in the air until the plane touched down in a field inside the busy St. Louis metro area. She'd expected Raven to follow them, but he hadn't.

"With any luck, Vessler will bleed to death," Mace said.

"Well, my luck hasn't been dependable lately." Nor her instincts. She was going to kill Vessler. It seemed impossible, but she'd actually planned to murder him. Nikki put a hand to her temple where a headache pounded.

To Mace, nothing stood in their way now. But Nikki wasn't who she used to be. When they touched down and he reached to steady her, she pushed gently from him.

"What's wrong, Nikki?"

"Everything, Mace. You don't know what I was going to do."

"Michael told us he'd met you last night."

When he moved to get closer to her, she stepped back. "I was going to kill Vessler. It's sort of a blur now."

"I know you've had a huge internal monster to fight, but Nikki, I think Vessler was poisoning you." Mace shook his head. "Or drugging you."

She frowned.

"Raven told me that Omega can inject a serum that will cause a violent creature to be docile. Maybe it would work in reverse too."

"And I'm the creature."

"I'm just saying. You were pretty obsessed with that designer water Vessler gave you. Could he have been dumping something into them?"

"Could he? Sure." But her actions couldn't be completely blamed on some unknown drug. She'd wanted revenge. Had been desperate for it. So much so it made her crazy inside. No, she couldn't simply blame drugs. She had to be responsible for her actions. Actions that almost included taking a life.

"You're alive, Nikki. You're okay now, and you're a Halfling. It changes everything." Mace looked so full of hope, it made her want to cry. Mace always believed the best. Especially of her. But once again, she would set him up to fail, because she wasn't who she once was, and she saw no way to go back. Vessler's promise haunted her. "This isn't over."

Mace used his thumb to rub away the worry lines on her forehead. "It never is."

"If Vessler lives, he'll continue his quest."

"But you know what you are now. He can't have you."

"I'm spoken for?" If it were only that simple. She'd changed forever in the last few weeks. Who knew if Mace would even be interested in the new, damaged Nikki she'd become?

"Exactly."

"Well, don't think you're going to get the blessing of my legal guardian."

"How about if I'm your guardian?"

"No."

He flashed a frown.

Her headache lessened enough to allow the tiniest smile. "You're way too bossy."

"Is that right?"

She nodded. "And you're always trying to protect me instead of teaching me how to defend myself."

He raised his hands in surrender. "I promise to help you learn to defend yourself. Although what I just saw in the airplane would suggest you need little instruction."

"I need a partner, Mace. Not a boss."

"Okay, okay. I get it. If I was over the top, it's just because I love you."

Oh.

"You were saying?" He gestured with an upturned hand for her to continue.

"No more damsel-in-distress heroics?"

"No more. You've been called to be a leader, Nikki. I owe it to you to help prepare you."

"Still, I don't think of you as my guardian."

"No?"

"You're my angel."

He led her to a river's edge. For a long time they listened to the cadence of water against rock. "Think we can rest now?"

she asked, but she knew she wouldn't. She needed to discover who this new Nikki was. Maybe Mace could still love her. But she doubted it because ...

Because she was too much like Raven.

A week after Zero reported Nikki was safe and back with the other Halflings, Raven stretched back, resting his hands on his stomach. The sky looked different from his ruins. Closer somehow, and more like an ally than a distant onlooker. The North Star winked at him. He thought of Debra the horse and Adam Cordelle. Huh. His list of friends had been reduced to a pathetic guard and a mutant mare. *Wow, the depths one can sink to over a female.*

Female. Nikki. A Halfling. Could life be any more ironic? *I fall for a human, ready to give up everything for her, only to discover the human's been a Halfling all along. To top it off, now that loving Nikki won't lead to my damnation, I get to watch her spend eternity happily ever after with Mace.*

The rocks at his back bit into his flesh like tiny piranha chewing away at his strength, mocking his stupidity. It was easier when she was a human and the real threat was heaven or hell. He could have beaten Mace at that game.

But now everything had shifted. For Mace, Nikki had represented the one weakness that could send him to the pit. For Raven, she'd represented something to live for. He'd sink into darkness, of that he was certain. His eyes had been dimming into the blackness of the forever damned for years. Until Nikki. For all his unrestrained life, he'd allowed himself little time to ponder the hideous consequences of his actions. And he wouldn't now, either. Because this, this empty hole of an existence, was horrid in its trappings.

What could possibly be worse? The shrieking moans from those on the other side shot into his mind. And even now their tenor leeched the blood from his veins. No, there were things worse than a broken heart.

Maybe tonight would be the night. Maybe he'd awaken with the Dark Prince whispering a soothing lullaby of revenge into his ear. Maybe *he'd* be the one to hunt the Halflings ...

Raven clamped his arms around his head and shut his eyes tight, interlacing his fingers and squeezing out the demonic influence. With solid intention, he threw his eyes open and stared up. The North Star again, once a symbol of a promise, was now a small-but-guiding drop of radiance. "Help me," he whispered.

He'd prayed on many occasions. Hey, he served the Throne. When you're packing fully automatic weapons, you don't reach for the hunting knife. But Raven had never prayed for himself. It felt weak, somehow, to petition the One who'd commissioned him. A lack of faith in the omniscience of the Great Stabilizer.

A fisted hand fell to his heart; the physical pain, dull but constant, surprised him. Could he talk about Nikki to the quiet sky? Would his voice hold or shatter like ice under too much pressure?

She'd be at Viennesse by now. Will had moved the group there once again, opting to keep them in Europe until the dust cleared around Vessler. Another week, maybe two, then they would probably head back to Missouri. Raven hadn't gone with them, but he'd felt her leave; a strange sensation, one he could only liken to having a section of skin ripped from his body.

And so he'd followed. But he stayed at the castle ruins rather than go home.

"Look, I try not to bother you too much."

Silence.

"I, uh …" He was surprised at how hollow his voice sounded, how spent. "I just need to know that she's going to be okay."

Nothing.

His lungs filled and emptied. Filled and emptied. "So, is Nikki going to be okay?"

A dazzling light whirred before his eyes, and for a moment Raven thought someone must have snuck up and whacked his head, though he felt no pain. He leapt to his feet, hoping the blood would move with him.

In the center of the light, a being took shape. It was clothed in layers of glory, and he knew it had been at the Throne.

For once, Raven's voice was gone.

The angel was the size of Will, but smelled like the place where life particles danced until the One called each to an individual purpose. He'd only dreamed of such a location, but knew of its magnificence and power somehow inherently. For Halflings, the midplane was the closest they'd ever get to heaven. For most, it was enough.

The angel stood toe-to-toe with him, eyes alight with the fire of the One he served. He was … waiting for something.

"Uh," Raven uttered. "Why are you here?"

"To answer your question." There was little emotion or inflection in the being's voice, just pure, smooth, and resonant words.

A question? What had he asked? What was he even thinking about? *Nikki.* "Is Nikki Youngblood going to be okay?"

The angel's answer sparked and ignited a fire of fear throughout Raven's being. "No."

Raven's mouth dried instantly, as if all moisture had been drawn from his body with the single word. He needed more information, but the angel was turning away like he intended to go.

Raven leapt forward and seized him, arms closing on the angel's waist. But the magnificent being flicked him off. This was not an evenly matched confrontation. *New plan.* "Why not? Why won't she be okay?"

"Because a Seeker has been released from the pit."

Raven's knees buckled and crashed against the rock-strewn ground. Fear and urgency pinched his lungs into crumples, making him unable to pull even the smallest of breath.

A Seeker.

Released to hunt Nikki.

Suddenly, the angel was offering the same hand that moments ago brushed Raven from his garment. Powerful golden fingers drew him to his feet.

Still, Raven was too stunned to speak. The angel turned once more, this time slowly, as if awaiting another ambush.

"Wait," Raven finally mustered, throwing his remaining oxygen into the plea. "Why did you tell me?"

Was that a slash of a smile that appeared? "Because you asked."

And then the angel was gone.

Raven was left with one hammering thought. He had to get to Nikki before it was too late.

Check out this sample from book one of the Halflings series.

Heather Burch

Halflings

What if Following Your Heart
Meant Losing Your Soul

Chapter
1

Fangs sank into Nikki Youngblood's leg, setting her skin on fire. A scream gurgled in her throat, but she willed herself past trees smeared by her jarred vision. Her jacket snagged on a branch. No, no, no … She jerked free, casting a glimpse backward at the gnarled faces behind her. The lead beast stumbled over paws caked with mud. She seized the moment to widen the distance.

Run. Her lungs burned. *Just keep running.*

Her feet, now numb, thumped against the dense carpet of the forest floor. Once a place of security, a quiet sanctuary of solitude and escape, her woods had morphed into a house of terror complete with four grotesque dog-wolves tracking her every step.

Despite her years of martial arts, of seeing herself as tough and in control, Nikki was completely helpless. But that didn't mean she had to die. Karate had taught her to stay calm in all manner of attack. *Though I don't think this is what you had in mind, Sensei.*

One minute she's perched against a rock, drawing. The next, she's running from … from …

She started to glance back, but stopped herself. *Concentrate on escape. Don't concentrate on your enemy.*

Besides, she didn't even know what those dog-things were. But one thing was certain: they were out for blood and Nikki was an easy mark for the vicious beasts.

Exhaustion squeezed each muscle, depriving them of strength. Likewise, it pushed at her consciousness, promising failure. When she thought her lungs might literally burst, a momentary, blinding flash of light sparked above her, as if the universe were snapping a picture of her dilemma. Within seconds of the spark of light, a sound descended. *Church bells?* The reverberation of a thousand muted bells soothed her nerves and curled around her like a warm blanket after a nightmare. The unearthly noise filled her ears, a beautiful hum closing her in. But the tempo rose higher and higher until it caused the backs of her eyes to throb.

The dog-wolves began to moan. She glanced back — the four monsters had crumbled to the ground, their taut, muscled legs folding beneath them. One raked his head in the dirt and grass, his massive paw clawing brutally at his ear. *The sound.* Convulsing and groaning, their desperate plea to escape the melodic cry of the bells filled the air around her. Nikki took in short puffs, knees nearly buckling beneath her where she'd slid to a stop. The first flicker of relief tried to manifest, but Nikki knew she wasn't out of trouble yet. Her mind reeled, searching for a feasible escape. But her eyes watered, causing her to press a flat palm to her temple where it throbbed from the wind song.

Wind song; that's all she could think to call it. And right now — whether causing a killer migraine or not — anything able to stop the ugly wolves ranked at the top of Nikki's new favorite things list. The pain intensified, but she still kept her attention riveted on the wolves. *Were* they wolves? She still wasn't sure. Each one was dark as a black hole, with hollow eyes she couldn't seem to look into directly. When she forced herself to lock eyes with one of the beasts, a cold river of pure fear streaked down her spine as if the wolf seized her very soul, choking out life and leaving a tormenting void.

The creatures' legs had folded and twisted into awkward positions, claws scraping at the ground, then at their ears. *Wait, that's not mud on the dogs. It's ... dried blood.* Her eyes blurred, causing her sense of survival to kick in. Head still throbbing like a bass guitar at a concert and with one hand at the side of her face, she ran. Through the tree line she caught a glimpse of silver. *Yes! The gate to the football field.* She'd make it to the other side and this nightmare would be over.

Was it just a nightmare? Some indigestion-induced dream? She could have fallen asleep in the woods while she drew the picture of ...

What had she been drawing? She couldn't remember.

But this was no dream. She was awake. Awake and aware of the spongy grass collapsing beneath her feet, aware of the scent of moist pine hanging on the forest walls. Aware of the searing sensation in her calf where *the thing* had sunk its teeth.

Eyes fixed on the fence, she tried to take a breath but managed only tiny gasps. *Get to the gate. Just get to the gate.* As if the deserted football field on the other side could somehow offer safety. Four dog-wolf-things had chased her through a quarter of a mile of woods; why would five feet of chain link stop them? She pushed on, leaping over rotting tree roots protruding from the earth like the twisted fingers of a witch. She imagined her

313

legs getting tangled in the mass of vines, imagined the weath-ered roots reaching for her as she bounded past. Determination swept into her soul. With sickening certainty, Nikki knew she was racing for her life.

And more. Things, big things, *world changing* things fac-tored into her circumstance. She didn't know how she knew it. But she did. And for the first time in her seventeen years of life, Nikki felt a destiny awaiting her. Fear and dread careening in her soul, and deadly hounds at her back, Nikki felt alive.

"Raven, the song is hurting her too," Mace said, anxiety creep-ing into his words as he peered over the rock ledge.

Raven scowled through his too-long bangs. "The Angel Song doesn't hurt humans. It only affects the evil within."

"Then you should be writhing on the ground with the hounds," Mace mumbled.

Raven chuckled and sank his hands into the pockets of his jeans.

Mace shifted his weight and slid his hands down his thighs. "It's time to intervene." If Raven thought he was going to tor-ture this girl for fun, he was dead wrong. What made him think he was in charge, anyway? Just because he'd been on more journeys, and was the oldest of the three Lost Boys? So what. Experience didn't make a capable leader. The best leaders were those who put the welfare of their soldiers before their own. Anyone who knew Raven knew he only looked out for himself.

Beside him, Mace felt Vine's apprehension rise. For a quick moment, he closed off the noisy world and quieted his own soul, tuning into Vine's heart rate. Mace's gaze narrowed slightly as he listened to the kid's breathing pattern. Inhale. Exhale. All in check. Just first-time jitters.

Assured Vine was okay and ready for the fight, Mace's gaze returned to the pretty teenage girl trying to escape a nightmare sent directly from the pit. Her name echoed in his head: *Nikki Youngblood*. He'd known her name instantly. They all had. One of the perks of being a Halfling. Her shoulders were narrow, arms thin, but looked tone beneath her snug windbreaker. A small, straight nose rested above full lips that remained parted as she panted with each pounding step. Large eyes stayed focused on the field before her. Maybe pretty was an understatement. There was something ... captivating about her. It wasn't her face. It wasn't the long train of golden-brown hair that trailed behind her as she ran. It was her absolute tenacity to outrun her pursuers, her determination to survive. He'd watched grown men crumble at the sight of a single hell hound; she was chased by four. And *crumbling* didn't seem to be in her list of options. She'd kicked free from the hound when it bit into her calf muscle, then with a limp bolted for the gate of the football field, and he could sense as well as smell her resolve. But a mere human girl against four hell hounds? Zero chance for survival there.

"Haven't you seen enough?" Mace spat.

Raven gave a noncommittal shrug and finger-combed his hair away from his eyes. "What's your rush?"

Mace glanced fifty feet below — first at the girl, then the hounds. "She's terrified."

"Yeah," Vine agreed. "She looks really scared."

Raven smiled, white teeth shining in the disappearing light. "So?"

"You're a jerk." Mace spread his arms and prepared to

descend. One of the benefits of being a Halfling: a fifty-foot drop was nothing. He snapped his wings open to swoop down, but before he could drop off the ledge something hit him square across the chest. Air whooshed from his lungs as he landed with a thud.

"She'll see you," Raven snapped. As he stared down at the girl, a surprising—almost tender—look crossed his face, only to be whisked away by his normal demeanor of cold detachment. But Mace had seen it, and the flash of compassion shocked him.

"You're not in charge, Raven." Mace said, rising from the rocky terrain. Once on his feet he dusted his rear end, partly to remove the dirt, partly to keep his hands busy so they wouldn't ball into fists and pound Raven into the ground.

"Be patient." Raven's voice lowered to a purr.

Mace's jaw clenched. He hated this part of an assignment. Yes, okay, sometimes it was important to let things play out a little, to not sail in and rescue too quickly. But the human side of Mace despised it. The angelic side of him ... well, the more journeys he completed, the less human he felt. Just as well. It was a world out of reach, and he needed to remember that.

He knew Raven would only allow intervention at the last possible moment. Mace felt the short hairs on the back of his neck rise along with the anger crawling up his spine. "Why would we have been sent if we weren't going to be utilized?"

Raven's eyes flashed fascination. "Maybe just for entertainment?"

Vine's mouth dropped open, his white-blond hair falling forward. "*Entertainment?*" He shot a quick, questioning look to Mace. "Does that happen? I mean, are we sent to just *watch* stuff like this?" Trepidation clouded those naive blue-gray eyes.

Mace sometimes marveled at the fact Vine was only two

earth years younger than him; his innocence glowed like morning dew, quickly visible and quickly trampled into the mud.

Raven's mouth twisted. "Our kind does it all the time." No dew softened Raven's stark features and face cut into strong angles. His eyes, once bright blue, had darkened to midnight in recent years, which didn't bode well. "You know, earth girls are hot when they're running for their lives."

That was it. Mace dove for Raven, sick of his antics and, well, sick of him in general. Raven sidestepped and in an instant the two were nose-to-nose, fists drawn.

Mace cast a glance to Vine. For the first time, the kid looked like a warrior. Ready to step in if the two older boys came to blows. *Go, Vine.*

Mace exhaled a long breath and lowered his hands. Adrenaline surged into his muscles and pulled every ligament into a tight cord.

Cool confidence oozed from Raven as he tilted his chin into the sun, as if daring Mace to strike.

"I won't fight you, Raven," Mace said. *Vine needs some sort of role model. Which he'll never have if I keep getting sucked in by Raven's games.* He forced his attention away from the Halfling and focused on the pitiful scene unfolding beneath them. A fist fight wouldn't help the girl either.

Long hair floated behind her. Strands matted across her delicate face where her skin glistened with a silky sheen of sweat. She smelled like fear. The scent curled into the wind and rose on pleading wings, calling to him.

When she reached the fence, her golden eyes flashed relief. Mace watched a moment longer. "Raven, there's nothing to learn. Look at her." He gestured toward Nikki Youngblood and the hell hounds no longer chasing her. The four beasts whimpered, trying to escape the Angel Song drifting around them. Nikki trembled at the gate to the football field, hands shaking when she spotted the padlock secured with a thick chain.

"She's here for a reason, Mace. We have to find out what it is." With a twinkle in his eye, Raven clapped his hands and the Angel Song died. "Time to party."

Sometimes the worst part of being a Halfling was standing aside and letting events happen as they're supposed to. Maybe that was the worst part of being any created being. Mace's eyes drifted shut. Without the Angel Song to torture them, the hounds would once again be on the hunt. And Nikki Youngblood would be as good as dead.

Talk It Up!

Want free books?
First looks at the best new fiction?
Awesome exclusive merchandise?

We want to hear from you!

Give us your opinions on titles, covers, and stories.
Join the Z Street Team.

Email us at zstreetteam@zondervan.com
to sign up today!

Also—Friend us on Facebook!

www.facebook.com/goodteenreads

- Video Trailers

- Connect with your favorite authors

- Sneak peeks at new releases

- Giveaways

- Fun discussions

- And much more!